Timothy O. Goyette

Timothy O. Goyette is the editor of the web-zine Quantum Muse. Many of his short works are found there. Other short fiction was previously published in the collection Quantum Musings available online and from book stores.

Read also

Quantum Musings - Timothy O. Goyette, et al.

Timothy O. Goyette

Lockdown

Cover design by Christopher E. Goyette
gemstonehelix@mail.com

Published by Quantum Muse Books

Visit us online at: www.quantummusebooks.com

Chapter 1 Kargan

The cold hard wind blew up the stone steps where dark and dirty figures shivered in line. They pressed against the wall of the old brick building for the meager shelter it provided. The wind cut through their ragged coverings, biting at their chins, cheeks, and noses. To their ears, it carried a sound.

"Help me, please?" a crinkled old voice driven to them on the relentless gale.

They looked at each other, their feet, and the door, but none looked towards the source of the voice. Samuel had looked once, had seen the bruised body and blood, the form of the old woman who had tumbled down the steps.

He gazed down the line of misery. Sniffling and coughing it wound its way down the edge of the building and into the garden. The garden in winter became a mass of ice-encased trees and statues. In less than an hour the woman would be one of them.

Summer came twice a year to Kargan City, ninety-two days of tepid relief. That day would arrive too late to save the old woman. Winter, even at the equator, consumed the land.

Except in New Kargan City. In the distance, the dome of the modern city shed a yellow hue, the city of eternal summer. The exorbitant entry fee kept their neighborhoods safe and beautiful. They would not even take in an old woman freezing in the streets.

"Would someone help me, please?"

Why doesn't someone from the end of the line help? He wondered. *They'll never get in. The shelter couldn't take in many more.*

Samuel looked up the line. Six more to go then he would be inside and this would be just another wretched memory he would strive to repress.

"It's just as well," someone said. "Weed out the weak old fools."

Samuel snapped around, scanning the line for the moron. He saw only sniffling and stamping feet. When the POW camp closed, he and the other prisoners descended on Kargan City in a wave. Those with money, family, or connections fled within days. The refuse left behind overloaded the city's emergency services.

He stood two away from the door when the sound reached him, a weak moan. He looked. She laid still, her complexion white as the snow marred only by brown splotches of frozen blood. Why should she die only a few meters from safety?

He couldn't help. Standing in line, he remained nameless, faceless, part of the herd. Stepping out would attract attention. Pulling his hood tighter about his face he joined the rest of the mass staring at their own feet. He kicked the wall, hoping a sudden shot of pain would distract his thoughts. Her body must have been numb, frostbite creeping into her extremities.

He rested against the doorjamb. Life giving warmth trickled through the partially open inner door. Little wisps of warm air caressed his face on their way out. Behind him, the arctic air snuffed them out of existence instantly. He placed one foot over the threshold, as a gust of wind beat against his back. It pushed as if driving him into the shelter. The blast carried only icy reminders of the outside. The voice crying for help was gone.

Scanning around, no one seemed to be paying any attention to him. To them, he didn't matter. Just the way he needed it to be.

Only a few people stood between him and the admittance desk. He waited a few meters from a safe warm bed and food. All he had to do was let an old woman die cold and alone on the street.

"Just great," he muttered under his breath. He turned out of the line. Avoiding eye contact, he let his shoulder length graying hair cover the sides of his face. He charged down the steps to the body. Kneeling beside the figure, he checked her pulse. Her skin, like ice, drew the warmth from him. The pulse beat weakly against his fingertips. That and the faint mist rising from her gaping mouth confirmed that she still lived.

He hoisted the slight body and marched up the stairs. All eyes looked away from his approach. He muscled his way between two grumbling men at the door and strode toward the admission desk.

A middle-aged man grabbed his shoulder. "Hey buddy, back of the line."

Samuel faced the cretin, staring him in the eyes. The man didn't look at Samuel's burden, just signaled to the back of the line with his thumb.

A man next to him, face wrinkled as much by age as weather, squinted at Samuel.

Raising his voice so all could hear, he said, "What if she were your mother?" He pulled away with a jerk.

As he turned, the wrinkled man stepped out of line. His deep blue eyes locked on Samuel's face. The man's jaw went slack and his brow wrinkled up even more.

Samuel felt those eyes drill into his back as he continued up the line.

The attendant stepped out from behind the desk. "Please be calm. We're processing as fast as we can."

Her demeanor changed when she saw Samuel's burden. She let out a tired sigh and called for an attendant. A man, overly large and underly kept, came with a wheelchair. Samuel helped them place the limp body in it. Water from melting snow and ice dripped from her hair, shoulders, and arms.

As Samuel set her in the chair her eyes opened. They locked on his for a second. Her arm rose slightly, trembling, and her mouth moved as if speaking, but no sound came out.

It lasted only a few seconds and she went limp, unconscious again.

“Do you know her?” The attendant asked.

He shook his head.

"Take her to the back and call Doctor Hood," she instructed the overly large man.

Samuel turned, heading for the door. He had made too much of a scene. Pulling his jacket tighter he prepared for the frozen blast that awaited him. If he hurried, he might be able to get into Domicile Seven across town. The roughness of the area kept all except the desperate away. The problem being, on a really cold night desperation ran in everyone. If he couldn't find a place, he would be relegated to the doorways and alleys that might offer some limited shelter.

Ahead of him, the wrinkled man stood out of line and pointed at him. Samuel thought he would have remembered those blue eyes. Quickly searching his memory, he couldn't place them. A woman's voice snapped him from his thoughts.

"Don't go away, mister. You've earned your stay, come back and we'll get you set up."

Samuel scanned the line as he turned. Steely eyes, harsh eyes, stared back at him. Retribution for line jumping usually came after the lights went out. Besides, they had all seen his face, looked into his eyes. He had to go.

"That's all right miss, I'll manage."

"We try not to turn anyone away on a night like tonight, but we only have so much space. One good turn deserves another." She flashed a smile. It had been years since he'd seen teeth that white. The smile brought her soft smooth face to life.

Murmuring grew from the line. He waited, lost in the smile. Her plain looks didn't distinguish her, but a kindness flowed through her smile. He didn't know what he felt, but it hurt.

"It's him!" an old voice shouted. "I was on Darnath. That's him I tell you!"

Broken from his trance, Samuel spun around. The wrinkled man spoke. Samuel marched quickly towards the door. He wanted to be invisible, to have the world melt away and be alone. But the voice grew louder, and the murmuring.

"Wait, come back." The woman had run to his side. She held his arm as he reached the door, and stared into his eyes. Hers were soft, brown, and glistened with concern. They were not made up, no goop or colors; simple, plain and honest.

He heard his name pronounced by the weathered man. It spread quickly until it reached the attendant. "Samuel Rochez," she rolled the words around in her mouth as if she'd bitten into an apple and found it rotten.

She looked up at him again. He looked away. As she let go of his arm, he pushed out the door. On the steps he took a second to look back. She stood just outside the door looking through him with a blank stare. The wind must have cut mercilessly through her light clothing.

Several men burst from the building behind her. Samuel leaped down the last three stairs and hit the pavement running. The sounds of men yelling and the crunching of ice beneath pounding feet grew behind him.

Using the little lead he had, he dashed around a corner and into a used clothing store. Ducking his head he wound between the piles of rags and remnants. As fast as he could, without drawing any new attention, he worked his way to the back rooms and the loading dock.

Pallets, greasy and black, rested in ill-organized piles. He dove behind one and started counting. He needed to leave enough time for them to run past and for some to return to check out the store and alley. If he timed it right, he could slip between their searches.

The seconds marched on. One hundred thirty seven, a commotion rose in the store. He slipped out and moved to the alley door. A simple metal bolt held the door shut. All he had to do was slip out and disappear into the night. He reached for the bolt while watching the doorway to the store.

The door banged against his hand. He jumped back. Someone on the other side was trying to get in, either to escape from the cold, or to find Samuel. He couldn't take the chance of opening it to one of his pursuers.

He scanned the room. The pallets were only good for avoiding a casual passer-by. Cement and brick made up the walls on all sides, solid except for the bolted door to the alley and the one back into the store.

"Hey Dodge, check out the back!" A voice rang from inside the store.

Whoever banged on the door could have moved along or could still be deciding what to do next. They would quickly give up on the door, but not the alley. He needed more time, but someone was coming through the store.

His fingers wrapped around the bolt's head. The chill and sharp flecks of rust pressed into his flesh. He held his breath and slid it gently back as the seconds burned by.

He put his arm over it to stifle the grating of rusted metal. With the bolt fully back he opened the door a crack. Two men surveyed a dumpster further down the alley. Luckily, their backs were turned.

A shadow appeared from the store as he slipped out.

He climbed over the railing and crouched behind the cement landing, squeezing himself into the corner. He became as small as he could, and as quiet. The sound of the dumpster banging echoed off the walls.

The door burst open. Samuel held his breath. "Seen him?" a voice close to him called.

"Not out here. Must have gone further up, or crossed the street."

Samuel pulled the hood over his face, holding the mist of his breath and body tightly to him.

"If you find him, holler," the close voice said. "He's mine."

"Get in line buddy. You can have a piece of the traitor if there's anything left when we're done. We lost our parents and sister."

The growling response sounded like a rabid dog ready to strike. The talk subsided into footsteps fading from the alley. Samuel peeked over the landing. Nothing but the snow, garbage and he remained. The street beyond seemed quiet, no shouting or sounds of running. Everyone, except for those searching, had the good sense to stay indoors. Most of those searching should give up quickly and head for shelter. He huddled back into the corner, hiding from the wind, and started counting.

Seventy two hundred seconds later he stretched his numb body out and stood up. He forced the frigid air into his lungs. The full dark of night enfolded him with its deathly chill. He paced, pumping blood from one cold area of his body to another.

To sleep was to die, he reminded himself.

Wandering about the confines of the alley, he examined garbage, cracks in the walls, and the patterns in the ice, struggling to stay alert. His eyes closed every few seconds.

He decided to move on, to find something to focus his mind on. From the alley he entered Kargan City where two moons and streetlights illuminated the wind swept streets.

He passed shops; their displays filled with hardware, flowers, clothes, even restaurant displays with replica food. He mulled each over in his mind, trying to latch onto anything, a random thought or idea, to keep his mind active.

A blue-gray holo-ad interrupted his thoughts.

He found it again. Wandering aimlessly through the streets, he ended up there many times. The creature of light that was the ad shone even brighter against the dark buildings and shadows of night.

It encouraged passersby to enter the military surplus store behind it. A handsome young man in camouflage posed smiling and laughing, a gun in one hand. "Independent forces! The life to lead. Free from worries, free from cares. Part of a team, bonded and solid." The recording repeated.

Independent forces was the euphemism for Mercenaries. Samuel shook his head. They burned out villages, bombed homesteaders, and pillaged defenseless colonies. They were more animals than men.

No, Samuel reminded himself, *not all of them*. He had met some with an acceptable moral code.

He reached into his left pants pocket through a hole and pressed three fingers in unison on bioelectric sensors melded into his body. Only his touch would open the compartment. A flap of skin hinged open.

The cache was only installed in secret couriers and some high level officers. If scanned it looked like a common bone implant.

Samuel had kept himself from opening it through the long years of prison camp. He removed a circular object, the only contents. In the streetlights, a clear crystal of Carlinium glinted at its center, the most precious material in the galaxy. The sliver, though tiny, represented a lot of credit. He could purchase a ticket off Kargan, but then he'd be in the same situation most anywhere he could go.

Besides, to get on a commercial transport he'd have to submit to a DNA scan. On the human planet of Kargan, that would result in arrest, trial, and execution, or a simple lynching.

Selling it would provide for a cheap apartment in the low rent area for a year or two. Once it became known, however, that a medal of honor had been sold in the city, it would lead to questions and searches and possibly to his unmasking.

As he thought about selling it his grip tightened unconsciously. Breathing out a long sigh, he relaxed his fingers a bit. His father had been at the ceremony. Three thousand men stood in formation as the Human forces supreme commander himself pinned the medal on his chest. It had been a good day, the sky bright, the weather warm. He smiled in spite of himself. He relished that memory as the last really good one he had.

He sighed.

"Hey, buddy," the hologram called. "Looking for a fresh start?"

He looked up. Its creators obviously programmed it to attract the released prisoners.

He looked back to the medal in his hand. The inscription read: Duty, Loyalty, Honor. The human forces Medal of Honor. He squeezed it until the crystal cut into his hand, and then bowed his head.

No, he would not prostitute himself to them, even if it meant living, or dying, on the streets of Kargan.

He put the medal away, turned and headed up the street. The spring returned to his step and lightness to his walk. Not because of the promise of the future, rather because he had faced a temptation and persevered.

"Until next time," he called over his shoulder.

He allowed himself a half smile. The medal brought him recognition and that brought him the Darnath assignment. Beautiful Darnath, it had been a respite, an island of peace. It felt more like home than any other world.

Thud, he collided with a tall man coming around a corner.

"Sorry," Samuel said and quickly backed away, noticing the two other men behind.

"It's him!" the man shouted.

"Great," Samuel said has he turned and ran. Before he got more than half a block, they tackled him. Hands grabbed at him, fists punched, feet kicked. Pain erupted in his body with each strike. Very quickly all went black.

###

The first thing that came with consciousness was pain; head, body, legs, hands. One hand looked and felt crushed; bits of pavement ground into the flesh.

The second thing was the stench of rotting. It surrounded him, filling his lungs, burning his eyes.

He struggled to get up through one searing pain after another. It took a few seconds for him to realize he'd been left for dead in a dumpster. The shelter probably saved his life. He lifted his head from the garbage and the pre-dawn light struck him.

Breathing hurt. Moving hurt. Living hurt. He fell from the dumpster screaming in pain. The cold ground leached his warmth and strength. Samuel decided to lie there, to go to sleep, and have winter take him.

He lay, drinking in the pleasures of stillness, he heard a voice. He dragged himself toward the street with his one good arm. *Why?* He asked himself with each jolt of torment. Better to die. His mind had decided, but something inside wouldn't let him just die.

Finally, he pulled his head from the alley. He filled his lungs, preparing to shout to the passer-by when he heard the words clearly: "Independent forces! The life to lead."

He let his head sink to the pavement.

"Hey, buddy, looking for a fresh start?"

Chapter 2 Cold

Samuel blinked several times against the light blazing into his retinas. Slowly the room resolved as his eyes adjusted. The white ceiling reflected a harsh light.

A variety of aches and pains came to his consciousness, although they seemed dull, or muted, as if he were feeling them from a long way off.

He lay in a bed covered by a white sheet. Stretching and balling his right hand, he found it slow to respond. It moved feebly. Starting the same procedure on his left he met with resistance.

He couldn't raise his head. His neck muscles felt like rubber. The effort caused the room to spin. Instead he managed to roll his head and see his hand in the grip of another. An old, bony hand held his. Although he could see the hand, he couldn't feel it. Medium length wavy gray hair topped the body attached to the hand. It looked like a woman, as best he could tell from the limited view. The head resting on his bed blocked his view to the rest of the body.

"Doctor Hood, this one's awake." A female voice sounded from somewhere on his right. He struggled to move his head but failed. The bed, the whiteness, Doctor; the meaning of it all slipped away as he tried to concentrate on it.

A moment later a hand pressed gently against his cheek and moved his head to face a man with dark hair, a graying beard, and glasses.

"What's happening? Where am I?" he tried to ask, but only mumbled gibberish came out.

A light flashed in his left eye and then the right. "Don't try to talk. We've given you some very strong relaxants."

Hands pressed at different parts of his body and some devices touched his skin in places. The contact barely registered.

"You won't be able to understand this until the effects wear off, but you had many broken bones and internal damage. The bones are knitting now and should be solid by morning."

"You're lucky to be alive, Harry." The stranger held something long and thin. He pushed it into Samuel's arm. "This will keep you still through the night."

His left hand moved and a quiet voice whispered, "Harry?"

"Yes, Lillian, your grandson is awake. He needs his rest and so do you."

Another voice said, "Nurse, will you see Lillian back to her bed."

Samuel struggled to focus his vision but it blurred. Something soft pressed against his forehead.

"Good night, my little Harry."

The next time he woke up the scene made sense. He rested in some kind of hospital. Balling and releasing his fingers seemed smooth and natural again.

Rolling his head from one side to the other, he took in the room. About a dozen beds lined the walls, a patient in each. A woman in white leaned over a man on the other side of the room. The elderly woman from before was nowhere to be seen.

"Um, Nurse?" he stammered then coughed. His voice strained in his dry throat.

The nurse came over and handed him a cup of water, which he gulped down.

Taking his wrist in her hand she pressed her fingers against his pulse point and looked up at a wall clock. Samuel blinked. There should have been a device strapped to his arm with read-outs of his entire system. Instead that woman used the most primitive means available.

"Where am I?"

The Nurse smiled briefly as she hauled over a machine that looked ancient. It stood about six feet tall, bulky with several read-outs and protruding arms. As far back as he could remember, even as a child, medical equipment had always been sleek and compact.

"You're in the downtown clinic." She arranged the arms over his body, moved a knob and pressed a button.

Samuel expected to hear the grinding of gears or something equally archaic, but it only hummed.

"You're lucky, you know. Over half the guys brought in last night didn't make it."

"What?" He shook his head.

"Oh, you didn't know?" She leaned in. "There's this rumor going around that Samuel Rochez is in Kargan City."

"Samuel Rochez." He repeated the name.

"Yeah, about forty guys matching his description were attacked." She sighed. "It's such a waste. All those poor innocent guys taken out by a chance resemblance to a traitor. I guess that will be a few more lives Rochez is responsible for." She emphasized the name with a sneer.

The machine beeped.

"Well," she flashed a brief smile, "you seem to be structurally back together."

Wheeling the machine away, she went off to another bed.

Voices grew from beyond the double doors at the end of the room.

"No, test them all!" boomed a deep voice.

"DNA identification is expensive and I don't have the equipment," responded a reedy voice. Samuel recognized it from the night before as the doctor.

"Then rent it from a real hospital." The deep voice rose in volume. "We must know if he is here. If we can capture him alive, so much the better."

"Look," the reedy voice rose in response, "My job here is to save lives and cure people. If you want to run the scans, get the money from your own budget, but stay out of my way!"

The door swung open and the doctor stormed in, launching himself over to the first chart on his left. Clasping his hands behind his back he concentrated, body rigid.

Samuel pushed himself up and regretted it. Dizziness hit him immediately and with the sharp pain in his ribs he fell back onto the pillow.

"You're going to have to take it a bit slower than that," the nurse said from the next bed.

She didn't miss much. A good trait in a nurse, he realized.

Raising his hand to his head he tried to steady the room. A moment later his perspective settled.

The doctor moved to the next bed as the door swung open again. One man led another in. The leader's dark skin, close-cropped hair and pressed suit contrasted the other's ragged hair and soiled, baggy clothes.

The ragged man plopped into a chair beside the door.

"Look around," the suit said in a quieter version of the voice he had heard arguing with the doctor. He turned toward the sitting man. "What are you doing? We've got important work here."

"I've been up all night and you keep running me around. I just need a rest, just a little one, that's all." He leaned back in the chair and rubbed his eyes.

"You want to find him, don't you?"

"Of course," the response came strong and hard.

"Well then, come on," the suit grabbed his shoulder and hauled him up. "This is the last place this morning. It's a shame the Loscar removed all images of him from the grid."

Running a finger over a chart, the doctor seemed to ignore them.

Having developed the skill of avoiding eye contact, Samuel examined the ragged man with peripheral vision. He knew the man somehow, he was certain, but couldn't place him. The mostly white hair framed a thin face with an unremarkable nose and bright blue eyes.

The eyes came back to him. He was in a shelter, he tried to leave, and that man recognized him.

Samuel looked at the opposite wall. He couldn't even sit up, how would he run away? Manipulating his body as best he could without inducing too much pain he rolled on to his side, turning his back on the men.

Mashing most of his face into the pillow he pulled the sheet up well over his shoulder and closed his eyes. His pulse picked up a bit as the footsteps sounded closer.

He steadied his breathing. Hopefully they would think him asleep and pass by with just a glance.

The two men whispered. As they came closer he could make out a little of it.

"Well, is it him?"

"It's hard to tell, they all kind of look like him. With the scars, swelling, and the bruises it could be any of them."

They sounded very close, when another, higher pitched, voice rang out, "Harry!" Its joy and light seemed to shatter the gloom in the room. The whispers, footsteps, and other quiet murmurings fell silent.

"Now, Lillian," the doctor said.

"Oh, posh," she shot back, more of a sound than actual words.

Samuel lay still, breathing rhythmically.

"Who is this?" the booming voice asked.

"Oh, Lillian Watson. She's here to visit her grandson, Harry."

His bed creaked with additional weight. "Harry?" came a quiet voice. He felt a light touch on his cheek.

Opening his eyes a bit, he looked up into the face of an elderly woman. It looked familiar. Opening his eyes fully, he took her all in. He saw her in his memory; white-skinned lying in the snow. He had rescued her at the shelter, he realized.

She gasped and threw her arms over him, sobbing gently. "I've been searching for you for years. For years now," he made out between her sobs.

Bringing his hands to her shoulders he prepared to push her away. She was a confused woman, if not delusional and didn't deserve to be deceived.

"Their faces are all bandaged or bruised or scarred. He could be any of them," the ragged man said in a hushed tone.

"You said that already," the suit responded.

"Oh."

Looking through her sliver locks Samuel watched the backs of the two men as they moved away from the bed next to his.

He would have to play along with Lillian until he could find a good way off of Kargan. He promised himself to help find her grandson when he got out of this, to make up for using her. Patting her back he whispered, "It's alright now."

###

Samuel and Lillian moved from the clinic to a shelter. After a few days, when Lillian seemed lively enough, Samuel took her to a library.

Desks with terminals filled the spacious building. Most had dirty figures asleep in front of them. The homeless used libraries for daytime refuge.

Finding an empty station Samuel sat down, Lillian looking over his shoulder.

"What you up to, Harry?"

"I'm going to try and find an old friend."

"Really?" Lillian's voice rose. "Is it a girl?"

"No," Samuel said shaking his head. "Where did that come from?"

She rubbed a hand through his graying hair. "You're not getting any younger."

Leaning back, Samuel pointed to the back wall. "There are books over there, Lillian. Why don't you see if there is anything you like?"

"Lillian?" she said, stern faced. "No matter how old you get, I'll still be your Gran. And," she pinched his cheek and smiled, "you'll always be my little baby Harry!"

Samuel rolled his eyes and shook his head while Lillian laughed.

"All right, I'll leave you to your stuff."

"Enjoy the books, Lill..." Her look cut him off. "Gran," he corrected.

Again he shook his head as she walked away. Wiping the smile from his face he turned to the terminal. "Alright, Harry, let's see what you're up to."

When the Loscar won the war they took control of the human grid and wiped all military data except for personnel records. Using generic officer grade pass codes Samuel found all the data available about Harry Watson. It took about half an hour to recover the data. Harry rose from private to lieutenant in three years and then volunteered for Hope Squad.

"Hope Squad," Samuel grimaced. Towards the end of the war, in desperation, crazy schemes were hatched to try and turn the tide of battle. All the missions ended in disaster for the humans.

Samuel sighed. Harry volunteered to join the crew of the David V. Chan at the end of the war. It fought at the battle of Quantara. No humans survived.

"Clear," he said to the terminal and the display blanked out. "Just wonderful," he said rubbing his forehead. Lillian spent years and all her resources chasing a ghost. If he told her, she would be devastated. Lillian thought she found her long lost grandson only to latch on to an imposter.

If he didn't tell her, he would be reminded every minute that he used another man's life like a cheap suit. He had stolen Harry's memories and family just to keep his own skin safe. If it were him, he'd want to know the truth. Samuel decided to tell her.

It would have to wait until he could find a better place for her where she could live out her remaining years in some comfort. He owed her that much for saving his life.

"Well, Harry," Lillian's voice interrupted his thoughts, "did you find your friend?"

"Yeah," he said looking at the ground. "He died in the war."

"Oh," she put an arm around his shoulder. "I'm sorry. I know it's hard, but we've got each other."

###

They stayed in shelters for the next month. Samuel found part time work knitting hats. Handmade pullovers were the rage among the trendy rich. With that and a little assistance from a local charity, they moved into an apartment.

It consisted of one room with a shared bath. It did, however, keep him out of sight of the populace.

Lillian had a knack for the knitting, or maybe experience. Some of the upscale stores asked specifically for her work.

"Harry?" she asked as he bundled up their week's work.

"Yes?" he looked up.

A crooked smile graced her face. "You know what tomorrow is?" She raised the pitch of her voice as she ended, as if trying to excite a child.

"Payday?" he responded with a touch of excitement, mirroring back her playful mood.

Her smile broadened. "No, silly. It's your birthday!" She squealed with delight.

Samuel shook his head. He felt guilty enough stealing the guy's identity, taking his birthday caused his stomach to twist.

"Gran, I appreciate it but we shouldn't do anything."

Her wry smile set and she turned around in a little shuffle dance as best she could with a cane, making it evident that she was more spry of spirit than of body.

He chuckled despite himself. "I mean, we can't afford anything but the basics for life. Maybe we can celebrate next year."

Lillian shuffled over, pinched his cheek and continued her smile.

She planned to do something that might put them back on the street. She might buy an expensive present or something. "I mean it. Don't spend anything," he said to her back. The food in the cupboard would last only a day or two if they stretched it. A few coins lay in one of the drawers. That plus the next day's payment would cover their rent. Their subsistence food came from a charity.

"Alright," she said with the wave of a hand.

"Gran," he moved over to look in her eyes. "This is serious. We don't want to end up on the street again."

"OK," she responded through a pout. Maybe the next day she would forget all about the birthday.

"Good." He started toward the table but turned back. "Look, I don't mean to hurt your feelings. We really just can't afford anything right now."

"Like your father. He was stingy too."

He sat down on the shambles of a couch he found in an alley. "Come on over. I'll read to you."

Lillian's smile returned as she cuddled up next to him. Resting her head on his shoulder, she sighed, a pleasant, satisfied sound.

As he read, she looked up to him with bright green eyes. He stifled a yawn with the turning of a page. They had but two books and had read them enough that he had them mostly memorized. Her body warmed him and the story no longer really held his interest. At some point along the line he fell asleep.

He awoke and leisurely stretched. Sitting up straight, he rubbed the sleep from his eyes.

He knew it was late due to the dead blackness outside the windows. He walked over to the small mattress on the floor that passed for his bed, right beside the real bed where Lillian slept.

Glancing over to wish her a silent good night, he noted that the bedding remained undisturbed. Maybe she had fallen asleep on the couch as well. Their room remained exactly the same as always except for the absence of Lillian.

He ventured down the hall to the bathroom and found it empty. She could have gone down to the lobby to the little sitting area in the corner. However, Lillian preferred their room.

Picking up the pace, he trotted down the stairs. She was nowhere to be seen. Checking the bathrooms on each floor he didn't find her either.

At the top floor bathroom he took a moment to think it through. Up till that point he had been reacting, grasping at straws. They had no friends in the building she would visit. Other than the bathroom, she would have no place to go.

She'd never done anything like this before, never letting him out of her sight for more than a few minutes as if she were afraid to lose him again. So what would change her behavior that day?

His mind brought up their conversation from earlier: Harry's birthday. She must have gone out to get something. If so, he thought she would already be back.

His pulse rose and his face grew warm. Lillian wouldn't stand a chance against a Kargan winter night.

Bolting down the stairs, he ran into their room and grabbed his jacket and outdoor gear. He stopped briefly at the drawer where they kept their loose change. She had taken it all.

Slamming the door behind him, he ran down the stairs and out of the building. The cold wall of air that met him at the threshold took his breath away. "Just wonderful," he muttered.

What would she have wanted to purchase for him? It could be a small piece of art, or article of clothing, or food. Birthday cakes were common amongst most human culture so he decided to search the local food stores first. None were open at that hour.

Maybe she lay in an alley too weak to go on, waiting in the frozen streets for him to save her again. The image of her shivering, pulling her cloak close around her drove him on.

Stopping at each alley he called, "Gran?"

Not wanting to waste precious time searching probably empty areas, he moved on after a quick glance.

Maybe someone found her and brought her to a shelter. She could be resting warm and worrying about him. That would be rich; they would laugh about it later. He'd have to search them after.

The first store was closed, as he expected. Dim lights illuminated the interior behind the window. Nothing moved, and Gran wouldn't be in a store after it closed.

"Gran," he said. When had he started thinking of her as that? She insisted he call her Gran, but he initially thought of her as the old woman or Lillian.

Pushing back from the building he continued on. A few alleyways on he saw it. A large lump, a form, lay on the ground in the flat walkway between the buildings.

He took a deep breath and steadied himself. It could be an animal or just debris. The streetlights didn't penetrate deeply. It lay in the shadows.

As he stepped closer he could make out legs in the darkness. He stopped and shook his head. It couldn't be. They were together just a few hours ago. As he got closer, the body resolved out of the darkness. It lay there; she lay there, stripped to her under garments.

He knelt beside the remains of the gentle old woman known to Harry Watson as "Gran." Fighting back emotion, he examined the body.

Pressing fingers against her neck, he found no pulse. He knew it before removing his glove for the test. Frost glistened over her skin. Frozen blood marked the ground near her right hand. A fingernail was missing.

She had put up a fight, he realized. They didn't just strip a dead body; they stripped an old woman of everything she had and left her to die.

Samuel jumped up and ran out into the street and made for the nearest intersection. Turning in a circle, he examined each building. Behind the windows murderers and thugs rested comfortably while she laid, hopeless, freezing bit by tiny bit.

"Are you happy?" he screamed. "Have you had enough? Maybe you want me? Here I am, come and take me too!"

Neither the buildings with their frost glazed exterior nor the cold-hearted people behind them responded. He hadn't expected a response. Wiping a tear from his cheek he pulled his jacket up around his face and stormed off into the night.

He hadn't intended to go there, at least not consciously, but after an hour or so of aimless wandering he heard a voice.

"Hey buddy, looking for a new life?"

He walked up to the hologram, ignoring its words. "Ok!" he yelled. Removing the medal from its hiding place he flung it through the man of light. "You win. I give up. Take it. Happy now?"

He pawned the Medal. There were lots of places that asked no questions. He took a pittance for it. It had no meaning for the scum any more than Lillian's life meant to the butchers who took it.

He answered a listing looking for a translator. The advertisement gave little detail. If anything, it would be nice to work with some decent non-human life.

Two weeks later Samuel waited on the edge of a snow field outside of town. The setting sun cast an orange pallor over everything. Out of the sky the rumbling of descent engines broke winter's silence. The ship landed outside the old city, a serviceable cargo ship, about three stories tall and roughly the length of a city block. Samuel had seen many like it. Inside it would have one large cargo hold taking up most of the volume. It could be crewed by as few as five people but usually held forty or fifty.

Samuel walked over to the hulk.

A hatch opened up and a voice called. "You Harry?"

Samuel didn't know why he kept the name. Maybe after they left the planet he would choose something else. He walked over and the young looking man extended a hand. Samuel didn't shake it.

"I'm ready," he said.

The other man looked at his outstretched hand for a moment and shrugged.

Samuel stepped toward the entry, but the other man didn't move out of his way.

"One thing first," the man said. "I'm Stagar Inmen, the leader of this," he waved his hand toward the ship, "Expedition. No one's coming along until I know exactly who they are."

He pulled a DNA reader from a shelf just inside the ship. "Besides, this costs an awful lot of money and I'd like to use it whenever I can."

Samuel stiffened for an instant. Why did he care? When this human found out Samuel's identity he would most likely kill Samuel where he stood. It would be just as well to be gunned down on Kargan than to continue running.

"Great," Samuel said. He extended his left arm, and inserted his index finger into the opening in the device. In only a few seconds the machine beeped and the man whistled. "So you're Samuel Rochez. I've heard of you."

"Who hasn't?"

The man rubbed his chin for a second. "Alright, welcome aboard." The man stood aside and gestured toward the hatch.

Maybe Inmen decided to butcher him inside, or sell him to some human colony. Samuel stepped forward and stopped with one foot in the ship. Taking a deep breath of the stabbing cold, he ripped off his hat and handled it for a second. Lillian had made it for him, the first one she knitted. He tossed it to the ground.

"Nice hat," Inmen said. "If you don't want it, do you mind if I take it?"

"Yes, I mind," Samuel said more forcefully than he intended. "It stays here."

Stagar shrugged again, followed him in and sealed the hatch.

Chapter 3 Jawell

Samuel towered over the dry grasses and brown shrubs in the open field. Little dust clouds raced by, swept up by the occasional gust of wind. He shifted his weight from one burning foot to the other. The ground called to him. Just a few minutes off his feet would be ecstasy. He took a deep breath and continued his vigil.

In a distant stand of trees the creature stood its ground as well. It rested in a covering of shade. Three serpentine legs wriggled and twisted around a branch, holding the cylindrical body erect. Samuel's skin crawled with the thought of tentacles slithering about his body. Its three eyes watched his every move, his every breath. The eyes framed the gaping black hole of its mouth, where shark-like teeth gleamed. Only the shiny sash running diagonally across its body seemed benign.

Wild grassland surrounded him along with scattered shrubs, some half as tall as a man and sprawling. Knee high slender shoots of grass filled most of the area. Samuel reached down and broke off a piece and looked through the hollow stem. Rubbing it in his fingers reduced it to a fine brown powder.

It seemed odd that on the borders of the parched field lush trees stood out from dense ground cover. All the plant life surrounding the dry patch of open space had a bluish green luster that called out life.

Taking a swig from his canteen he squinted at the native. Coal dark wings suddenly sprouted from the creature's sides, giving it the appearance of a giant deformed bat.

"Stay sharp now!" Samuel whispered to himself. He set his left foot back and secured his balance. The wings unfurled like giant flags fluttering from a walking stick. As the body lurched forward the wings cupped the air, and it floated towards him.

Samuel sucked in a breath and instinctively stepped back. In a single heartbeat the creature had closed half the distance. In another heartbeat it would be upon him and its intention would be made clear. Samuel glanced at a bush standing to his right. He bent his knees to be ready to jump for the flimsy shelter if the native proved hostile.

The native did not dive upon him from above, but passed over his head. No matter how maneuverable, there were physical limits on animal flight. Given the size of the wings, it seemed suited for long distance soaring rather than maneuverability. That should give him time to dive for cover

It made a wide arcing turn and lost altitude. Nothing blocked his way to the bush but simple grass. He bent his knees again and aimed for it.

Fluttering interrupted his preparation. Its flight had been nearly silent up to that point. It plummeted almost directly to the ground from a dozen meters. Just before crashing, its wings changed shape. With a woof, they billowed into twin parachutes. It settled to the ground about three meters from him. Its wings rolled up into its body and were gone.

The serpent legs slithered beneath it so smoothly that it appeared to float forward. Kitten-like fur of a golden hue adorned the cylindrical body, probably for warmth. The color clashed with the local vegetation, a trait tolerable for creatures at the top of the food chain. It did not have the mandibles or protruding jaw of a carnivorous predator. The eyes, evenly spaced around the top of the creature, were unusually human-like.

Its eyes shone with kindness.

No, he knew nothing of this species. Ascribing human attributes to other beings usually proved disastrous. The fur, though, seemed soft and gentle. Maybe the native purred. Samuel shook his head.

Where is the bush? Samuel wondered. He thought it should be important, but didn't know why. The thought flitted away as quickly as it came. The sweet little being before him deserved his full attention.

It approached just within reach. Samuel smiled and knelt. He stretched out his arm. It would be the sweetest feeling in the universe to run his fingers through the silky fur. Samuel's smile broadened as the whole of existence simply faded away. They were the only two souls in all of creation.

Reality crashed upon him like lightning and he fell back on his haunches. After blinking several times he focused on the scene before him. Four men in camouflaged uniforms were staking something down.

Samuel rose to his knees. A pile of golden fluff entombed in cords lay upon the ground. He tried to focus, thinking that he should know what these events meant.

"Hey, Roach," a voice rang from over his shoulder. He turned to Michael Lance. Memory came flooding back. It had been a trap for the native.

Lance slapped him on the back hard enough to knock Samuel back to the ground. He would expect Lance be the kind of mercenary who would spit in a starving man's gruel and take bets on the man eating it.

Lance laughed, "Maybe we should call you chum, because you make good bait."

A voice rang out which cut the outburst of laughter short.

"Mister Rochez!" Once again and it scattered the last vestige of fog that had enfolded Samuel's mind. Turning from the assailants, he focused on the voice. Stagar Inmen emerged from the trees behind them. His gaunt body was not adorned with the equipment he required the others to carry: utility vest, side arms, med. kits, and rations. Stagar carried only one item, a simple side arm, and a stun gun.

"Good work, Mister Rochez," he said, a thin smile breaking on his boyish face. "Get your equipment and let's see if this thing can talk."

Looking down, Samuel shook his head. "When we first stumbled upon this native I told you the folly of trapping it. To gain assistance we must develop a sense of trust with the native. After this assault, it will not be inclined to help us. Would you?"

Stagar took a deep breath and said in an almost fatherly tone although about twenty years the younger. "Look, Samuel, this is not a finesse operation. We have no long term objectives. We come in, do our job, leave and get paid."

"Our favorite is the pay part!" Kwanso Kim threw in. He struggled guiding the mess cart to a level piece of ground.

"Mister Kim," Stagar responded. "Perimeter guard."

"But, I'm just setting up..."

Stagar silenced him with a glance. Samuel nodded reminding himself why Stagar carried a stun gun. It inflicted a fair amount of pain and humiliation. Being non-lethal it proved a very effective disciplinary tool.

"Mister Harris, set up mess." Returning his focus to Samuel, he continued with a private voice. "We live by two very simple rules. First and most important, don't get killed. The second, profit from whatever you do. I understand how the last few years have been for you. I took a discharge rather than face their court martial. You are now and forever branded a traitor and a coward. They'll make no room for us in their universe."

"These ruffians," he said, moving his hand as if pushing away a bowl of bad fruit. "They want this life. I've known many guns for hire, some good, some not so good. The best never aspire to it, but learned to live with it." Stagar rested his hand on Samuel's shoulder. "You'll do well Samuel Rochez, just don't lose your focus."

Face flushed, Samuel pulled away from Stagar's hand and turned toward the native.

"Yeah great," he muttered under his breath. By assisting them he stood a chance of making enough from this one mission to disappear forever, to go where humans couldn't find him.

Looking down on the trussed up native, he shook his head. Stagar or Kargan, he had made his choice and would live with it.

"You'll get used to it," Stagar said in a quiet voice.

The native's unblinking eyes were focused on Samuel. He had made first contact with dozens of races like his, slaving to gain the trust of each. It had been that way on Darnath. He thrust the thought from his mind and turned again. The harsh afternoon whiteness beat on his back as he fetched the translation equipment.

###

Stagar stood leaning over the native, holding its sash, as Samuel returned. "Look at this," he said. White jewels flashed like sparks across its surface. "It stitched Carlinium into the material. Clever creature. Clever enough to lead us to its hoard, don't you think?"

"Yes," Samuel responded. "Weaving shows intelligence and suggests an early, possibly tribal, society with some division of labor, or at least some free time. The unevenness of the weave indicates a manual process. Most likely a pre-industrial civilization."

Stagar's face dulled, as does everyone's in a primitive technology lecture. It was the best way that Samuel knew to kill a conversation. "I'll set up the translation equipment."

The native accepted the neck ring and attachments without resistance. Samuel settled on the ground, crossing his legs and leaning forward, a position he would be comfortable in for hours. He switched the translation equipment into scan mode.

Blue, purple, red, random colors flashed, a rabid cacophony of images that beat upon Samuel's mind. His heart hammered in his chest. Pressing his eyelids tighter he struggled to block out the onslaught. He gasped and disconnected. The surroundings came back into focus. Shrubs and slender shoots surrounded him and the native. Voices drifted from behind him and the sun shone in his face. The native trained its unblinking eyes on him.

Samuel rubbed his temples and tentatively closed his eyes. When nothing happened he relaxed.

The equipment needed the abstraction ability of a human mind to interpret the images and build a vocabulary. The half-dozen other species Samuel contacted had all plodded along at a slow but steady pace. This being; however, blasted everything at him in a single, blazingly fast stream of consciousness.

Samuel decided to connect for only a second or so and do the analysis off line.

He reconnected. Flash, a woven mat of some type appeared for just an instant, followed by several natives on the mat. The mat rested on a tubular structure that stretched out, twisting and entwining itself. Home, Samuel knew, and family. The pace stayed steady, just slow enough for him to keep up.

A few minutes passed and Samuel stood up.

"Stagar."

The leader looked up from a steaming can of mulch called excursion rations. Most people would be pleased to be distracted from such a wholesome meal. Stagar's brow furrowed.

"Is there a problem, Mister Rochez?"

"We are ready to communicate."

"That was quick. Doesn't it take quite a bit longer than that?" Stagar walked towards him.

"I know." Samuel said smiling. "It's an amazing subject. I've never heard of anything like this little fellow before. It's as if it already knows how to communicate."

He reached out to pet the native, but pulled his hand back just short. He didn't know how it would react. He needed to take his time and approach the native carefully.

The movement reminded him that he had tried to touch it when it approached him. His memory of the incident seemed dim and hard to recall. That simple act violated all of his training and experience. He looked at his hand and wondered why he had done it.

Stagar broke him from his thoughts. "Thank you, Mister Rochez. Proceed with the interrogation."

"Hey, Roach," Lance called as he approached. "You showed some backbone out there. Hardly what we expected from the traitor of Darnath."

Samuel looked at the others. Their steely eyes fixed on him.

"Thank you," he said, echoing Stagar's mock politeness.

"You sold out our race and our civilization. That's something we don't forget easily."

Lance leaned in so close that Samuel smelled his sweat. His voice dropped to a whisper. "I warned Stagar not to take you on. Once a traitor always a traitor. Just a matter of time till you turn on us. You'd better be very, very good."

A black hand clamped down on Lance's shoulder. "Don't waste your time on that grub lover," said the gravelly voice of John Harris.

Wherever Lance went, his lap dog followed.

Lance rose up and glared at Samuel for a moment before turning to Harris.

"I hear grub lovers taste just the same as grubs if you spice them right," Lance said.

"Is that boiled or baked?" Harris asked.

"Skewered, of course!"

They both roared out laughs and headed back to the others, talking jovially.

Samuel turned away from the men and focused his attention to the subject. He switched the equipment into communication mode and spoke to its mind.

A black void swallowed up Samuel's consciousness. Shock set in as he felt emptiness surround him. He strained to reach the mind he had been working with but found nothing. The equipment couldn't be defective. Bad equipment left the user completely unattached, not dropped into an abyss.

That just didn't happen. At the xeno-work conventions, there were no reported experiences such as this. A vision of the convention floor jumped into the void and was sucked away. Other random thoughts, images, the full sail of his sand glider, the sweet aroma of his uncle's pipe appeared and then flew from him. Samuel grasped at the next, the Copernicus, the first deep space ship he served on. It slipped away. He remembered the color of his mother's hair, what the ocean sounded like. The next memory shot waves of bitterness through him. An old woman lay on a street, glazed in ice.

He recoiled from the memory and popped out of the link. Covered with beads of sweat, he gasped for breath.

"Are you alright?" a voice behind him asked.

"Leave me alone!" he barked without turning. He sat and fumed as the sun arced lower in the sky. It would be easy to give up. He would be beaten, but maybe they'd leave him alive. If so, he would be deposited on some other compost heap of a planet. Or maybe, they'd leave him here. No human within seventy light years.

His spirits began to pick up. A wide variety of vegetation grew around them. It would seem reasonable that something would be edible. Raw material for building shelter grew all around. They were close enough to the equator that winter might be mild.

No, he reminded himself, a survey team was on the way. Soon the planet would be awash in mining operations and colonies. He needed financial security to ensure his retirement from humanity.

He looked back to the native. "We're going to have to work this out between us."

Samuel took a deep breath and reconnected.

The room felt familiar, white nondescript walls and a pale floor. From his frame of reference the native sat on a mat just out of reach. The room would fill in as their bond strengthened. The connection enhanced affinity for the participants. Hyper friendship it had been named, and had disqualified many potential translators. Falling in love with another species tore away the objectivity necessary for the work.

"Hello, my name is Samuel Rochez."

The response came softly floating back. "It is in peace that I greet you Samuel Rochez. May the voices of the sky sing you joy. I am the one called Jawell." The peaceful feeling invaded his being. All tension drained away and his body slumped forward. It could have been the calm of sitting out in the open, or the occasional breeze singing rest to his soul, but the past years of tension didn't exist any more. Samuel fought the urge to sleep.

"I sincerely hope we have not offended or hurt you in any way," Samuel said. "Are you injured?"

"It is kind for you to ask. I am most well. You must indeed have come from a great distance. Our memory does not recall your other-kind. Where is it that you have departed from to grace this land?"

"We have come from far beyond the eastern sea, and it's a pleasure to be visiting your land."

"I am filled with sorrow because this is not the land of the home-kind, and I am unable to welcome you and your other-kind as it is our custom. Perhaps you would be so kind as to allow me to guide you to the land of the home-kind. There we will be able to properly celebrate your arrival."

"Report, Mister Rochez." Stagar's voice ripped Samuel out of the ebb and flow of the conversation like a sudden violent breaker.

Samuel leaned his head back, stretching his neck muscles. Blinking, he looked around for Stagar. The darkness confused him as he tried to pick Stagar out of the shadows.

"It's night already?"

"Yes, Mister Rochez, our eight hours of daylight are up. Now report."

"He seems very friendly and cooperative."

"It's a ploy, Samuel. Gain the trust of your captors so they'll lower their guard and make a chance to escape. Best thing to do if captured. Remember it. How about the Carlinium?"

"Haven't gotten that far yet. We've just started establishing a relationship."

Stagar looked down at Samuel. "Mister Rochez, we don't have time for relationships. The survey ships have already left. We have ten days to strip as much of the stuff as we can and clear out. Every minute is vital. Start interrogating it. I must know if this thing can lead us to a stash or if I need to send out recon teams. You have till morning."

Samuel paused a moment to prepare another approach. "Um, listen Jawell. Could I ask a favor of you?"

"It would be most kind of you to allow me to keif opetat."

The words could not be translated. "What is a keif opetat?"

"Is it something that you have no knowledge of?" There was a brief pause. "It is the rendering of assistance by one to another who has asked for the aid."

"That is a very specific definition for a simple word. Are there other words that you use for helping?"

"It is the custom among the home-kind to use the five base words, but the true total accumulates to seventeen."

Every culture has its customs. The things that are most important to them have the most words. On Kargan the simple act of snow falling had quite a few names: Snow shower, blizzard, and others. A culture with seventeen words for help is no less strange.

"OK, here is the keif opetat. The material stitched into your sash, we call it Carlinium. Do you know if there is any nearby? We are looking for a great deal of it on the surface of the ground so we don't have to dig."

"There is a great amount of it in a large hollow. It is very close, within one day's travel. It would be an honor if you would allow me to lead you there."

"That is good."

Samuel disconnected. The dim glow of the food-heating unit stood out as the only light in the area.

"Stagar," Samuel called out.

A groggy "yes" echoed from the darkness.

"It's about a ten hour trip from here and Jawell will lead us."

"The grub has a name? Anyway, good work, Mister Rochez. We will set off at first light."

Samuel connected to thank Jawell and say good night.

"If I may, it would be most pleasant if you would answer a question for me."

"Go ahead and ask."

"Why is it that you have come to get some of this Carlinium?"

We are a raiding party, come to illegally strip your planet of some of its natural resources. Samuel thought to himself. *He'd really be impressed with that*. "We have to bring it back to our people who need it."

"I see. Your other-kind have such faith in your ability that they have selected you to acquire this material for them. I am doubly honored to assist you in this great endeavor."

Though the sun had set and a cool breeze flowed, Samuel's face burned. "Uh, well, that is nice of you to say. But I think that's enough for tonight. Good night, Jawell."

Samuel stripped off his rig, throwing it to the ground. Turning his back, he left Jawell staked to the ground, exposed to the night.

Stars filled the sky, a billion glowing hearths. In the stillness of the night, the abyss, he stood alone. The feeling filled him. He could be alone in the world or the universe.

The snort of someone snoring broke him from his escape. Ahead and to the left the noise picked out a rhythm adding to the squeaks and mutterings of the night animals. He had somehow failed to register their sounds before.

Directly ahead glowed a dim, reddish light. Though the mess table rested just a few meters away, the light was barely discernable.

Since the discovery of fire, man and most intelligent diurnal beings gathered around it to ward off the dark. Samuel shook his head, another primitive culture lesson. He strode to the table.

"Rochez, hi."

The slight frame of Kwanso Kim stood at the far end of the mess table.

"They've eaten all the franks."

Samuel scooped some of the rice onto a plate. Wisps of steam carried the buttery herb aroma up to him.

"You like this stuff?" Kim asked.

Samuel shrugged as he picked at his food.

"Where're you from?"

Samuel raised his eyes to meet the young man's, and then turned back to his plate. Maybe some conversation would be distracting.

No, he told himself. This was Kim's first mission. He'd latch onto who ever didn't hassle him. Samuel didn't want a puppy.

Kim obviously considered the gesture as an invitation to continue.

"I grew up on MP437. It's so far away from everything that we didn't know there about the war until the Lockjaw's showed up to collect their tribute. They actually took a little less than the Human Empire."

Samuel dumped most of the rice along with his plate into the recycler. The machine would clean the plate and sanitize the rice. Remains were processed, flavored, and dumped out in food bars. The bars were nutritious, if not tasty. They were much like the excursion rations.

He leaned against the table. It made no sounds but Samuel felt the vibrations against his hand.

"Wonderful, isn't it?" Kim said with bits of rice falling from his mouth.

Samuel could join the slumber party, lay down watching the stars, or continue ignoring Kim's onslaught. He could even educate the kid on leadership tools for manipulating morale, such as providing hot, tasty meals in the field.

He headed back toward Jawell. Lying down, he worked himself into a comfortable position. Staring up at the stars, he felt that he liked the view better further away from the men.

Chapter 4 Standoff

Samuel blinked his eyes open.

"Wake up."

A hand shook at his shoulder.

Turning his head to the voice, the smiling face of Kwanso Kim came into focus.

"Since we missed the franks last night, I showed up early and got us some sausages." The kid held out a steaming plate.

Samuel rubbed his hands over his face. The kid's smile brightened as Samuel looked at him. Samuel sat up and accepted the plate without really focusing on it.

Bonding with a member of the group helped new people meld in. Understanding the kid's motivation didn't make Samuel any more inclined to take him in.

The kid seemed nice enough at that point, but he had chosen to join with mercenaries. His innocence would wear off eventually and he would be indoctrinated. Samuel decided that Kwanso Kim would have to find someone else to lead him down the path to the darker realms of humanity.

"Look, kid, I appreciate the food. It's kind of you. I have a lot of work to do and this work requires tremendous concentration. So please just leave me to it, Okay?" He purposely kept his tone cold and uninviting.

The kid's smile snapped to a frown. "Okay."

That complication gone, Samuel turned to his plate. It held eight sausages and a massive pile of scrambled eggs, both their rations.

"Hey Kid," Samuel called out. "Come back and get your half. I can't eat all this."

A mildly enthusiastic smile grew on the kid's face as he turned and started back.

Samuel's stomach forced its way up a bit. The same sort of feeling as when Lillian had claimed him as her grandson washed over him.

He tucked Lillian's memory back where hopefully he'd never recover it again.

If the kid wanted a father figure he would have to choose someone else.

"Why didn't you get two plates?" Samuel asked as the kid knelt down.

"I tried to. Harris said that if you wanted any, you'd have to come and get it yourself."

Samuel leaned back to see beyond the kid. The pack of men mulled at the table, stuffing their faces, talking and laughing.

Samuel leaned back, letting the sun warm him. It had taken the sun only a few minutes to evaporate the dew. The grass surrounding them regained its dry and brittle state.

The kid did better with the sausage than the rice of the night before. They quickly whittled the plate down to one sausage.

The kid opened his mouth to speak, but Samuel cut him off before he could utter a single syllable.

"I have to get to work now," Samuel said

"Hey, Kimmy!" a voice boomed from the distance.

The kid's face fell slack and he diverted his eyes from Samuel. Harris called from the mess table with Lance behind him. Lance's lips pressed tightly together as his eyes bore down on the kid.

"Clean up the mess table and prep for travel."

Kwanso was young, which made him the kid; he was new, which made him the low man in the pecking order; and he hadn't been in a firefight, which made him a virgin.

With this group, it would be hard to break out of the mold. His best chance would be to gain some experience and then find another band.

Standing, Samuel turned his back on the kid and the last sausage. He came to Jawell and donned the gear.

"Good morning, Jawell."

"It is a day worthy of the greeting, Samuel Rochez. Are your other-kind ready for this day's journey?"

"They'll be ready in a little while."

"How many of you are there?" Samuel asked.

"There is only one of me. What is the number that is contained within your being?"

"Sorry, I phrased that wrong. How many Home-kind are there?"

"We consist of all, the Home-kind, everyone."

Samuel nodded and smiled. Difference in cultures often led to that sort of conversation. "Where are the Home-kind from here?"

"Our place is a day's flight away, and is to the north of here.

"We have seen that Some-kind are always traveling. Their journey is the result of search of food, water, or another place for sleep. Is this the case with your-kind?"

Samuel set back, brushing his hand through his hair. "You know, Jawell, we've traveled so far for so long, I think it's the only thing we are good at." He lay back letting the sun warm his body.

"Have you made things, tools, something you use to make the sashes?"

"Yes, the home-kind have made a great variety of useful things. One of those that is most useful..."

He felt the mental squawk like a pressure wave. "Oh, dear," the translator interpreted.

"Come on, little grub. We're going for a walk." Samuel heard from outside the link.

Pulling off the equipment Samuel looked around. Lance released Jawell by violently yanking his rope towards the stake and slipping the knot over the top. Jawell's body slammed against the ground with each pull. Bound, he couldn't brace against the pummeling.

"What is your problem, Lance? He's agreed to guide us. Thrashing him around won't help!"

"Mister Lance is releasing tension." Samuel turned to see Stagar approach. "One of his passions is interrogation. He's a bit miffed that the grub gave in without any coercion."

Samuel watched as Lance slammed Jawell down again. He fought back the impulse to attack Lance and turned to Stagar. He looked from Samuel to Lance and back. A strange glimmer shown in his eyes, although his calm remained face.

Samuel reached for his pulse pistol. Intent on his entertainment, Lance didn't notice. It would be easy to drop him, just shoot him through the head. Samuel rejected the thought as soon as it entered his mind. Blatt. The shot went through the rope and hit the ground. A small pile of ash was all that remained of about twelve centimeters of rope.

Lance stared at him from the other end of a slack rope. His mouth hung open for just an instant, before he snapped it shut.

Stagar flashed a quick smile as he turned to the men. "Come on, People! We're moving out."

A razor smile cut across Lance's face as he tossed the rope aside and strode towards the others. "You heard the man. Let's get a move on!"

Samuel wrapped his arms around the bundle of ropes that encased Jawell and picked him up like a child. He wouldn't carry him like a rag or drag him.

Samuel lifted the native easily. Jawell's weight reflected his locomotion. Flying required great amounts of energy for each gram of body weight. Most flying life forms were deceptively light for their size.

In the few moments it had taken Samuel to gather up Jawell, the camp had broken. The last few men stuffed blankets into back packs.

The nine men lined up in front of Stagar. The kid bustled about the mess table, sealing compartments in preparation for hover.

Walking up behind the kid, Lance slapped him in the back of the head.

"Speed it up, Kimmy!" Lance yelled. "You're holding up the entire outfit. My dead grandmother could tear down faster than you."

Kwanso ran to his pack and bedding, stuffed the pad and blanket in without rolling or even shaking them out.

On Samuel's first field assignment as a biologist, he was a junior officer. The hazing he received paled in comparison to the enlisted mens'. In this undisciplined gang he expected it to be a real challenge for the kid.

Kwanso sprinted to his position. The men formed up in two uneven lines. They stood with none of the snap and polish of a military outfit.

"Mister Rochez," Stagar called and Samuel jogged up to him.

Putting a hand on Samuel's back, Stagar turned him away from the men.

"Where to?" he asked in a conspiratorial hush.

"Towards the rising sun." Samuel responded. "Jawell says there are some obstacles, but they are simple to get around."

"Good." Stagar snapped around.

"Men, we march to the east!" He turned to Lance. "Mister Lance, move them out."

"All right you bunch of grubs, let's make some time." A twisted smile emerged on his face. "Harris, get Kimmy and take point."

Harris's smile matched Lance's. "You got it."

Rolling his eyes, the kid ran over to Harris.

Stagar again turned to Samuel. "Travel with the mess table, Mister Rochez. The grub can ride on it."

Samuel nodded and left for the table.

After they got under way Samuel asked Jawell, "Why are you so cooperative?"

"It is true that no kind would ask for assistance unless there was some real need. To lend assistance is of the highest honor. In the way that you have taken me, it is clear that your need is most great. So very great that you had to insure it with violence. I am honored to the skies to be able to assist."

The table took up its place in formation just before the rear guard. The column left a path the table could follow.

The mercenaries cut through the line of trees with energy beams. Trees toppled right and left as if a giant were pushing his way through. Squawking animals fled from the devastation, some flying, others scampering.

The musky odor of the vegetation mixed with the smoke of smoldering stumps. Branches, leaves and shrubs packed the sides of the path like a wall. In the shade of the man-made canyon, the temperature dropped several degrees.

Before Samuel's eyes fully adjusted to the dimmer light, he emerged into open grassland again.

Samuel bent down and ripped up a hand full of soil. The completely dry clod crumbled easily in his fingers. "Jawell, why is the country crisscrossed by forested lines?"

"This area does not resemble the land of the home-kind. Three days of flight to the south would bring one to a vast expanse of sand. This area is referred to by the home-kind as the land of dryness. Very few plants grow in that land.

"Four days of flight to the north is the land of the Home-kind. Water abounds there, springing from hillsides and flowing into the valleys of the land.

"The land in which we are traveling is called of the Home-kind, the in-between. The large variety of plants grow from their long roots which reach deep down to the water that flows not on the land, but beneath it."

"That makes sense, but how do you know there is water under ground?"

"There are a great variety of animals that dig down to the level of the water. The larger of these simpler-kind provide the help of digging water holes that the Home-kind use when traveling in the in between."

"Which way?" Stagar interrupted.

A hill brown with dry grasses and shrubs loomed before them.

"Jawell, where do we go from here?"

"The way that is easiest is from the air. However you other-kind, being not blessed with that skill, will have to travel on land. From here, travel around the base of this rise to the north. There a flow of water runs along the surface. It is this that will lead you, Samuel Rochez, and your other-kind, to the dazzling rock that you seek."

"North, around the hill to a stream."

"Right," Stagar said as he headed off.

They passed through several lines of trees. Creatures twittered as small shadows moved among the upper branches.

Jawell identified a couple of edible plants for him.

As they passed through a line of trees, Samuel spotted one of the water tunnels. It was about a half-meter in diameter and twisted and turned. Lying on the ground Samuel peered in, but heard and saw nothing. He stuck his arm in up to the elbow. Droplets of condensed water vapor developed on his hand.

Samuel rose and wiped down his arm with an anti-microbial towelette.

“Keep moving,” a gruff voice sounded.

Samuel nodded to Heinricks, one of the rear guard. “Moving out,” Samuel said, and then jogged to catch up to the table.

The seventh line of trees was deeper than the rest. A full fledged river must have flowed under it. They broke out into the light after about 20 minutes.

"Would you look at that," he heard one of the men say.

Samuel looked up the hill. The stream broke through the overgrowth in jagged ribbons of silver, waterfall after waterfall.

"This spot is very much like an idealized location on Earth," Samuel responded. "This particular terrain is much like a tropical paradise on Earth. It's only natural we're impressed with it."

A couple of the men turned to Samuel with a side-long looks.

"Yes, it's very nice," Samuel said nodding his head.

"No post cards, ladies," Lance called from ahead. "Keep a move on."

Breaking through the next stand of trees, they emerged into an oasis. A silvery pool surrounded by soft mossy growth with shade trees looming overhead. On the far side the pool extended into a swamp of sorts. Some vegetation grew up out of the stagnant water.

Samuel hadn’t heard an order given but most of the men stopped and were resting on the ground.

A splash caught Samuel’s attention. Harris had stripped off his vest and jumped in. Immediately, unsnapping and zipping sounds filled the grove.

"Wait," Samuel yelled.

The kid and Lorenzo stopped one step from the water's edge.

"We don't know what type of animals or micro-organisms inhabit that water."

Samuel looked to Stagar for support. The leader of the mercenaries stood impassively staring at the water.

“Look,” Samuel continued. “Our respiratory and digestive systems are protected by medi-bots. The only path open to micro organisms is through the pores in our skin."

He pinched some skin on his arm for emphasis.

Lance turned to Samuel, his arms folded over his chest. "Ya telling John he's got to get out?" His spoke with a pleasant tone and smiled broadly.

"I've seen what non-Terran contagions can do to humans. I wouldn't wish it on anyone, Lance."

"Look," Samuel pointed across the pool. "There is a swamp over there. It's a natural breeding ground of all sorts of thing. The waters commingle right over there." He pointed again.

"Hey John," Lance called; still looking at Samuel. "The Roach here says you've got to get out of that nice, cool water. Ya going to take it from him?"

"I don't take orders from no insects!"

A chorus of laughter rose from the men. However, the kid and Lorenzo stepped back from the pool.

"But you will take them from me," Stagar said. "We need everyone at full strength. Harris, get out of there." Then to everyone, "Purify the water and fill your canteens, we move out in five."

The laughter ended and the men busied themselves collecting their gear. Lance's face was stone. With an arm led by his pointing finger he stabbed the air in Samuel's direction. "Stagar, He's a new guy. Got no seniority, got no rank, and he's a traitor to boot. He's got no business giving orders. Treating him like an officer is a slap in the face!"

"In this case though..." Stagar paused for an instant," he is right." Stagar turned and strode off, dropping his canteen for the kid to take care of.

Lance strode after him waving his arms in emphasis. With hands gripped behind his back Stagar walked in silence.

None of the conversation drifted back to Samuel. He bent over, collected his canteen and made his way to the pool.

They continued on, each foot fall became heavier. Having not taken time to acclimate to the lower concentration of oxygen in the atmosphere, the trek wore on all of them.

Samuel took his lunch with Jawell, a few meters away from the others. He looked at Jawell and considered giving him one of his food bars. His rations, however, might not be digestible by the little native.

"Are you hungry, Jawell?"

"It is very kind of you, Samuel Rochez, to be concerned with my well being. It would be most useful to eat now. I have gone beyond what is a normal period for the home-kind to eat."

Samuel looked about the trees and vegetation. Tall, leafy, tendril plants, vines that seemed to grow straight into the air. Others were more traditional tree-type plants, although all of the vegetation had a bluer hue than Terran plants.

"What can you eat here?"

"The thin tree that is directly across from us has delicious fruit that grows at the top of its height."

"Right," Samuel said and headed for the tree. He struck at the base of the vine-like tree with a utility knife. A sharp crack echoed though the clearing as the blade skidded off the tree. His hand stung from the collision. Upon close examination he found a slight nick in the plant where the blade struck it.

"Great, this stuff is like metal," he mumbled.

Looking up and down the tree it didn't seem to have any weak spots. It was like a rope of iron rising straight into the sky. If a knife couldn't cut through it, he'd have to take more drastic measures. Pulling out his gun he fired at the base of the tree.

Crack! The plant tumbled through the upper vegetation, crashing to the ground.

Before it hit, the others were up, armed, and advancing.

"What's going on Mister Rochez?" asked Stagar.

"Just getting some food for Jawell."

Stagar paused, but Lance spoke up. "No, we keep the grub hungry. Promise it food when we get to the Carlinium. That'll keep it motivated."

Samuel stared at Lance for a moment. He embodied all the worst traits of humanity. Taking a deep breath Samuel responded. "It's part of his culture. It is morally unacceptable for him not to help us."

Lance pulled out a knife and stepped menacingly towards Jawell. "I can give it a lot more inspiration than morality."

"All right, Mister Rochez, feed your pet," Stagar said.

"What?" Lance spun around to face Stagar. "You can't give up an advantage to that grub."

"It won't hurt us or our mission. There is no reason not to. Besides, it may help Mister Rochez develop a sense of trust."

Lance lowered his voice so the men could not hear, but Samuel just caught the comment. "Are you sure this is the decision you want to make, Stagar?" Lance stared intently at the smaller man.

Without focusing on Lance, Stagar let his hand rest on the handle of the stun gun.

Lance strolled away as if nothing had happened.

The group spread out, most to finish their meals. Samuel got the fruit.

"Hey, Samuel."

Samuel turned to see the kid. "Is that stuff edible?"

Samuel took one of the fist size fruits and tossed it to him, "Test it."

"What?" he said, screwing up his face.

"In my pack is a toxicity meter. Set it on solid, stick the needle in and wait for the readout."

The fruits were round, purple and red, with a sweet odor. Samuel put one in Jawell's circular mouth. His razor-like teeth quickly sliced it up while the mouth contracted, mashing the bits to pulp. It wasn't pretty, but quite efficient.

"Is it okay?" the kid asked bringing the meter over.

Samuel glanced at the data. "The readout says good, but that's only half the battle." Samuel took the fruit, broke it in two, and gave half to Kwanso.

The younger man rolled the fruit around in his hand, examining it from all angles.

"You're sure it's okay?"

"The meter doesn't lie."

The kid held up his half. "Here's looking at.... well, somebody that isn't here."

Samuel bit into his half. Grisly tendrils ran through it like a sponge. They were hard to chew. The juice sweetened his mouth and tasted of toasted grain.

Samuel sucked the juice out and swallowed, feeling the slippery texture running down his throat.

The kid scrunched up his face and followed. "You know, it's sweet enough, but the texture's pretty bad." He pulled a lumpy string from his mouth.

Samuel took another bite. *Familiarity is the tool of appreciation*, he thought.

Kim sucked the juice from his portion and threw the bulk away. "Harris and the others don't like you much."

Samuel locked his gaze on the young man but didn't respond.

"It's because of the war, I know. They all believe you're a traitor. I'd like to know what happened."

"Ask them. They'll happily tell you." Samuel leaned against the meal cart.

The kid snorted. "I'm not that young. There's a point of view for every side. What's yours? I'd really like to know."

Samuel plopped another fruit into Jawell's mouth and stared into the distance.

"Harris says that you like grubs better than humans. That you turned traitor at Darnath because you hate humans and wanted us to lose."

"Please, they are not grubs. They're natives, aliens, or non-terrans. And yes, they are, in general, better than humans. Only humans consider genocide a strategic ploy."

His voice grew quiet and cold. "Before Darnath, I hoped the Human Empire would win."

"Since then, I'm not sure anymore. There is wonderful nobility in our race, there is also great evil. I wish that the evil part of us wouldn't win out over the nobility so often."

"Hey, Samuel, come on, no reason to feel so down. This is Kwanso Kim, remember?" He sat down, resting against a tree facing Samuel.

Samuel met the kid's eyes for a moment before shaking his head and looking down again. No matter how badly the kid wanted it, they were not friends. The kid was the most benign of the mob, however. Samuel shrugged. "I'm sorry. Man is one of the most complex beings out there, and I'm apparently no exception."

"So, what did happen?"

Samuel sighed and looked up. The canopy blocked out the sky, shading them from the sun.

"Darnath was the key planet in a strategically vital quadrant. I had been in charge of it for about two years when Admiral Chessman arrived with his fleet.

"They had a simple plan. Let the enemy conquer Darnath, then blow it up.

"You see," Samuel said pointing to Kim. "The Loscar used the same tactic each planet they conquered. Hold their fleet in tight orbit to protect their gains until they could establish control and defense, then move on to the next.

"Chessman figured the blast would take out the landing forces and most of the fleet. They would easily pick off any survivors."

"Sounds like a good plan," Kim said.

Samuel scratched his chin. "Yeah, great, unless you're one of the billions of sentient beings living on the planet."

The kid whistled.

Samuel nodded. "I worked with the natives to sabotage the detonation. When Chessman pressed the button nothing happened. His rage got the better of him and ordered everything he had to attack the orbiting fleet, leaving nothing in reserve."

"No one stopped him?"

"Well," Samuel shrugged, "several of the ships' captains tried. He had each relieved, and went in guns blaring. He had surprise on the initial attack and inflicted a severe blow. But the enemy got their heavy ground-to-space artillery on line and it ended very quickly.

"The enemy found the detonation devices and the sabotage. Soon everyone knew I was responsible."

"That's not the way I heard it," said Harris.

Samuel, focused on feeding Jawell, hadn't noticed Harris approach.

"Yeah," said Lance as he strode up from behind. He leaned against the tree the kid rested against. "Your friend here, Kimmy, he took plans for weapons, ships and systems and whatever else he could get his hands on and gave them to the Lock jaws at Darnath."

The kid looked from Lance to Samuel with wrinkled brow.

"Chessmen figured out what was going on and ordered the fleet to attack to stop this traitor from giving all our military secrets to the enemy."

Samuel shook his head. "Really, is that the official story?"

"What do you mean story?" Harris moved forward stern faced. "You think we're going to take the word of a traitor?"

"Gentlemen," Stagar stepped into the conversation. "Decorum.

"Tell me, Mister Harris, how often did you trust the word of our government in general?"

Harris looked to Lance before responding. "Well, they're politicians; you can't expect the truth from them, unless it's to their advantage."

"So," Stagar continued raising his voice slightly, "I would assume that Mister Rochez's version is much closer to the actual truth." It appeared that he wanted to make certain all of the men heard it. He nodded to Samuel when he finished.

Samuel ignored him and fed another fruit to Jawell.

"Well," Harris stammered, "At least Chessmen was a man about it. When the treaty was signed, instead of surrendering he took a small fleet of ships and took off."

Harris knelt and grabbed the kid by the collar. "Now, Kimmy, what are you doing over here?"

The kid looked up sheepishly, "Talking."

Harris avoided Samuel's gaze. "I can see that. But you need to take your talk over there with the humans. We don't want none of these grubs rubbing off on you."

A bit of quiet desperation shone in the kid's eye. Speaking up for him would only make it worse for Kwanso.

Samuel turned from the mercenaries and fed Jawell another fruit. The crunching of undergrowth indicated their departure.

Through the rest of the afternoon Samuel and Jawell talked. The slow rhythms made the day pass quickly. Samuel felt a kindred soul in Jawell. The type Samuel hadn't met since Darnath.

Jawell showed him more of the home-kind food. Some was edible, but none tasted as good as the fruit.

They arrived with the sun near the horizon. A great, jagged scar crossed their path. The angle of the ravine walls kept the star's light out. It looked like a black void running roughly north-south.

On the opposite side, the line between light and shadow worked up the side of the ravine. Yellow and blue vegetation glowed gold and purple in the refracted light. It twisted in the breeze like a single organism undulating up the ravine.

Through gaps in the rippling vegetation flashes of pure white shot out like tiny explosions: Carlinium crystals.

"Over here!" someone called.

"What have you got?" asked Stagar.

The man moved from behind a shrub. "There's a big chunk of Carlinium sticking right out of the ground."

"Good!" called Lance. "Everyone fan out, there's bound to be more."

Samuel looked down at his little friend. In a few short minutes Jawell would be winging his way back to the Home-kind. Samuel squashed down his regret.

"Over here!" Harris shouted. He held a sparkling trophy above his head. Bedlam ruled, mercenaries ran from one place to another, ripping crystals from the ground and throwing them in a crude pile.

"Yahoo!" another man yelled, turning his scanner to anyone who passed him. The material played havoc with sensors. The wildly random readings indicated that they were standing on a buried mountain of the stuff.

"Jawell, thank you for this. You have no idea what this means for me."

"If I have brought you pleasure along with assistance, then I am filled with joy as well."

A hand pressed firmly on Samuel's shoulder. He looked up into the smiling brown eyes of Stagar Inmen. "Well done Mister Rochez, look at all this. The shares will be enough to retire on."

"Heck!" Clark threw in. "Buy an island on Isabel and live like a king."

Although any of them could turn in an instant, it seemed Samuel wouldn't need to watch his back for a while.

"Yes," he said in a matter of fact tone. *It is a good day. It will be a better one when I don't have to deal with mercenaries again.*

"Mister Lance, do the grub." Stagar's voice brought silence.

"Yes, sir," Lance responded with a broad smile.

"Wait," Samuel called and lunged at Lance. He grabbed the barrel of the rifle and pushed it away from Jawell.

"Why Stagar? Jawell led us here. He deserves a better reward than death."

Stagar stepped closer. No spray of emotion washed across his face. "No can do. We let your little friend go, and he could come back with hundreds or even thousands more grubs. We'd run out of ammo slaughtering the little beasts. Not worth the risk. Besides, we can't leave witnesses. You talked to him; someone else could, too.

"Mister Lance."

Dressed and waiting for slaughter Jawell sat, his innocent gaze happily watching his captors, waiting to help fulfill their next desire.

"Jawell, they're going to kill you!" Samuel yelled.

Stagar shook his head. "Mister Lance, now."

Lance spun. A lightning fast elbow slammed into Samuel's skull. He crashed to the ground, reeling in pain. Looking up he saw Lance smirk, his eyes shining with pleasure.

No! He wouldn't let that animal kill Jawell.

Samuel fumbled at his vest. Groping, his hand closed around a plasma grenade. If Stagar wouldn't listen to reason, he'd listen to force.

The smirk dropped from Lance's face. He turned the weapon on Samuel, but he was too late. Samuel stood up, with the grenade raised over head.

Most of the pack scurried for cover behind a large boulder. Kwanso Kim stood staring a few meters away.

"Kwanso," Samuel said. "Better get to cover with the others."

Kim didn't move. "You'd kill all of us for that?" he said pointing to Jawell.

"You'd die rather than let him go?" He couldn't allow any distractions. Lance would seize any opportunity to take him down. "Besides, I like grubs better than humans, remember? Get to safety while you still can. Only those out in the open are in danger."

Kim backed towards the boulder.

Through the whole exchange Stagar stared at the ground as if unaware of the threat.

Lance obeyed Stagar, which made him the only one who could save Jawell. Samuel had to make him see that killing Jawell would be more trouble than freeing him.

Stagar came to life with the muffled growl of a dog: "Bloody hero." His voice rose as he continued. "You know what a hero is? No of course you wouldn't. A hero's someone stupid enough to try something no thinking human would even consider and manages to survive. That's what got you here, and you're doing it again. Putting your life on the line for a creature.

"Look at it, Samuel. It's a disgusting, little, wretched life form. It probably has a gruesome death waiting for it tomorrow. Today we kill it quick and painless. Come on man! Figure it out!"

"He's an intelligent, sentient being who brought us a fortune. You can't want to just kill him." Samuel considered why he fought. Jawell, so far as he could tell, was happy to go along. The home-kind with their warped sense of honor would revere him for it no doubt. One primitive being on one planet out of the entire universe. What did it matter?

He looked at Stagar wondering if this was how he started down the path that led him to become what he became.

"No!" Samuel declared and pressed a button on the grenade. With a "zeep" the grenade announcing its activation.

"Mister Rochez! If you don't give it up right now you will not see a credit from this mission! Keep in mind; we are your last chance. Anyone else would kill you on sight. Remember Darnath? You did the moral thing there, and see what that got you. It's hard," his tone softened, "I know, but you have to get beyond it."

A moment before Samuel basked in thoughts of safety in exile. Now he stood facing Stagar and his pack. If they didn't kill him they would send him back to the streets, to another death.

What kind of a loathsome rodent offers up his friend to a ravenous drooling monster? He looked to Stagar, aching for the cut-throat to back down. Stagar's empty eyes waited. He was giving Samuel what he considered a chance. He wouldn't wait very long before unleashing Lance. "My friend," Samuel whispered, breaking the harsh silence. "He's my friend."

He felt as though a billion fingers were pointing at him, the traitor. A black depression flooded his mind as he heard their condemning roar. Just as he began to lower his arm and deactivate Jawell's only hope, Stagar spoke.

His spoke softly. "Samuel, sometimes friends have to die." He said it with a strange shimmer in his eye.

Samuel blinked and looked closer at Stagar. The man would willingly sacrifice a friend. From his tone and look, he had done it, maybe more than once.

Stagar's form twisted in his mind, instead of a boy-faced man doing a dirty job, he became a robot with a demon at the controls. He would kill his whole family if it suited his purposes. At last Samuel reached a unified crescendo of decision. It was evil, and to go along with it was to become evil.

He dropped the grenade and dove for Jawell. With 5 seconds to detonation he had to hurry. The only thing that mattered was getting to cover with Jawell. *Two seconds, there's a boulder*. A dive might crush him. *One second.* Instinct took charge. They dove behind the stone. *Just in time*. The heat from the blast swept around their primitive shield. The hot wind lapped at his hair and clothing as the deafening roar of the shock wave blew by them. As soon as it blew past he pulled out a knife and cut away Jawell's bindings.

"Jawell, you must go now!"

"Is it that you no longer have need of me now that you have found what you came for?"

"No time! Leave now! Go to your home-kind and don't look back."

Before another meandering response could begin he ripped the communications rig from Jawell and thrust him away. He flopped once, then twice. The thumping sounds of feet came from the blast zone.

Jawell! Hurry! He thought

Tied up for nearly two days, Jawell's muscles must have been cramped. Samuel watched as he struggled to take wing.

"Just great," he murmured.

Jawell had no hope in the open, unless Samuel provided Stagar's pack another target.

Samuel leaped from his hold and sprinted northwest keeping inside the tree line. Jumping over shrubs and dodging around trees he ran. He heard the tick of projectiles as they sliced through plants to his right. An energy beam vaporized a branch just above his head.

The indistinct shouts grew closer. The younger and more fit men of the pack gained on him. His breath came short and hard. He'd have to stop soon.

As he ran he scanned for defensible positions, but nothing obvious came into view.

A large gray-green log lay across his path. As he prepared to vault it, a sharp pain erupted in his shoulder. Carnivorous flames ate at every bit of his body. The scenery faded in a blaze of whiteness.

###

"Ugh," Samuel spat. A violent wave of nausea crashed over him. Consciousness came slowly, and uncomfortably. Searing pain cut into his wrists and ankles. He was staked down and couldn't focus past the blinding whiteness of the setting sun.

"You're awake, Mister Rochez."

It seemed that Stagar had let him live so he could enjoy a little more torment.

"I don't see why you did this to yourself. Samuel, you had everything going for you: talent, knowledge, and training. You did your job well. You even handled the rabble's ribbing, something they can respect, as much as these dogs can respect anything. They would, in time, learn to look up to you. You were coming around so well. Why did you have to throw it away for a grub?"

"Something you wouldn't understand."

Stagar's voice softened, "Honor. You think I don't struggle with decisions? I said we are alike, and I meant it." He dropped down to one knee and looked into Samuel's eyes. "You're the only other one here that isn't a jackal.

"But, we have to choose our battles. You can't make good decisions tomorrow if you get killed today. There was no chance here. Samuel, you've thrown your life away for nothing."

Face tense, he stood and turned to the twilight horizon. "We could have worked well together, rising above this riff raff. Now, you will die here."

"This is an execution to keep your reputation intact. It's a way to keep those dogs from turning on you." Samuel pulled at the unyielding rope.

Walking to Samuel's right foot Stagar kept his gaze fixed on the distance. "That's what command is about."

"No! You use Lance to bully them around as individuals, but you're afraid to stand up to them. Command is about leadership."

"You don't understand. I don't enjoy this." He pointed finger toward where Samuel assumed the men must be. "I would like nothing better than to dump these people." He said the last word with a sneer.

"And Lance..." he started but Samuel cut him off.

"You have a choice, Stagar."

Stagar rubbed his hands together for a moment before responding. "And, I've made it. No matter what I may have done, or what you think of me, I am still a good, decent man. We are both good, decent men. And because of that..." Stagar left the rest unsaid.

He kicked at the post Samuel's right foot was tied to. It became loose, very loose.

"Stagar, what are you playing at?"

Without a word he repeated the operation at the right hand.

"Is this some-kind of a trick? I'll be able to get out in a minute. You want me to escape?"

"In an hour or so, Mister Lance will come to check on you. If you're unfortunate enough to be found, well..." Stagar trailed off with a shrug. "If not, the Carlinium around here makes the trackers useless. We won't be able to mount a full scale search without abandoning our profits."

"I suppose you want thanks."

He said nothing. His lifeless eyes came to rest upon Samuel for a moment. Then he turned and strode away, leaving stillness in his wake.

With an hour's head start he didn't expect to get very far, especially the way his stomach rolled and head pounded. Samuel would have to make the best of it.

Pulling himself free, he staggered off into the growing darkness.

Chapter 5: Flight

Snap, another twig broke. Samuel froze. The sounds of pursuit had faded hours earlier, but they could have switched to a stealthy hunt.

The sound came from some distance away, however, exactly how far was impossible to tell.

Nocturnal animals chattered and called. Trees moaned when the wind kicked up and somewhere in the distance a stream gurgled. The varied noises made it impossible to pick out sounds of pursuit from the background.

Blackness, not darkness, enveloped Samuel. The canopy above blocked all light emanating from the night sky. Samuel listened intently into the darkness. He focused on distinguishing each noise and attributing it to a source.

As he did, his half-open eyes closed. He snapped his head, suddenly alert. He turned his head from side to side to hear better. A chill ran down his neck, pricking up the hairs. Darkness pressed in like a hunter closing on his prey. Hearing a snap he turned again. The feeling of danger welled up in his chest, imminent and with savage intent. A crackle and a low hum, he turned again, this time from the front. Sounds came from all directions.

He took a deep cleansing and calming breath. They weren't the sounds of Stagar's pack he decided, but the local wildlife. Since arriving on the planet the only large life-form they had encountered was Jawell. There didn't seem to be any dangerous predators. He had a lead on the mercenaries and Stagar wouldn't let them search for long. They came for the Carlinium, and chasing him wouldn't fill their pockets. Samuel drew upon logic and reason to fight his doubts. His mind cleared, but his chest remained tense and heart raced.

He groped into the darkness and forced his body forward yet another step.

###

Dawn was a relief. With the gray light, maneuvering became easier, each step more sure. The trepidation of the night before gave way to exhaustion. The background sounds changed as the nocturnal wild life went to sleep and the day time crowd woke up. Keeping the rising sun over his right shoulder, he trudged through the sea of brown grass stalks. The next line of trees enticed him forward. Once he reached them, he'd rest. He had made the same decision for the previous two tree lines, but had found the strength to continue. "Just over the next hill," he whispered with a tired smile.

He raised one foot and pulled it forward; the trees grew closer. Sixty three, he counted. The rising sun which he had welcomed began to beat down. Rolling up his sleeves he pushed towards the shade of the trees.

At two eighty seven he reached the first of the trees. Stretching out his arm, he rested his weight against a wide, smooth barked, tree. Not edible, he reminded himself. As if the thought had sparked it, his stomach began to rumble. Pulling himself into the trees, he scanned for wild food. He found thickets, pitchy pears that were toxic, iron rope trees with fruit out of his reach. Rubbing his stomach he rested for a moment. Looking down he saw a sprig of bluish vegetation. It had wide leaves with a central vein, the edges serrated; a dozen or more leaves sprung from a shoot only a few centimeters tall.

Samuel fell to his knees and gripping the twig, he pulled. The stem remained fast. He adjusted his position directly over the plant and gripped it even tighter and drove his fingers into the ground, ripping out clumps of the soil. The pinkish white flesh of a tuber poked from the dirt. Gripping the top, he tore it from the ground. Wiping it clean he bit off a piece, crushing it between his teeth. The bitter syrup oozed into his mouth. He gagged and coughed and with a deep breath forced it down.

The second bite he spat out. He tossed the remnant away and scanned the area for anything good. In the time he had with Jawell he had only learned a handful of edible plants, and just two that were palatable. Nothing else in the area looked familiar. Survival would require days of foraging before he would be able to move on.

He sighed and leaned against a tree. "How far to the Home-kind?" he wondered. They flew, and so covered more ground in a day.

A movement, a flash of green and white, caught the corner of his eye. Samuel dropped to the ground following the blood that seemed to drain to his feet. A mercenary had emerged from the last row of trees. Samuel rolled behind the tree and peeked around it. He noted the pursuer's wide chest and muscled bulk. It had to be Lance. He wore something over his eyes. Samuel strained to make it out. Lance's neck was bent as he scanned the ground, plodding along.

"Infrared." Samuel knew he was done for. The Infrared scanner would be clear enough at close range for tracking. Unless he ran over a huge outcropping of Carlinium or through a river there, Lance would be able to run him down eventually. Besides, Lance, 20 years his junior, was in much better shape and carried weapons. The two bites of root threatened to come up.

Keeping the tree between Lance and himself he pulled himself up. Sticks and dirt, maybe a rock, made a weak defense against Lance's personal arsenal. Lance was arrogant, over confident, and cruel, but he wasn't stupid or careless. Working his way into the trees he scanned for anything that might take Lance down.

He entered a small mossy clearing. It would have made the perfect place to stop and rest if he had time. Off on one side lay a small pile of overturned dirt.

He ran to it. A hole, a bit wider than a hand's breadth lay exposed on the other side. He scooped up soil and hurled it into the woods. Panting he forced his muscles on. Falling down he stared at the canopy while catching his breath. Beyond his gasping and heart beat the woods remained quiet; no sound of Lance.

He rolled over and pulled up to his knees. Staggering to the edge of the clearing he ripped up a mat of moss and wadded it over the hole. He laid it in, carefully smoothing it out. Rising fully to his feet, he lumbered into the trees. Kicking up dirt here and there he continued his search. He scanned the distance when his dragging feet stubbed against something hard.

Again he dug into the ground. This time he unearthed a pair of rocks; one the size of a child's fist, the other of a large potato. He took the potato and scurried back to the clearing.

Expecting that Lance would sneak up behind him he arranged it so that the covered hole was less than a meter behind his upper back. Samuel waited.

He heard the first muffled foot steps a few minutes later. At first he thought they were his imagination. They grew louder, closer. Samuel opened his mouth taking deep slow breaths. Rapid chest movement might alert Lance to his ploy. Each step seemed impossibly close.

Lance might wake him up in any manner of ways. He could kick him in the back of the head or smack him with a weapon. Of course Lance could just shoot him in his sleep and be done with it. But that didn't seem like Lance. He would want to savor the look on his victim's face before taking his life.

No, Samuel was certain Lance wouldn't kill him without relishing it.

The footsteps stopped right behind his head. Samuel tightened his grip on the rock. The silence dragged on for minutes. Samuel constantly reminded himself to relax, lie still, and look asleep.

The scraping sound of boot against dirt came from behind. Samuel tensed.

Whatever it was, it was coming.

A bolt of pain struck the middle of his back. Flung over onto his face he landed hard on the rock still clutched in his right hand. He sat up, stopping several times for the pain to ease and keeping the rock out of Lance's view. The barrel of a multi-rifle pointed into his face, on the flame thrower setting he noted. A particularly nasty version, it projected a flame out fifteen meters and spit out a stream of talyerite crystals.

Beyond the barrel shone the face of Michael Lance. His smile beamed as his whole face glowed with sadistic bliss. Samuel held back the urge to look at the trap; it might warn Lance. However, he was certain Lance stood astride the hole.

"Been looking forward to this have you?" Samuel asked.

"Sure have. Roasted roach," Lance said. "Just like mom used to make."

He had to make Lance move laterally and he only had a second to do it. So he looked right, a feint. Lance fell for it and moved the muzzle in that direction.

Good, thought Samuel as he rolled left, getting his feet under him.

Before completing the maneuver Lance recovered and had his bead on Samuel again.

"Not good enough," Lance said with a laugh and adjusted his stance to face Samuel. As he did his foot fell into the hole. With a snap Lance's body plunged forward.

As Lance hit the ground a burst of flame erupted from his weapon. Samuel hopped to his right to avoid the blast but the stream of flame caught him in the right calf. The pant leg ignited. He dove at Lance before the pain hit.

Lance threw up an arm to block the blow. The weight of Samuel's body; however, crushed the defense and the rock connected with Lance's skull.

"Aaaaaa!" Samuel screamed as he rolled off Lance. Reason fled as his flesh burned and training took over. Sitting up he madly ripped soil from the ground and buried his leg and the flames.

His calf throbbed. Needles of searing heat drove deeper into his leg. Every instinct yelled for him to take it out of the ground, to nurture and protect it. He clenched his teeth, pounded the ground, and ticked off seconds.

Once heated the crystals reached critical temperature and dissolved through a chemical process, which kept them blazing hot for thirty seconds or more. Even if the fire from the flame thrower were extinguished the crystals would continue to burn into flesh or reignite if exposed to air.

"Eighteen, nineteen, twenty." Samuel gingerly brushed the dirt aside with one hand. In the other hand he held a clump of dirt to smother any sparks before they could burst into flame. Luckily, none appeared.

Scootching on his bottom he worked his way over to Lance. The lacerations on Lance's forehead disappeared into the blood stained hair over his temple. Blood ran down most of his face. The flow from his forehead ran around his eyes and dripped off his nose.

Samuel gently touched Lance's neck and searched for the carotid artery and found a pulse. Moving his hand to Lance's face, he felt breathing. Lance would likely survive. Glancing at the hole he saw Lance's ankle at an odd angle. He may be limping for a while, but he should recover.

On the back of Lance's vest, Samuel found and removed the med kit, and set it aside. He then rummaged a knife out and ripped out the seam on the burnt pant leg from the knee down. Gently he uncovered the blistered and pocked calf, revealing a mass of blood and dirt. He slowly washed it clean using Lance's canteen, pausing to deal with the pain of the process every few seconds. Minutes later, satisfied with the job, he stopped and examined the red and swollen calf.

From the med kit he took a canister of un-burn and sprayed the injured flesh until the gooey medicine started dripping off. He then sprayed on a sealer, forming a black cast around the calf. It was flexible, and held the healing salve against the wound.

He turned his attention to Lance. The large man's body lay sprawled. The blood around the cut had clotted. Samuel removed Lance's utility vest and took all his weapons, placing everything a few meters away by a tree.

He sat down against the tree where he could keep an eye on Lance and tore into one of the meal packs. The artificial, reconstituted beef jerky tasted tangy and sweet. It had never tasted delicious before. He savored every bite. Only the water tasted better. Boring old water was transformed into ambrosia. He finished the meal pack in less than a minute.

Resting after the meal, a sweet numb feeling enveloped him and his eyes began closing. Before sleep fully overtook him, Samuel splashed some water in his face. It would be folly in the extreme to fall asleep this close to Lance. Using the tree and his good leg he pulled himself up. He wavered a little, probably from trauma.

He fastened on the vest and all of Lance's equipment. After a last swig from the canteen he scanned the tree branches for anything that could be fashioned into a crutch. A forked branch looked perfect. It took two blasts with the pulse pistol to bring it down. A couple more and he made it into a serviceable crutch. The crude device scraped under the arm pit. He smoothed it some with a knife to make it tolerable.

Lance still lay unmoving, breathing regularly. Samuel spared him one last glance, turned, and limped away.

"You just going to leave me here like this?" Lance's voice came from behind

Samuel paused, looking back. He opened his mouth to speak but thought better of it and started away again.

"Stupid Roach!" Lance called. "Leave me alive and you'll regret it. You know I'll come after you and you'll beg for death by the time I'm through with you."

Samuel turned raising the pulse pistol. "Are you asking for death, Lance?"

"You can't kill me. You're a weakling sap." Lance gingerly touched the wound on his head. "You're smart. I'll give you that. But you're too stupid to kill me. Wimps like you make me sick"

"You know the difference between us, Lance?"

"I'm strong and you're weak."

"You represent the worst of humanity. All the vile and cruel tendencies the better of our race have tried to purge out have come to fruition in you and your like."

"Save me the lecture. You're a grub, just like those little parasites you love so much. You just happen to look human." Lance hissed.

"Why thank you," Samuel said with a grin which he immediately replaced with a scowl. "I'd much rather be associated with them than the likes of you."

Samuel turned his back and stumbled away, ignoring the threats and curses Lance flung after him.

Chapter 6: Eye-Storm

Samuel measured off a piece of tape and pressed it down firmly along the length of the cast. It sizzled and grew into a bubbling, green seething mass where the tape had been.

Noxious vapors rose in a mist from the chemical reaction. Samuel jerked away from the vile fumes.

The sizzling faded and a strip of skin lay exposed where the bandage had dissolved away. Squeezing his fingers under the edges, he pried the material from his calf.

For the first time in three days, none of the small wounds bled. Most were little white splotches of new skin; a few were scabbed over. A complete examination of the leg revealed no bleeding or open wounds.

He broke out the sterilizing spray and applied it to the injured skin. The open air felt cool and refreshing against the exposed flesh, much better than the burning and itching of the cast. His leg would be safe from infection now that the wounds were closed.

Planting the base of his walking stick into the ground, he pulled himself up. The staff, cut from an iron rope tree, easily held his weight. He rubbed his armpit and winced. It was tender from the crutch he had thrown away the day before.

Shielding his eyes he looked out into a bright day. To the north, rolling hills ascended from the plain. The in between still lay before him for another day's journey or so.

Leaning on his staff, he stepped from the sheltered shade of the tree line. Every day since the fight with Lance walking became easier, except in the morning. The recovering muscles seemed to contract during the night and fought against movement until he'd walked for a few minutes.

Beads of sweat gathered on his face as he trudged under the blazing sun. Taking out the canteen, he shook it. The light splashing indicated near emptiness. He allowed himself only a mouthful.

As Samuel continued on sweat soaked through his clothes. It seemed that he constantly wiped it away from his eyes.

Wet? He thought. On every previous day perspiration evaporated almost immediately. He stopped and looked around. The environment looked the same as the past few days. He couldn't have traveled into a different climate zone. The weather pattern must have changed, bringing in moisture from some large body of water. He regretted not studying the lay of the geography before landing.

Oh, well, he thought, *can't do anything about it now.*

He turned in a circle to get a full view of the surroundings and stopped part way through. Large black clouds billowed in the southwest sky. As if on cue, a wave of wind rolled across the grassland and washed over Samuel.

Ecosystems vary widely between planets and even within regions on a single planet. He couldn't predict whether this storm could plod along or race across the landscape. Samuel, about midway between two tree lines, turned his back to the storm and picked up the pace. First and foremost, he needed shelter.

The wind grew and whipped the dry, brown grass. Just a few more steps and he'd be under trees. He glanced over his shoulder. The darkness of the clouds covered about one third of the sky. In a few minutes, maybe an hour and he'd be engulfed in rain or hail or whatever the storm brought down.

The trees loomed just before him. As he went to step forward they wobbled impossibly. He shook his head. They couldn't bend to the ground and stand up. The colors faded and blushed, grass, trees, and sky.

The walking stick wavered as well. The storm would be on him soon. He wondered if it were some kind of pressure effect?

He forced his feet forward. With the first step the disorientation faded. He paused for just a moment. It would be an interesting effect to examine if he had more time. At the moment he needed shelter, and so he lunged into the wood.

His breath came easier, his chest stopped heaving and the pulse beating in his ears faded. Life was good, he felt.

A smile grew upon his lips, and he chuckled. What did it matter?

A rustling came from the distance. In the upper branches a form moved. Samuel dropped to his knees and held his arms out wide.

Tentacles wrapped about the trunk of a nearby tree. Golden fur shone in the shafts of light that filtered through the vegetation.

It was the soft, kitten fur he had seen shortly after his arrival. Peace flooded him, and he welcomed it. He could barely think.

As the native moved closer, Samuel watched, unable and unwilling to resist the advance.

The native stretched out a whip-like tentacle. Samuel held out his right hand. Soon he would feel the gentle fur.

The tentacle wrapped about his wrist. Neither cold nor clammy, it pulsed with pleasure and comfort.

"Are you the one called Samuel Rochez?"

The question dissipated the fog filling Samuel's mind. "You are one of the Home-kind? Do you know Jawell? Is he all right?"

"It is nice of you to ask about my brother traveler. He returned to the home-kind as you told him.

"We have all heard of you."

Samuel suddenly realized that he was speaking to the native without the translation equipment. "I can understand you. How is this possible?"

"I am sorry. I understand that your-kind's preferred means of talk is through some strange tool. But, you do not seem to have it with you. Please forgive me for the direct contact. It is the only way the home-kind can talk with other-kind."

Samuel laughed out loud.

"Ah, Jawell did not tell us that you other-kind could be merry. Your-kind is only the second the home-kind have found that can speak."

Samuel wiped a tear from his eye. "I used the equipment because I didn't know Jawell was telepathic. It would have saved me the better part of a day."

Instead of the replicated words of the translator, this communication carried feeling. Not the human inflection of voice and body language, but raw emotion flowed from the new native.

"What is your name?"

"I am named Jahara. It is joy to meet one so noble."

Samuel hung his head and shook it. He took a job that led him to kidnap one of the Home-kind and nearly got him killed in the process, and they called him noble.

"Have I said something wrong, Samuel Rochez? It was not what I meant..."

"It's all right. My kind doesn't like to be praised or complimented." The Home-kind sense of honor would keep him silent on the subject from then on.

"I understand. It will be hard for us, with one such as you among us, but it will not happen again."

"Come," Samuel said, "let's set up camp before the storm gets here."

"What is this camp that you speak of?"

"I'll show you. Come along."

As Jahara's tentacle unwrapped from Samuel's wrist, the world fell back into focus. The presence of the little native still calmed his mind, but the overwhelming positive force had dissipated.

Samuel forced his way through the undergrowth while Jahara swung from branch to branch using his tentacles as a gymnast would his arms. Samuel's route was full of thorns and branches.

After a few minutes Samuel came into a small clearing and dropped to the ground panting. Worn from the days of marching and the extra effort of outrunning the storm he laid there just breathing and feeling his muscles begin to relax.

The first wisps of the approaching clouds appeared overhead like the advance scout of an army.

Samuel sighed. Jahara stayed up in the trees, hanging upside down under a wide branch.

"So that's how you stay dry," Samuel voiced to the quiet figure dangling like a large fruit. He smiled.

Shrugging the vest off his shoulders, he let it fall to the ground. He stretched his arms and back, letting the cooler air blow across him.

From a rear pocket he removed a grapefruit sized globe. Around the center were eight pairs of eyelets and hooks. Lance must have used it a lot. The eyelets hung floppy from the sides, instead of being pulled tightly to the body.

The clearing was a bit higher than its surroundings. It had some small vegetation, but no worse than his accommodations of the past several nights.

Trees ringed the clearing, leaving roughly a two-meter circle. Samuel walked to the nearest. Grabbing a hook he stretched the material around the tree and locked the hook into the companion eyelet.

Taking the opposite pair he stretched the material across the clearing, hooking it up to another tree about a meter off the ground.

Jahara glided to the ground and followed Samuel.

The blue material easily stretched, forming a line across the clearing. Samuel continued with each eyelet-hook combination until the clearing was covered.

Crawling under, he propped his walking stick up as a tent pole. Jahara followed him under the shelter. Linking up Jahara spoke.

"A portable roof is nothing the home-kind have ever seen. This is truly a work of wonder."

"It's very useful for my-kind. There are even fancier ones than this. The type that change colors to match their surroundings."

"Truly, this would be a marvel. Your-kind have a great many types of tools. I am most pleased to see some of them."

Samuel sat up to face his guest. But the canopy blocked his rise. Pushing up with one hand, he made room to sit up. When he let go however, the material molded around the top of his head down to his ears.

"There's only one problem," Samuel said, "It's too low. Poor assembly, I'm afraid. It needs one more pole to make it comfortable. I'll be right back."

"Hurry Samuel Rochez. The eye-storm will soon be upon us."

"Eye-storm?"

"An eye-storm will be over us in a very short time. I am certain, because the air feels like it. You must remain here until it is past us."

The hair on the back of Samuel's neck pricked up. It was suicide to leave the shelter. "What is it Jahara, what's going to destroy me?"

"There are bright flashes of light which are harmful for the Home-kind's eyes. Bad, loud sounds follow each. In the land of the Home-kind we hide in the caves until the eye-storm passes."

With each word Samuel's heart beat faster. Dig a hole. He could dig a hole to hide, like those creatures that burrow down to the water. Would that be deep enough?

There was nothing to dig with, maybe a grenade. Samuel sat back to look around and Jahara removed his tentacle.

Samuel pressed his hand against his chest and forced himself to breathe slowly. He felt all of Jahara's emotions as if they were his own. He must strive to remember this when linked in the future so that when the native burned with fear he could remain rational.

It dawned on him that this effect caused his euphoria when he met each of the natives. This race deserved more investigation. They would make a very interesting case study.

His pulse rate diminished. Just a lightning storm; Samuel had been through many on a wide variety of worlds. They were virtually the same on every planet. Just in case something unusual happened he'd make certain to return to the camp before the fireworks began.

The wind beat the woodland. Trees swayed and creaked. Branches and leaves rattled. They all combined with the roar of the wind to form a violent symphony.

It would be easy finding an iron rope tree; they wouldn't be swaying in the breeze.

A flash of light lit up the sky above the trees.

"One, two, three..." Samuel counted. "Nineteen," and the clap arrived.

He wandered off in the cloud-induced twilight. It took just a minute to find his quarry. Using the pulse pistol he blasted out a section that roughly matched his walking stick for the second tent pole.

The top of the iron rope tree fell into the clearing beyond the tree line. He thought it would be nice to bring some fruit back to Jahara.

He stepped out into the plain, the clouds boiled and churned with feral energy. The wind, unrestrained by the vegetation, blasted him full force. He leaned into it. Balancing against the blow, he stood drinking in the forces whipped up by the advancing storm and breathed deeply of the biting wind.

Lightning flashed, not a jagged trail, but a full sheet, like a curtain coming down. The countryside lit up brighter than under the sun.

He blinked, but it was still there. Slamming his eyes shut, he covered them with his hand, but it was still there, etched on his retina.

"Absolutely wonderful," he yelled. It was foolish. It was dumb! Knowing nothing of this planet, it was stupid to treat a storm so lightly.

His vision might clear up, given enough time. But he would have to survive until that happened. Despite the cooling air and wind, Samuel wiped the sweat from his palms.

The vest, and all of its gear, lay safe under the tent back at the camp. All he had with him was a gun. What value did a gun have to a blind man in a storm? Samuel felt the handle of it just to verify that it was still there.

He reminded himself to think. "The mind is the most powerful tool you have." The phrase had been drilled into him from instructors and mentors throughout his life. He, in turn, passed it on to others.

Samuel took a few deep breaths. The camp was a short walk behind him. Turning, he reached out and took a tentative step forward, no trees, nothing to trip on. He hadn't moved far into the field. It should not take more than one or two steps to reach the tree line. He stepped again, but still no trees.

The wind beat against his back. It must be the correct direction, unless the wind changed direction while he was distracted. He might have taken a few steps. He tried to go over it in his mind. Had he turned, stepped or moved at the moment he blinded himself? His stomach rose, blocked by the lump in his throat.

"Think Samuel," he told himself. He had come out to cut down a tent pole. An iron rope tree lay on the ground, and one end rested in the trees. He knelt down and stretched his hands out through the brittle shafts of grass.

Working hard to keep his feet in one location, he moved around, reaching out in a circle. Nothing but grass, not even a small shrub. A shrub wouldn't have helped. He hadn't taken time to review his location before the lightning strike.

Jahara couldn't help. He would be under the shelter trembling with fear.

Samuel laid out flat on the ground and stretched. Working out in a spiral, eventually he'd find the trees or the iron rope. He scurried around in the dirt as the first drops of rain splattered on his back.

All of the rain gear was in the vest back at the shelter. A brilliant planetary researcher wouldn't have left the shelter with a storm approaching. An experienced one would have stayed close and returned quickly. Only a rank novice waits transfixed as destruction approaches.

He squeezed his eyes tight and opened them again. There was nothing but the cloudy image of the lightning.

Rain dropped around him, splashing bits of mud all over. He spat out a bit that landed on his lips.

The roaring sound of the approaching water fall told him he had only a few seconds to find shelter.

His hand latched onto something round, slick, and hard, the iron rope tree!

Pulling himself closer and up on his knees, he reached up one way and then the other. The end was out of reach. He worked his fingers underneath it and curled them around the shaft. Lifting one end and then the other, he went to the heavier end, following it hand over hand.

The rain poured on him as if from a bucket. In two seconds he was soaked. His waterlogged clothes pulled on his arms and body.

The ground became ankle deep muck. Pulling one foot from the mud sunk the other deeper. The wounded leg throbbed. After only a minute he was breathing hard, sucking the rain swollen air into his lungs.

He pulled himself a step further and the rain changed. Instead of small drops, great globs of water bombarded him. Stepping back, the rain returned to the continuous pelting of thousands of smaller darts of rain. It had to be the trees. The leaves would collect the raindrops and dump them when the volume built up.

He worked a few steps forward. Under the canopy, very few globs struck him. The echoing of millions of rain drops against leaves and branches filled the air. Only the occasional thunder broke through the din.

With each step he stretched his arms, reaching for the trees. A few steps later his fingers brushed a rough vertical structure. He pulled himself in, hugging the large tree and breathed heavily into its bark.

If that were the start of the monsoon season he could be trapped for days. However, the vegetation did not match the established pattern for monsoons. One mistake would be enough for that day; he wasn't going to make another by assumption.

Resting his weight on the trunk, only the occasional drip struck him. If he could see, he would build a primitive shelter. No, if he could see, he'd go back to the camp and wait out the storm with Jahara.

Blind and pulling himself through the muck he'd never find the camp. He turned and leaned against the tree. The bark scratched against his back. He shuffled around to find the least uncomfortable position and tried to sleep.

The night went on and on. The rain stopped but the branches and leaves above him continued to drip for hours.

He first felt the warmth of the sun on his feet. It worked its way up his legs in a slow steady march. The storm must have passed. If it were overcast he'd feel little to no warmth. He relaxed into the light. The radiant heat began evaporating the moisture from his drenched clothes and limbs.

As he lay enjoying the warmth a rustling came from his left. He jerked his body up and turned in the direction of the sound. That would scare away any creature that wasn't looking for a fight.

Whatever it was, it continued to rustle its way closer. Before thinking the gun was in his hand and pointing in the direction of the sound.

It could be Jahara, Samuel realized. He removed his finger from the trigger, but kept the muzzle pointed towards the noise. Unable to aim, there was little chance the gun would save him unless he proved very lucky.

A breeze swept over his right shoulder. He leaned into it slightly, letting it caress the back of his head. It was going to be a glorious day.

The peaceful feeling filled him, and in its essence the presence of Jahara made itself clear.

As the tentacle wrapped around his arm, he was transported into the world of his mind. Jahara sat across from him in a nondescript white area.

"Is your body injured, Samuel Rochez?"

"I ignored your advice and walked right into it. I'm sorry, Jahara. I should have listened. The eye-storm blinded me!" His frustration must have filtered through because Jahara cringed. The feeling of panic fed back to Samuel. The tentacle snapped away from his arm and plunged Samuel back into nothingness.

"Jahara," he called. What was wrong with the native? Both Jawell and Jahara had bubbled over with friendship. What would cause the native to pull away just as Samuel needed him?

Minutes passed while Samuel listened. The feeling or sound of Jahara did not come back. Samuel might be on his own until his vision cleared or he died.

Dying felt like a bad option. "Jahara," he called again. The native must have some form of auditory sense. Nothing but the wind blown leaves responded. He strained to hear any sound that indicated Jahara was near by.

Animals chattered over head. The last of the rain dripping off the vegetation splashed on the ground. The sun continued its warming journey up his legs. A dull yellow fog made up his visual world.

Stumbling blind across the landscape would be pure folly. It would take a miraculous amount of luck to stumble upon the camp. In his condition he couldn't identify many edible plants. Would starvation be his final fate, he wondered.

He shook his head. There must be some way to survive. So far, the weather hadn't turned cold enough to kill. He hadn't come across any large predators. So, food and water were the critical items.

He needed sight to identify any local food plants, except iron-rope fruit. He'd cut down the trees to get fruit for Jawell before. The one he'd intended to make a tent pole from should be a very close.

His muscles complained as he leaned away from the tree. He spent a few seconds stretching his back, and then reached out to his left. Just at the length of his reach his fingers wrapped around the prone tree.

Working his way down the trunk he found the tufts of leaves at the end. It only took a moment to find one of the round fruits. He allowed himself a smile. The iron rope trees could keep him alive until his sight returned. The tree is common and easily identified. He would just have to grope around the stand until he came upon them. As long as the power held out in his gun, he could blast them down as needed. He reached down and felt the handle of the gun again.

The sweet juice filled his mouth as he savored every drop. The sun warmed him. The left side of his body became uncomfortably warm, which meant that he faced south.

He ate another and pocketed the other two for later. The base of the fallen iron rope was within the trees. He would follow it along the ground to get back into the woods. He headed hand over hand, down the prone tree. Reaching out he felt the skinny twigs of shrubs, the rough and smooth bark of wide trunked trees.

A few vestigial drops of water echoed through the wood. Occasionally one landed on him.

Minutes passed. Iron rope trees seemed plentiful the day before. More minutes passed. His arms were scratched up and aching.

After what seemed like hours he came upon a wide tree with smooth bark. Taking a deep breath he heaved himself over and sat against the tree, listening to the environment. He wiped sweat from his brow and wished for a cool breeze.

As he munched on one of the fruits, he felt Jahara. Turning his head from side to side, he searched for the sound of approach. Nothing but the normal woodland sounds came to his ears.

Something flopped as a blast of wind rushed over his head. From the sound, something landed directly in front of him. He guessed that the beating of Jahara's wings had caused the wind.

Reaching out, his fingers rubbed upon a woven fabric. His vest, Jahara had returned his vest.

"Yeah!" Samuel called out. He pulled out a food bar, leaving the bigger food stuff for later, and ate it quickly. It wasn't sweet like the fruit, but felt more substantial in his stomach. Finding the canteen he took a swig and put it back with a satisfied sigh.

A rush of wind and thump in front of him indicated that Jahara had landed.

Samuel held his position, unmoving. He didn't want to scare the native away again. Doing anything might be the wrong action.

The sounds of movement grew louder. The peaceful feeling mildly touched against his mind, but it was weaker than in times past. The best word for it would be reserved.

Jahara took longer than at any other time, an approach of caution. The tentacle gently rested on his hand, instead of wrapping firmly around his wrist.

"Samuel Rochez, are you feeling any better now that you have the outer clothing?" Jahara's voice whispered as if blown on the wind from a great distance. His representation in Samuel's mind was ghost-like.

"I'm doing well, considering."

"Then, you have recovered from the depression you were feeling earlier."

"I'm not happy with the situation: and, I'm very disappointed with myself, but now that it's happened there is nothing that can be done about it. Just make the best with what we have to work with."

The tentacle wrapped tightly around Samuel's wrists and Jahara's presence was fully represented.

Chapter 7 Ordeal

They trudged on, each footstep higher than the last, climbing, always climbing. A brief descent would have done wonders for Samuel's calves. His legs moved on their own, simple repetition: up, down, right, left. It all melded into a blur, the last minute like the last hour. Time didn't seem to pass in his darkened world. The only sign of an outside was the moving feet and the voice. The smells meant little to him, nor did the sounds, except for the voice. The air had cooled, though he still perspired with the effort. The only things in his world were the trudging and the voice.

"Foot of a tree at your next step. Please, step high over it," Jahara said.

Samuel gave up responding hours before. Breathing heavily, he dragged his feet forward. He steadied himself on trees, vines, and his staff as they struggled through the wooded areas.

"You seem to have become tired of body. Is it not time for us to rest until the dark-time?" the voice said in his head.

With that little bit of encouragement Samuel came to a full stop and gently lowered himself to the ground. Massaging his calves, he wondered when the trekking would get easier.

Samuel felt through his pockets and came out with a food bar. Maybe twelve remained in his vest. One didn't make a full meal, but it would be enough to satisfy for the night.

"Samuel Rochez, would it be helpful if I brought back something that you would like to eat?"

"About the only thing I know I can eat is the fruit on the iron rope trees."

"Yes, those are liked by the Home-kind. We have been blessed with many of them in the Home-kind's land. I will go and get many for us. It is a great honor to help in this way. The giving of food is one of the highest forms of helping."

"Then I will be honored by your helping. And thank you for all your assistance. I'd probably die out here if it weren't for you."

Samuel smiled as Jahara's pride and happiness flooded into him. "There is nothing here to be a danger to one as large as you. The only is the lack of eating and drinking, which happily I will help you with, my companion."

With that the air swirled around Samuel as Jahara's wings beat close to the ground. The breeze felt thankfully cool. Goosebumps rose up on his exposed arms. Samuel laid his weary torso back with a sigh and munched on the bar.

###

Samuel awoke. Slowly he came to full consciousness. He sat up and groped in the grass around him. His left hand found his cane while the right found the half eaten food bar.

Something rubbed against Samuel's leg. He instinctively pulled away, but it stayed there.

"You have been asleep for well into the light-time. Is this normal for your-kind to do this after every dark-time?"

"Jahara, oh, sorry I was a bit disoriented. Um," he stammered getting his thoughts together. "Yeah, we tend to sleep longer than the Home-kind. Why didn't you wake me? We could have started off at first light."

Samuel felt the amusement seeping in from the little native. He hadn't told a joke, but he couldn't keep a slight smile off his face.

Jahara's voice seemed light. "Samuel Rochez, that would not be of a help to you in any way."

The question was silly, Samuel realized. Jahara explained as to a child who had asked why they can't have desert before supper.

"If Your-kind has a need for a longer amount of rest than the Home-kind, then it is the rest that you should be getting. I could never force you from your rest. It would not be helping."

"Well then, we should get going."

"Perhaps it would be wise for you to have something to eat before we begin the journey for this light-time."

Samuel, now fully awake, felt his stomach emptiness. "Sounds like a good idea to me."

Jahara spoke amid the sound of rustling grass, "I am rolling the fruits that I gathered over next to your leg."

Samuel began patting the ground beside his right leg.

"I am sorry, Samuel Rochez, for not being clearer. The fruits are near to your other leg."

The native's embarrassment seemed to push his words out. "That's okay, Jahara. You've done nothing wrong. You have brought food to a blind person. You have greatly helped."

Jahara swelled with pride. Could the Home-kind share feelings? Jahara could certainly transmit to humans and Samuel seemed to be able to affect the native's mood.

"Forgive the question, but may I ask why you are not with Your-kind, but out here seeking to meet with the Home-kind?" Jahara asked as Samuel bit into a fruit.

"Jahara, I want to warn the Home-kind."

"What is it you wish to warn about?"

"Another-Kind is going to come to this land. They are called the Loscar. There will be many, many of them. They are different from the Home-kind and My-kind.

"They are coming for the crystals, and they will take most of them away from here."

"It is certain that the Home-kind will help in this work. The crystals have no value for which the Home-kind need them."

"Yes, but in this case, however, they will not need any help. In fact, they may be a danger. I must talk to the Loscar before they meet the Home-kind.

"To do that, the Home-kind must let me know when the Loscar arrives and avoid them until I have spoken to them."

"Samuel Rochez, what is the danger that they could cause to the Home-kind?"

"Well," he paused, "worst case, it's possible that they may use the Home-kind for food."

"For food?"

Samuel felt the confusion emanating from the native.

"But, that cannot be. The Home-kind is not food. We do not grow in the ground."

Samuel leaned forward. "Is there no kind on your planet that eat other kind?"

Samuel felt the shock and horror strike him, and couldn't keep his breath from shortening and Pulse racing.

"Samuel Rochez, this thing cannot be. All kind only eat plants. It is very strange where you come from. We must move quickly to avoid this danger. Come, we must go."

"Jahara, wait. They are not here yet."

Samuel tried to push some calming emotion towards his companion. It seemed to work as the tension dropped almost immediately.

"When is it that these Other-kind will be here?"

"Don't know exactly," Samuel massaged his recovering calf. "Stagar thought we had about a week. They'll do an orbital survey, of course."

Mentally ticking off the days spent on planet with probably time for research before landing, he calculated an estimate.

"Five to ten days," he said. "And, it will take a while before they start exploring the country side."

"That is not a very long time, Samuel Rochez."

"No," he shrugged, "but it should be enough. They'll want to come to the richest cache, just like we did. So, the odds are they'll set up somewhere near here.

"I've had dealings with the Loscar before and should be able to make a smooth introduction."

Jahara seemed satisfied with that and they started off.

###

Samuel zipped up his vest against a chilling gust of wind. The higher the elevation, generally, the cooler the temperature, he reminded himself. It didn't seem that they had climbed high enough to account for the temperature change.

"The cold, Jahara, is another storm coming?" They'd need shelter if it was. Wet and cold were a deadly combination.

"It is not to be, Samuel Rochez. It is simply the type of clouds that come with cold air. It should only be with us for up to two light times."

Samuel checked the vest with his free hand; weather jacket and blanket were there. Lucky thing Lance packed properly.

"No," he mumbled. Lance forces someone else to do it, and chews them out if any little thing isn't right. Knowing Lance, he'd chew them out even if it was perfect.

"What is it that you say 'No' about?" asked Jahara. "We are moving slower as you have asked."

"Sorry, Jahara. I was thinking about something else."

"What is it that you were thinking about? Most of the time your thoughts are a cloud to me."

"It was about one of My-kind. There are important things that I need to tell the Home-Kind about."

"I would very much like to hear about it. It would be very kind if you were to tell."

"Okay, some of My-kind are not nice, and this one is very unkind."

"This is very strange. How can it be that you are part of Your-kind and you are very kind? Is not this other of Your-kind?"

"Just because one of My-kind behaves in one way, it doesn't mean that any other will act in that same way."

"But, is it not true that you are all One-kind? How can one act differently than another? It is not the way the winds created Kinds."

"Each person of My-kind is actually their Own-kind."

Jahara didn't respond immediately. Samuel could feel the native's confusion as he tried to work through the concept.

"Your-kind all come from the same dwelling place, you look to be the same-kind, you work together as if one-kind. How could it be that you are all different-kind? It does not seem that it could be possible."

Samuel's right foot caught on something. His weight already being forward, he fell. Gripping the staff with both hands he managed to slow the fall and land on his side rather than his face. The thud knocked the wind out of him.

"Jahara?" he called. There was no response. Quickly dropping the staff he stretched out, feeling for his companion. Under his knee he felt the soft fur and firm flesh of Jahara.

Lifting his leg he gently extricated the native. The tentacles moved about. It could have been death throes or just the result of stunning, as far as Samuel knew. But soon Jahara roused.

"Jahara, are you alright?"

Samuel sat and held Jahara in his lap. The tentacles continued writhing.

"Jahara," he called, but again no answer. He sat there cradling the native as the cold wind wafted about them. Finally a spark of light lit in Samuel's mind. Slowly, it grew until Jahara returned.

"Are you hurt?" Samuel asked.

"I do not appear to have any significant injuries. Have you suffered any injuries yourself?"

"No, I'm just happy you're okay."

"Jahara, I think it is best," he paused reflecting on his word choice, "Helpful for both of us, if we keep our conversations to a minimum while we travel. I don't want to see either of us hurt."

"There is wisdom in that, Samuel Rochez. I will be more watchful."

They trudged along further up into the hills with one of Jahara's tentacles wrapped around Samuel's leg.

###

Samuel stumbled to his knees. The soft mossy ground welcomed him. His aches melted into sleepiness. He disconnected from Jahara and flopped to the ground.

Jahara's voice drifted in, "We have traveled a great distance today. Continuing on, as the sky's wish, it will take us but seven more light-times to reach the Home-kind."

"It will be nice to see Jawell again. It would be nice if I could see by then." Pulling off his glasses, Samuel rubbed his eyes. "What?" he muttered.

With the glasses on, the world was black as death. With them off however, the world was a very dark gray. To test the observation he removed and replaced the glasses in quick succession. Each time he detected the difference. A smirk came to life on his face as a chuckle escaped.

"I can see! Jahara, I can see." Reaching out, he caught his companion in a hug.

"That is good for you, Samuel Rochez. You must certainly be happy."

"Well, not fully, you know, like normal. But I can tell the difference between light and dark. Is it still light-time?"

"For a very short time, yes it is light time." For the first time Samuel couldn't recognize Jahara's emotional state. Perhaps his friend had been learning, too.

###

"Wake-time," said the voice in Samuel's head. He rolled over to a more comfortable position. "Wake-time," the voice persisted. It was dawning on his sleep soaked mind that Jahara was speaking.

"A bit more time, Jahara, please?"

Tentacles wrapped around his shoulders and he was rolled over onto his back.

"Aw," Samuel complained. "I thought it was the ultimate goal to help others."

"It is, Samuel. I'm helping you to wake up."

"Why don't you fly off and get some food while I rest a bit longer? We need to eat before we start anyway."

"No, I can't leave you while you are asleep and cannot protect yourself."

"I thought that nothing around here could hurt me?"

"Perhaps you'll move in your sleep and hurt yourself. You make many strange sounds while sleeping."

Resigned, Samuel sat up and forced his eyelids open, darkness. Lately, he'd been able to detect daylight when the black shadow etched in front of him turned grayish. But this was completely black. It must be the barest glimmer of light that started Jahara.

Samuel blew out a slow breath of air, probably creating a fine mist in the cool morning air. Still, the temperature continued to rise as they made their way down the mountains. The field blanket, undoubtedly, had saved his life the past few nights.

Samuel rose. Jahara took his normal position. Over the previous several days, it became a reflex. It required no thought. They both fell into their allotted roles.

They trudged on to the north, continuing their descent from the hills. More and more time was taken up moving around vegetation and stepping over roots and logs.

A rumbling sound came from ahead. It was faint, a constant drone. As they continued, the rumble became louder. Often it was drowned out by the wind blown leaves, but whenever the air fell slack the rumble returned.

Other than that the day wore on as on all previous days.

###

With another step the rumbling sound that underlay the previous day's travel overwhelmed the wind and dominated all sound except the words of Jahara.

"What is that?" Samuel asked.

"It is water that is moving."

"It must be a good sized river by the sound of it." Samuel moved his head side to side and determined that the sound came from in front of them. "And we are headed directly for it."

"Yes," responded Jahara in a very mild tone. "Once we pass over it will only be two or three light-times to the Home-kind."

Samuel put his hands on his hips and stretched his back. "And, how are we going to cross it? Is there a bridge or something?" Because the natives flew Samuel believed it unlikely they built and kind of walkway over the river.

"Have not Your-kind a means of passing over moving water? It would seem that All-kinds would have this ability in some way."

Samuel paused. Jahara's response was more analytical than he'd heard before. Hopefully he wasn't rubbing off on the native.

"We build things to cross over rivers: boats, bridges, or some others."

Samuel pondered for a moment.

"There could be a natural bridge, either rocks or a fallen tree. Can you see the river from here? Do you see anything like that, a walkway across the river?"

It was a moment before Jahara's response. "Yes, not too far out of our way a fallen tree amongst rocks."

Kneeling down next to the native Samuel rested a hand on its side. "Does it go all the way to the other side?"

"No. How close does it need to come to the other side?"

"Pretty close, actually. How close is it?"

"Close," came the simple response.

It was another situation where the differences in understanding broke down communications.

"If I could see it," Samuel stated, "Then I'd know if it is passable."

"But you can see it!" Jahara's being filled with excitement. "You can see through me."

"I'm sorry, what?" Samuel pulled his hand away.

"It is a way of teaching the very young. We could do it here and now."

Samuel felt some reluctance. "Does this work with Other-kind and will it cause harm to either of us?"

"It will not harm, but will be of help. Please let us try?"

It seemed the best of the options open to them. "Ok, then, what do I do?"

"Just relax."

Another tentacle wrapped about his ankle and in a moment he felt disoriented, like he was revolving head over heels. He tried to reach out to steady himself but his body ignored the impulse.

A green light exploded before him and then developed into a scene. Other colors resolved in until he recognized a hillside looking down into a valley with a river running down the center. The colors were off and the center of his field of view stood out, magnified more than the peripheral, but he could see.

Turning his head left and right, up and down river, he found the log. The close end wasn't on the bank but in still water, so he should be able to mount it.

As he focused on the log it came into even sharper relief. The Home-kind had an interesting vision system. About half way down the log it passed through the white spray of the rapids. That would be difficult to get by. Most of his body would be underwater right where the current raced the fastest. The end of the log extended past the middle of the river, but not past the current to the still water near the other side.

"No," he decided. It wouldn't work.

They had been disconnecting several times a day over the past week or so, but breaking this more complete connection took a bit longer and he had to steady himself to keep from falling over.

"That one won't work, Jahara," Samuel said with a sigh.

"What'd you expect?" came the curt reply.

"Jahara," Samuel asked, attempting to stare at the native. The response didn't sound like the native at all.

"Yes? Well, do you think you can make it?"

"Are you all right?"

"Of course, why wouldn't I be? You going to try to cross or what?"

Jahara sounded like a slightly annoyed human. Samuel hoped the effect would wear off. He hated to think he had permanently damaged his little friend. "Jahara, I think we should disconnect for a while so I can contemplate the options."

"If you must." Jahara cut the connection quickly.

After a few hours they reconnected and Jahara had recovered his previous personality.

###

"Jahara, I can feel that you're hungry. Go and eat, I'll be fine." He continued trying. It was impossible for Jahara not to feel his frustration.

"No, Samuel Rochez, I must remain with you. You may discover many forms of danger, injured as you are."

Samuel took a deep breath. As each hour passed, Jahara became more and more unreasonable. "If you starve to death who will guide us to the Home-kind? If you don't eat, I'll be left alone, lost in the wilderness."

Jahara's response came after a long pause. "I fear for you, Samuel Rochez."

Samuel jostled his glasses, rubbing the sore spots behind his ears. It hadn't taken Jahara any time to accept that logic just that morning.

"This is what we've been doing for days. Don't start worrying for me now. You need to eat. If you're too weak, you'll be the one needing help. Don't worry; I've got food for myself."

Samuel cut the connection. He hated being so forceful with the native, but it would be better than waiting for him to starve.

He felt the tentacle unwind from his leg, only to be replaced by one on the exposed flesh on his hand. Keeping his mind empty gave Jahara nothing to hold on to.

The pressure on his hand increased, making it a challenge to keep thoughts out. The hand throbbed from constriction so strong that it cut off circulation.

"Augh," Samuel opened his mind. "That hurts!"

A succession of feeling flooded out of Jahara, none stayed long enough to recognize. Finally it settled on whimpering shame, and Jahara left.

Samuel lay back on the ground, nursing the hand. The impressions on the skin were clear to the touch. Jahara was losing control of himself.

###

"Jahara, how long will it take to get to the Home-kind?"

"We have traveled quite well, and I believe that it will be another three light-times."

Samuel stretched the muscles in his back. "How long if you were to fly?"

"I would not fly away to leave you unassisted in your state."

"I know but out of curiosity, how long would it take flying?"

"It does not matter. As I have said, I would not leave you here."

"Well then, if another of the Home-kind were with us, how long would it take them to fly to the Home-kind?"

"Leaving at this point a home-kind would arrive well before the end of the light-time."

"Would they be able to get back before the end of light-time?"

"It is not possible, I think. The distance is too great."

"How about if they left at the very beginning of light-time?"

"The Home-kind would have to fly very fast, but it may be possible."

Samuel paused. Now came the tricky part. "It's not going to be easy to cross that river." He pointed toward the sound of the river.

"It has been very hard traveling for both of us. This is but another challenge. We will be able to pass it, as long as we are together!"

"Look down there!" Samuel demanded, "How is a blind man supposed to cross that. Do you know how heavy I am? And remember that I can't just fly over it." Samuel struggled to force down his frustration. "With some extra help..." He paused trying to find the right words. "A few more Home-kind..."

"All I try and do is help," Jahara cut him off. "I treat you with honor and respect, and assist in all things you need. Your complaining does not help."

Samuel had never heard Jahara, or Jawell for that matter, angry. Not only the native's voice, but his raw emotion barreled out. Taking a deep breath he steadied himself. "I'm sorry, Jahara. I shouldn't have become angry like that."

"I have reason to apologize as well. I have failed you."

Sincerity flooded over Samuel like a tidal wave. The exchange troubled Samuel. He dredged up a happy memory, focused on it and felt a shadow of the happiness. Rolling back his head, he laughed. It was forced, but enforced the positive feelings.

"Jahara, how do you feel?"

"I am happy we no longer share the blackness."

Samuel's mood sunk. Their form of telepathy showed some drawbacks. Being alone with an alien being for so long apparently wore on the native. He needed to get Jahara back to the Home-kind, and as soon as possible. Hopefully, they should be able to help him.

Jahara spoke up, breaking Samuel from his thoughts. "I am concerned about how we can cross the river below."

He reached out to Jahara, resting his hand on the native's side.

"And we can't just sit here."

As he moved his hand, he felt a bare spot.

"I will help you through every thing..."

Samuel cut him off. "You fur is coming out in clumps." Feeling over the native's body he found five other bald spots. "I don't think this is healthy."

"No, Samuel Rochez, you are mistaken. There is only a little. It is not worth your concern."

"We should join again, so that we can find a way across this river."

Samuel remembered times when he had been manipulated. With a twinge of guilt he recalled times he had used others. He let out a good long sigh.

He forced doubt from his mind. This had to be done to save Jahara. Squaring his chin he let resolution fill his being.

"Jahara, you can fly to the Home-kind."

"No, Samuel Rochez, it would not be good to leave you here alone."

"You can bring back help." He focused on an image of Jahara the hero.

"Are you very sure it would be safe for you, Samuel Rochez?"

The positive attitude seemed to affecting Jahara. "Everything will turn out well, because you can do it!"

"Yes, it would be possible I think. It is but one light-time, the sky willing."

"It is only a short time Jahara, easy for you."

Samuel felt determination build in Jahara. "You will do it, Jahara. You will save my life. You will have helped the supreme helping."

"Yes, I am off, Samuel Rochez, and will be back before the end of the light-time."

With that the link was broken and Samuel felt a gust of wind as Jahara took to flight.

Samuel dug into a pocket and removed a food bar. He assumed that Jahara wouldn't return until the next day. The Home-kind wouldn't let him return in the night. Hopefully Jawell would come and they'd keep Jahara, if they could help him? At least he'd be able to catch up on some sleep.

Quickly finishing the food bar, he washed it down. With some effort, he dislodged the blanket from its pouch. He had been unable to fold it properly by touch, and Jahara was little help with it. The sun warmed him as it melted into his body, giving him a comfortable calm feeling. It was time to make up for all the short nights.

Weariness faded to numbness as his thoughts drifted. Relaxing into sleep, Samuel closed his eyes.

"Samuel Rochez, you cannot sleep in the light-time."

Samuel bolted up, "what?"

"You are not a young-one, Samuel Rochez. It is not required for you to sleep during the light-time."

Samuel felt like he had just closed his eyes.

"Have you been to the Home-kind already? I must have slept through a whole night."

"No, I have been gone only a short time. I realized it was wrong to leave you. I will never leave your side again."

Chapter 8 Arrival

Stagar rested in the shadow of the ship, a light breeze cooling him. The air was still humid from the previous day's rain. Stagar wiped the sweat from his face with a handkerchief. All about him green shoots sprung up between the dead brown stalks of vegetation.

Scanning the area, his eyes came to rest on the well worn track leading from the ship, rutted from the wheels of the transport carts, and the feet of the men who ran them.

A cart lumbered along the trail kicking dust up into a ruddy-brown cloud. The work trudged on slower than Stagar hoped. The cart held no more than ten to twenty kilos.

Stagar ordered deliveries every hour to keep all the men busy, and in case of emergency. He smiled. Moving even small amounts meant that if they had to cut and run, not much Carlinium would be left behind. As the brains of the operation he did well, no detail too small.

There were three hundred seventy nine orders, each for two kilos. Each buyer believed they were purchasing what a single government inspector has managed to smuggle out of the carlinium storage facility at Tobos, Alnda. Of course, with the current rate of extraction not all the orders would be filled, but enough to be rich beyond all care. The buyers who lost out on the delivery would be the real winners.

Soon, very soon the price of Carlinium was going to crash. What they'd extracted so far was about one twelfth of the known supply. Thousands, maybe millions, times that amount rested in the crust of the planet.

Once news of the find got out, their stash would be no better than a load of standard ore. Stagar smirked.

"Donaldson, it's not break time, move it!" shouted Lance in the background.

Stagar looked back to the path. Lance, leaning heavily on his cane, had Donaldson by the collar, shaking him vigorously. Donaldson's canteen lay open on the ground.

A change had come over Lance after his hunt for Samuel. He limped into camp four days after leaving, scratched, bruised, and with a bad ankle. He immediately began terrorizing the men. Kim, the first to ask about Lance's injuries, ended up on the ground bleeding. The scene had been memorable. Stagar smirked briefly. Lance stood over the crumpled form, muscles tensed ready to pounce on the next person to comment.

Always a good intimidator, Lance had become more of a bully. He even belted the med-tech when he had the nerve to offer to repair the ankle. Even if the smaller intricate bones were broken, a simple procedure would have made it good as new.

But Lance settled for a cane and a limp.

Over the last three years Stagar had grown to ignore Lance's idiosyncrasy. The men, however, prone to gossip and speculation, traits of small minds, talked constantly about what may have happened. But the only thing the men said to Lance after that point was, yes.

Stagar looked back to see Donaldson picking himself off the ground and hurrying the cart towards the cargo doors, while Lance hobbled back towards the dig site. Lance would get this job done, and then Stagar would cut him loose.

He'd cut them all loose and go into semi-retirement, hand picking simple lucrative jobs. It would feel good to mix with a better group of men, where he wouldn't need an enforcer like Lance. He'd select jobs without the need for murderers and thugs.

Stagar allowed himself a small, satisfied smile. Maybe he'd even rub elbows with higher society.

Of course his appearance, name and history would have to change. He'd made a few too many enemies along the way.

"Stagar," a voce called from behind. He turned to face Roy Epstine, leaning out of the access hatch.

"Yes, Mister Epstine?" Stagar always used proper names. It instilled respect in the men serving under him. It's the details that matter.

"One of the long range buoys has picked up something."

Stagar followed him through the hatch. The interior odors burned at his nostrils. Pungent oils mixed nastily with ozone and metal. Why hadn't he upgraded the ventilation system before the mission? However, after a few minutes on board the smell just fades into the background. Humans could get used to just about anything.

Conduit and ductwork lined one wall of the passage. The other wall was bulwark against the outer hull.

"It may be ships," Epstine said, "at the edge of the buoy's sensor range."

"Then you're not certain?" They passed through the inner hatch into a hold filled with boxed up Carlinium

"No, not certain. But if it is, they'll be here in just a few hours. I thought you'd want to know as soon as possible."

Stagar always hired the best technicians he could get his hands on. It often meant the difference between success and failure. Stagar patted Epstine on the back. "You've done well, Mister Epstine."

They trotted up a flight stairs and entered deck three. Past four doors down the hallway they entered the sensor room. In the center of the room a low, flat-top console sat with a continuous bench around it. The walls were covered with displays and read-outs. Stagar wrinkled his nose upon entry. The room was filled with the regular ship scent plus musk and sweat. One look at Epstein's greasy hair introduced one to his personal hygiene. Epstine often slept in the sensor room rather then his quarters. Stagar suspected that it was to minimize the chances of running into Lance.

Epstine didn't seem to notice the smell. Stagar decided to set up extra air purification for the room; after all, comfort kept moral high. Even if Epstine didn't appreciate it, the rest of the crew might.

Epstine led the way to the center console and sat. Stagar stood over his shoulder. "See, Stagar, they're too far out for a clear reading."

The black display had the local solar system laid out. Planets, moons and asteroids as varying size dots with identification information. In the upper right area was a ghostly shape moving ever closer.

Stagar pulled out his transceiver and punched up Lance. "Lance, bring the men to the ship. There's a problem," he disconnected, not waiting for a response.

"Mister Epstine, can you get this any clearer? We need to know what's coming."

Epstine touched the blur on the display and a focus control pad popped up. The technician made adjustments but the image remained ghostlike. "Nope, not until they come closer. The passive sensors are limited. And if we use the actives, they'll know we're here for sure."

"Are they using active sensors?" Stagar asked.

"Nope," Epstine tapped another display above the one they were watching. "This board will light up if they do."

"They believe they are the first here, yes. Why run active scanning when they're too far away to get the resolution they need? That gives us a window of opportunity.

"Watch those blips, Mister Epstine, and let me know the instant you have resolution on them."

Stagar quickly made his way out of the ship and waited as men started coming out of the trees. It took a few minutes for them all to make it. The last man stumbled out with Lance yelling at his heels.

The men milled by the side of the ship as Lance and the straggler arrived. Lance called out: "What's up, Stagar?" It was the most he had said to Stagar since he came back. Which was another reason to cut him loose.

"The survey ships are early," said Stagar.

The men erupted into a mingling mass of voices. Lance yelled over them. "You said we had two more days."

"My informant must have gotten it wrong. There's a first time for everything. That doesn't matter now. We have less than two hours before they can see us clearly."

Lance immediately started calling out orders, "Simmons, Kim, you're fast, go get the last of the crystal. Be back in five or get left behind. The rest of you secure the cargo and prep..."

"Stop," Stagar yelled at the top of his lungs.

All faces turned to him.

"We are not leaving the planet. We need to clean up the..."

Lance ran up to Stagar, "What do you mean, not leaving?"

"If we take off we'll almost certainly be spotted. They can catch us on passive sensors, they're that close. When they get the first faint image they'll switch on the actives, and we'll be tagged. They'll have task forces waiting at every civilized planet."

"Not if we keep the planet between us and work our way to the local sun. We can keep that between us until we're out of range."

"Lance, the risk is too great. The planet doesn't have enough sensor shadow to make it to the local star. If they tag our ship, we will not be able to put in to any port and we'll be hunted down."

Lance stepped to within a meter of Stagar. "We have to take the chance. I'm not going to be put in any lockjaw prison."

"You won't. We'll hide. There's enough Carlinium to mask the ship. S. O. P. The Loscar always do an orbital survey; report back and in a week to a month a ground team comes in. Just a little patience and we'll get off free."

"No, no! Stagar. You've been making one bad decision after another on this operation." Lance began poking Stagar in the chest. "I should have cut you loose a long time ago. I've only kept you around to play nice with the customers. Now, we're doing things my way. We take the chance, we leave."

Lance turned around. The men were staring open mouthed at the scene of the two men arguing.

"Get moving," Lance hollered.

The men started for the cargo bay.

Stagar drew his stun gun and placed the barrel in the small of Lance's back.

"You wouldn't dare," Lance growled

"I make the rules, you enforce, that's the arrangement we made all those years ago. " Stagar wiped his brow. "You want to cut me loose? Well, okay. But, after this mission."

"Stagar, you're a convenience. Don't ever get the feeling you're anything more. You lead because I let you."

"That being as it may, we've made good money together. And, we've had our share of close calls. You remember Narclon four? This is just another close call. We'll make it. Trust me one last time."

Stagar removed the gun from Lance's back. "This is the only sure way to keep us out of prison."

Lance turned. His muscles tensed like he was holding back a raging bull. He poked Stagar in the chest to punctuate his words, his voice barely under control. "If that's the way you want it. But, this is the last time, Stagar, the last time."

Lance stormed off after the men in the hold.

It took half an hour of their dwindling time to clean the dig site and move the ship directly on top of the Carlinium deposit. Lance drove the men with malevolent efficiency. The rest of the time was taken collecting vegetation and draping it over the ship to camouflage from visual scanning. It added extra realism to the standard camo.

The men milled about the cargo bay. Stagar stepped out of a higher deck and addressed the crew. The men turned to face him and went silent.

"Gentlemen, we now go into stealth mode. The Loscar will be using active scanners, so we will remain in the ship for the duration. The ship's hull will hide our bio signs. Some of you may feel that the Carlinium outside would shield us. Besides electronic scanners, they use optical scanning, and Carlinium does not interfere with the visible spectrum of light. So we will remain safely inside.

"Also, they may be able to pick up any form of energy generation. Ship's systems have been completely shut down, and will remain down for the duration.

"And finally, we will subsist on cold rations alone. The food cart is locked up and will remain so for, again, the duration.

The murmurings of the crew reached Stagar. He could only pull out a few words, "cardboard, garbage," and a few other terms critical of the taste of the cold rations.

Stagar cleared his throat loudly to get attention. "Anyone who breaks these rules will be turned over to Mister Lance for discipline."

The men grew quiet again.

"Gentlemen, this is the state of affairs for the next several weeks. There is nothing we can do to change the situation, so make the best of it."

Stagar searched the group until he spotted Epstine. "Mister Epstine, meet me in the sensor room as soon as you can."

Stagar turned from the men and went back through the hatch into the crew section of the ship. Lance was waiting for him.

"Quite a stirring speech. I have one question, oh leader: considering we can't use passives, how are we going to know when the lock jaws are gone?"

"Mister Epstine," Stagar said calmly as he started down the corridors with Lance in tow.

Lance scrunched up his face. "Fatso? How can he help? He can't use any of his fancy toys."

Stagar nodded his head. "Mister Epstine has more resources than you know."

A few moments later they entered the sensor room.

"What a pig!" Lance said, just as Epstine burst into the room gasping for breath.

"Mister Epstine, thank you for coming so quickly." Stagar didn't wait for him to respond. "You have a device that we need, an optical lens device."

"Telescope?" panted the sensor-tech.

"Yes."

Epstine noisily pushed aside some boxes in front of a locker, and removed a long rectangular box. Placing it on top of the sensor console, he pulled out a cylindrical object with what could only be an eye piece sticking out of the side on one end.

"Mister Epstine," Stagar said, "you are to teach the entire crew how to operate the telescope. Set it up at the porthole in the mess hall. We've left that area clear enough to see through."

"Mister Lance," he continued, "I want the men on two hour shifts through the nights, logging every sighting, time and duration."

Lance slapped Epstine on the back. "So, you're not completely useless without your tech-toys."

Epstine, recovering from the blow took a step away from Lance and responded, "Apparently not."

Chapter 9 Crossing

Bonded and looking through Jahara's eyes, Samuel stepped into the river. The cold drag of the water pulled urgently at his legs. The frigid bite of the river would fade into numbness soon enough. Jahara came alive with terror as they entered the rushing river. Samuel struggled to block Jahara's panic.

His hands seemed distant as he saw them through Jahara's eyes. Groping out in front, he strained for the log that crossed the swiftest part of the river. The slightly greenish tint of Jahara's perception made colors less vibrant, but the image was much sharper then his own vision. He picked out small details of the surroundings, even in the distance.

Taking a deep breath, he focused on the task at hand.

Jahara retained a vice-like grip on Samuel's shoulders; his mind jumped from one horrible death to another.

Samuel struggled to fight back his own fears. With Jahara's on top of that, it was all he could do to keep moving forward.

Hip deep in ice water, he approached the log that straddled the river in the middle of a run of rapids. At one point the log lay submerged entirely in white foam.

Touching the log, he felt the driving force of the river vibrating through the mighty fallen tree.

Holding the end, he pushed off the slippery rocks to get his chest on top of the log. Jahara's weight shifted to one side and almost pulled him back.

Bracing his feet on the boulder supporting the trunk, he pushed up and got his hips on the log. Crawling forward, he used his hands to pull the combined weight of the two of them onto the log.

The splashing water soaked through all his clothing in just a few seconds. Jahara's fur must have been plastered flat against his body. Samuel wished he could see. It would have been his best chance to see what the body form was beneath the fur. He gave a wry smile. Their lives hung in the balance and he took the time to ponder alien anatomy. No wonder grunts hated techs.

Samuel righted himself, straddled the log and took a moment to gain back some composure and strength. Jahara's emotions appeared, thankfully, overloaded. The native seemed just shocked into silence.

Samuel moved his feet to try and feel them. The chilling water had done its work deadening his lower extremities. His feet wouldn't be out of the water again until they reached the other side. As long as he could control his legs and grip the log, they stood a chance of reaching the other side.

He had known cold on Kargan, but this exceeded that. On Kargan people could conserve body heat. The water dragged away internal heat as it was produced, washing it down river. If it were not for the baking sun he would be in the early stages of hypothermia.

He leaned forward and transferred his weight to his arms and scooched his hips forward.

In a few minutes they reached the point where the white water shot up over a boulder and crashed down on their bridge. Samuel reached into the crush of water and felt the trunk. Not only had the force of the water torn away the bark, but had also polished the wood smooth. He tried to put his hands directly on top, but the crashing water pushed them off.

Leaning down, he placed his chest on the log and wrapped his arms around. The log's size kept him from clasping his hand together on the opposite side.

Sitting up again, he removed his belt and wrapped one end around his right hand.

Lowering his chest to the log again, he reached around grasping the belt and looped it around his other hand until he had a tight grip on the log.

"Jahara, we're going to get very wet," Samuel said as they moved towards the fall.

As he came under the spray, he leaned into the current, letting it press him tighter to the log, rather than ripping him from it.

He would be able to hold on to the log. The danger was if he slipped and ended up under it. There would be no choice but to let go to the mercies of the raging torrent.

Slowly, like an inchworm, they came under the full force of the water. Jahara's emotions jumped from panic to sorry to depression and back. Each change struck Samuel like a slap to the face. He had to stop moving forward to contend with Jahara's feelings.

Samuel found it hard to breathe. They were mostly submerged with the falling water compressing them against the log.

Pushing on, a centimeter at a time, they finally emerged from the shower. As they cleared it, Samuel sat up and took stock of his body. Legs: cramped, Arms: trembling, Teeth: chattering, Feet: still numb. The water level reached above his knees.

Having made it past the worst spot on the transit, Samuel began to feel more hopeful that they'd make it.

Forward progress continued until they came to a large branch protruding up into the air. Samuel leaned all his weight into it, but it didn't break. Then he rested his weight against it, and relaxed his legs a bit. The fact that the branch hadn't been broken off in the log's tumble downstream indicated its strength.

Pulling his legs from around the log to get beyond it seemed too dangerous. His only option left was to blast it off.

Samuel looked around using Jahara's eyes. They only had one minor rapid to go, then ten meters to get out of deep water. The log lay low in the water, nearly submerged. The current's strong tow still pulled at his legs.

Moving back a bit he examined the distance to the branch. Too close and they might be hit by splinters or the falling branch. Too far and he might miss and weaken the log. The flash might also startle Jahara. He pushed back a bit more.

Concentrating on Jahara's sight he reached behind him to get Lance's rifle. Just then, Jahara moved and their collective center of gravity changed. Samuel tried to grip with his legs, but the numbness kept them from responding quickly enough. The water enveloped them.

The churning water tossed them down stream. The roar, muffled while underwater, broke anew as he surfaced.

His vest had inflated to drag him up out of the water. He put effort into seeing through Jahara's eyes, but saw only the sky as a light haze. Everything else was black. Reaching back he only felt the vest, shirt, and the butt of the gun, no Jahara.

The current overcame the buoyancy of the vest and dragged him under. He popped back to the surface a few seconds later, coughing up water.

Without Jarhara's sight he could only make out the horizon.

He splashed around until his feet were downstream of his head. As rapids came up he used his feet to push off to the right, always the right. They had been closer to that bank when they fell in.

He came to the first rapid. As his feet hit the boulder, his knees buckled and he launched head first over the rock.

The cascade of water dragged him down to the riverbed. The water pressed him hard against the gravel bottom. Straining against the force of water proved futile. Grasping with his hands and kicking his feet, Samuel tried to wriggle free. His right hand brushed something large. Bringing his other hand to bear, he found a crack in the boulder and wedged his fingers in.

His lungs burned as he pushed and pulled. Putting all of his strength into one massive push he managed to move enough that the current around the eddy pulled him free.

He popped to the surface, hacking and grasping for breath. Water crashed around his head. Energy almost gone, he struggled to get his feet downstream again.

He could no longer feel his fingers. Two minutes, maybe three, then his muscles would freeze and he'd drown. The vest might keep him alive a bit longer, but without the use of his limbs, he wouldn't last long.

He felt the impact in his hips as his feet struck a rock. Locking his knees he beat his arms against the water and managed to slide around the right side.

His arm struck an exposed rock on his right as the current picked up force. Then his left arm rubbed against another rock surface, as if he were in a chute. Rough stone rubbed each arm, and occasionally his feet. Faster he accelerated and the walls moved in on either side. He struggled to keep his feet in front of him.

Suddenly, the current thrust downward. Samuel felt himself falling for a brief second before he submerged again.

When the vest popped him up to the surface this time, the current wasn't as strong. The roar of the river didn't press in on him as much. He started swimming to the right as fast as he could, struggling with the clubs that were his hands and feet.

When he felt bottom he tried to stand, but his limbs failed and he fell face first into the water again. Using his upper arms and elbows he crawled out of the frigid water onto a bank of loose stones.

The sun's warmth did little to stem his shivering.

For the first time since entering the water, he had the chance to think of Jahara. Alone in his mind again, he felt a sense of loss.

As he lay shaking with cold, he found himself mentally reaching out for Jahara. As with most flying organisms the Home-kind were deceptively light for their size. Jahara may be buoyant enough to float. However, no amount of buoyancy could save him from a large eddy that he might be pulled into.

Samuel could almost feel the panic, the utter loss that Jahara must be going through. When they had first met Jahara was curious and strong. Jahara's breakdown over time wore on Samuel.

His influence on Jahara had been unhealthy for the native. Would this be the fate of all the Home-kind once the planet was overrun with mining operations?

"I'm sorry, Jahara," Samuel said

As he focused on Jahara, he felt water all about him. Samuel splashed with his arms to get righted in the river. Through the corner of his eye he saw leathery wings, and for a moment this didn't startle him as he concentrated on navigating through the rapids.

Somehow Jahara pulled him in. With the more buoyant body it took much less time to swim to the riverbank.

As soon as Samuel/Jahara pulled himself out of the water, Samuel snapped back into his own consciousness, shivering on the bank.

The first order of business, survival, Samuel fumbled at his vest for a food bar. His fingers, still numb, bumped uselessly against the pocket flap. Using his forearms he pressed against the bottom of the vest pulling it up closer to his head. The vest buckled and folded as he continued his efforts.

Raising his head, he attempted to grab the flap with his chattering teeth. Several times he missed, and gave up.

Dragging himself up the bank, he eventually made it past the rocky bank onto an area of dusty soil. He pushed his hands into the dirt, hoping the sun-baked soil would reinvigorate his dead hands.

He lay on the ground, with constant sunshine, but he shivered still. Every few minutes he tried flexing his fingers. Slowly, they started to respond.

Regaining control of his body, he rolled over to let the sun bake his front for a while. He successfully got a food bar and unwrapped it. Between the sun and his chewing, his face warmed up enough that his teeth stopped chattering.

Sitting up, he flexed his toes to check the recovery of his lower extremities. He gingerly rose to his feet, checking his balance along the way. When he felt reasonably comfortable that his legs would hold, he paced around in a circle to get the blood flowing.

Feeling somewhat himself, he unslung the rifle and felt the safety, making certain it was on. Then, holding it in his right hand he used it as a cane, scanning the ground in front of him for obstacles.

Lance would be infuriated to know his gun was used in this way. This gave some small pleasure to Samuel as he made his way back toward the roar of the river.

In his present condition he wouldn't be able to find Jahara. But if he were close enough Jahara could make himself felt, if the poor little native were still alive.

Feeling ahead with the gun he found where the ground fell away before him. That had to be the lip of soil, below which was the rocky bank. This undoubtedly was the high water mark for the river. He stayed off the rocks to keep his footing, but checked for the demarcation every few steps.

After the constant barrage of Jahara's breakdown, Samuel enjoyed the solitude as he walked.

The heat of the day waned and the sun lowered to the horizon. Samuel could make out the orb of the sun and the horizon, but nothing else.

As he considered whether to stop for the day, as his muscles urged, he felt something familiar. He froze and concentrated on his feelings. He definitely could feel something.

"Jahara!" he called.

The feeling grew, but had no real strength, like a dim candle. Either Jahara was too weak or too far away to respond strongly.

Samuel quickened his pace. The feeling grew stronger. It began to take form in Samuel's mind: sorrow, loss, abandonment, and death.

"Jahara, I can't see. You have to guide me to you."

Samuel continued his quick march. Luckily the ground was even. He stopped. The scene was just too strange. He looked up at himself from some distance. He could clearly make out bruises on his face and arms. Like before, he had no sense of himself. He was Jahara.

He dragged himself forward with his wings. The tentacles didn't seem to work. The rocks, though smooth, felt harsh against the fine skin of the wings. Samuel lost track of time in the slow crawl back to his body. Finally he reached himself and when he touched his leg, he snapped back into his own body.

Squatting down he rested his hand on Jahara's body. He seemed smaller, frailer, than Samuel remembered. Far from being cold, Jahara's body seemed hot compared to Samuel's hand. In a human it would indicate a fever. In Jahara it could be completely natural.

"Jahara, can you travel? Can you fly or walk?"

Although the feelings of despair were gone, no other emotion replaced it. The little native must be nearing the end.

"Jahara, we need to get you to the Home-kind as fast as possible. We need to merge. Can you do it?"

Samuel shouldered the rifle and picked up the native, cradling him in his arms. He gently wrapped one tentacle around his neck.

"Come on, Jahara, you're strong, an example to all the Home-kind." Samuel hoped his desperation wasn't making it through. "You can do it. You can help us make it to the Home-kind!"

A little spark of pleasure flitted in Samuel's mind. "That's it, Jahara. We're going to make it."

Samuel again found himself seeing through Jahara's eyes. He took off at a dead run for a line of trees a couple hundred meters away.

When they made the tree line, Samuel shot down the first iron rope tree he came to with fruit on it. Ripping one off, he shoved it into Jahara's mouth.

Slowly Jahara's mouth began to move, just bruising the fruit, but the juice began to trickle down his throat. Experienced through Jahara, it tasted sweeter and fuller.

The juice stimulated Jahara enough that he began chewing in earnest. Seeing this, Samuel sat down on the fallen tree and plucked a fruit for himself.

According to Jahara's estimates they still had a couple of days travel to get to the Home-kind.

As they traveled, Jahara remained hot, and didn't form any cognitive communication. Samuel navigated a course as straight north as the lay of the land allowed and trusted that the Home-kind were wide ranging enough to run into one or more as they got closer.

In the afternoon of the second day Samuel felt a wind gust on his left side. When he looked through Jahara, a Home-kind rested on the ground beside him. He must have been too wrapped up in Jahara to feel its approach.

Samuel sat down and offered his hand to the new Home-kind. The native responded by placing a tentacle along Samuel's wrist.

They connected immediately but it felt more formal than Jahara had been.

"My name is Samuel Rochez. This is Jahara, he needs help."

"You and Jahara have been alone together for some time, it would seem. Come, I will lead you along the way to the Home-kind. I am the one called Caltia, and it is my honor to help you in finding your way to the Home-kind."

"It's lucky you found us. Jahara is unable to communicate to direct me. I could have marched right past your village."

"Then it is very fortunate that you come at this time. I and many others are out around the area of the Home-kind. It is always so, when we are preparing for war."

The native broke the link and moved off through the underbrush.

Chapter 10 Lockdown

Lance marched through the dim innards of the ship, the dull thud of his footsteps offset by the sharp tap of the cane's metal tip. Without main power, only the emergency bio-lum cartridges cast their bluish pale within the ship. Moisture condensed as time went by, making the deck slick. It would only get worse until they could turn on the ventilation system. The open cargo bay hatch did little for the rest of the ship.

As he rounded a corner a dark figure came into view. He slowed down until close enough to recognize the chiseled body of John Harris. They met each other's gaze with a nod.

Harris bared his perfect white teeth in a smile. "Oh yeah, I'm going to enjoy this." The smile left his face. "Where's Stagar?"

Lance spit, which splatted on the damp deck. "His lordship is up on the bridge, hiding from the peasants. You know he doesn't like to socialize with the underlings."

"But he does occasionally make a good will tour."

Lance snorted and Harris' smile returned.

"I think we have a day or two before he descends again."

"Right," drawled Harris.

"Remember, Harris, we need to be subtle."

"You subtle, Lance? That's like putting flowers on an invasion barge."

"Listen," Lance said with a growl in his voice. "We need the men to be on our side when we take down Stagar. Even if we only have half of them it'll be enough force to keep the others in line."

"They're sheep. There's not a man among them who'll stand against you."

"I'm not concerned with any one of them. It's a group that can cause a problem. And, you never can tell who's going to grow a back bone.

"Kim's young," Lance said rubbing his chin. "And the young can be more idealistic than pragmatic. We'll need to keep him on a short leash. Stay close to him, Harris."

"What about Epstine?"

Lance shook his head. "Spineless slug. Even with Stagar backing him up, he wouldn't stand up to a fly."

"We need him, don't we?"

"At least till we get back. We'll have to watch him. As I said, he'd never stand up to me, but it is possible that Stagar could get him to do something behind our backs."

"Once we have someone else we know we can trust, we can set a watch on Epstine."

"Yeah. This is going to be by the seat of our pants, so keep your eyes open."

Lance struck the other man in the shoulder with the right side of his fist in a sideways chop. The other man returned the gesture.

"Head on in," Lance said. "I'll give you a couple of minutes." As Harris turned to go, Lance paced up and down the hall

After a few minutes, Lance entered the mess hall. The light from the portholes temporarily blinded him. He blinked the room into focus. The crew sat quiet, lounging about the tables in their own stink.

"Whoa, welcome to Epstineville. Which one of you girls forgot to shower this month?" Lance asked with his teeth showing.

No one responded, although they all looked up.

By one of the portholes Kim stood taking notes beside the telescope.

Lance strode over and slapped him on the back with enough force to knock the smaller man off his feet. However, Kim managed to brace his hands against the table and retain his footing.

"Good," Lance said under his breath, and then out loud. "What's the bad word, Kimmy?"

"It's hard to catch anything with this thing during the day time," Kim gestured to the telescope. "As far as I can tell, they're still following the same pattern. They're beyond the horizon. They should be back in about five hours." Kim checked his watch, "after Dark."

Lance grabbed Kim by the collar and yanked him close. "Spare me the play by play. The only thing that matters is: are they gone yet?"

"No," Kim said meeting Lance's eye.

Lance let him go and turned on the other men. As he turned, he noticed Kim rubbing the spot that had been slapped. Lance smirked.

"Are you idiots enjoying Stagar's little holiday? Nice little vacation. Just sit back, breathe the same old air, smell the same moldy armpits, eat dried food from a can."

At this, the men averted their eyes as if they didn't want to face the things Lance threw at them.

Lance reached the counter and pulled out a can of coffee crystals. He poured a hand full into a cup and added water from a faucet. The water trickled out.

"Oh, what's this?" Lance said in mock alarm. "Water pressure's almost gone?"

Taking a swig from the cup, he chewed the moistened crystals with his mouth open so the sound echoed around the mess.

"Ahh," he sighed, "Just like mother used to make."

"What about the rest of you slugs? Want some of the gourmet elixir?"

He straddled a chair one table away from the other men and looked each one up and down. "What a sorry state you're all in," he said between crunches of black crystals. "So, nice vacation, no?"

"No," Harris chimed in. "Festering dead monkey in a can. Stagar's lost it." Harris's voice rose in pitch and volume. "We should have run while we had the chance!"

"We would be spending our fortune by now," another voice added.

"Yeah, we could be lounging at a resort or something," another man threw in.

"Destalgo," a voice called out.

"Destalgo," several men repeated with nodding heads and smiles.

"No, man," Epstine jumped in, "Destalgo's is too hot. Give me George's mountains on Henum three."

"What, George's mountains? Great place if you want to sleep and do nothing. Now, the casinos of Chimil, that's where the fun is."

Lance caught Harris' gaze and nodded quickly.

Harris spoke over the other men. "But we're here living in our own stink. Like dogs, we roll in it every day."

Marius laughed. "During the war I was on a ship that crash landed on Belus two. We spent eight months trapped in the carcass of the ship. This is nothing. If Stagar's right, we'll be off this rock in a week, two tops."

Lance gritted his teeth and looked sternly at Harris.

Harris shrugged and said, "So, you like the accommodations? We could leave the ventilation system off in your bunk."

The group laughed. Someone threw in, "You could bunk with Epstine." More gruff laughter arose from the men. "The rest of us'll shower and avoid you."

"Hey Kim, you're quiet over there. How you gonna spend your cut?" Andrews asked.

"Casini four," Kim responded.

"Casini four, Casini four, what's on Casini four?"

"Family," Kim shrugged.

Lance balled his fists. It wasn't going the way he wanted. The weaklings needed to be angry with his highness.

"But," Lance said with enough force to bring silence, "it doesn't matter. The only place we're going is prison or the grave."

Silence overcame the room as the men looked at each other. After a moment, nervous laughter broke the silence.

"I tell you no lie," Lance countered.

Kim spoke up. "How do you know? We've escaped detection so far."

"Ah, what's the matter Kimmy, you don't get it? Stagar sentenced us all when he let the Roach escape."

"How does that put us in jail?" Andrews asked.

Harris shot back, "Don't try and think Andrews, you might forget to breathe."

Lance let the men stew it over in silence for a few seconds. "What happens when the Loscar come to mine their treasure? They'll find the Roach."

"He won't talk," said Kim.

"All they have to do is threaten one grub and he'll cry like a baby."

Kim's ears turned red.

"Oh, so you thought he was your friend? Remember he was willing to blow us all away for that little grub."

"There's no way he'll survive long out there on his own," called out Epstine.

"You idiots really are dumber than dirt. Roach may be a grub-loving freak, but he's not a moron like you dogs. Alien planets, plants, and grubs are his specialty. While Kimmy was in diapers Roach was evaluating planets for the corp. Biology, geology, and botany, and twenty plus years of experience are on his side. The Roach is a field scientist with military training. He has a better chance of survival out there than we do in here.

"And who do we have to thank for our situation?" Lance continued with a sneer, "Stagar. The best we can hope for is a life on the run, laying low. No resorts or pleasure domes. It'll be the cesspools of the galaxy for us, or prison."

Lance looked each man in the eye till they looked away. "We all signed on for the wrong trip, with the wrong man: Stagar Inmen."

"But," Andrews ventured, speaking to the men around the table. "Why would they care about the pittance we've got, while they have a planet of the stuff?"

Lance flung his spoon like a throwing dagger. It made a satisfying thwack on Andrew's head, skittered across the floor and banged into the wall.

"Now I have to spoon feed you babies? You'd think this was the nursery.

"The Loscar won't care about the Carlinium. They'll care about the knowledge of this place. They're the most secretive race in the galaxy. You think they want everyone to know of this treasure planet? Word gets out and it could be another war. This time with all the races teamed up against them, instead of just us humans.

"In that way, we are loose ends to tie up." Lance drew his finger across his throat. "Get the point?"

"Then, we have to find Rochez," said Kim. "Take him with us."

"Hey, Pig Pen," Lance called to Epstine, "Can any of our tracking equipment locate Roach?"

"Nope," came the immediate reply. "Too much interference. Visual scanning could take months and we'd have to be really lucky."

"So, which one of you ladies knows how we can find him? Go wandering off blindly into the wilderness? Let me remind you, we don't know how much time we have after the survey team leaves."

A few of the men turned pale. Once it seemed that no one had any other theories to shoot down Lance crunched down the last of his coffee crystals, tossed his cup at the sink, and strode towards the door. As he reached it he turned and addressed the men one more time. "Wrong mission, wrong leader." He turned and left the mess.

###

Lance sat on a sealed crate of Carlinium in the hold, his back against the hull and his legs stretched out across several crates. The grinding swish of his knife across the whetstone faded into the cavernous room. The footsteps did not concern him as they drew closer. Only one person approached.

"Hey, Lance."

He recognized Harris' voice, but didn't look up or respond.

"You laid it on pretty thick in the mess. We really in that much trouble? I mean, I don't want to live on the lam. I've done that before and it's pathetic."

Lance smiled. "Don't worry. Even if Roach talks; there are places to hide that are comfortable. Also, there are a number of ways to change our identity. Stuff that'll even fool a DNA scan."

"Whew," Harris said resting his weight against the hull, "you really had me going."

"Well," Lance said examining the edge of the knife, "They weren't biting at the discomfort approach, so I had to bring out the big guns.

"Besides, if they don't know the right place to go, the right people to see, they'll be hunted down like dogs."

"And you're not going to tell them." Harris smiled, and Lance smiled back.

###

Stagar and Lance stood behind Epstine as he warmed up the passive sensors.

"Are you sure, Stagar?" Epstine asked.

"It's been forty eight hours with no sign of the survey ships. I think we can risk it." Stagar added a reassuring smile to encourage the technician.

Epstine flipped a switch and the console in front of him lit up in a pale blue light. Moving his hand over the display and touching and dragging his finger about the surface in a dancelike movement, he ran through the full range of scans. "No active scanning in our hemisphere. I'll check with our long range probe and see what it has to tell us."

Rolling his chair to the right, he hit a switch on another console. This one was multi-colored with an overlay of the solar system. Three white dots were moving quickly towards the edge of the screen.

Epstine let out a sigh of relief, while Stagar snickered and slapped the technician on the back. "Way to go, Mister Epstine."

"Lance, assemble the men outside. They could use the airing out."

Lance turned to go without a word. He hadn't spoken to Stagar in anything but single syllables since their confrontation.

"And Lance," Stagar called as Lance reached the hatch, "take out the food cart, too."

"Mister Epstine, why don't you go out with the men as well? It'll give you a chance to get out of this sweaty tin can for a while."

"Thanks," said Epstine leaning back in his chair, "but, I want to run some additional scans. You know, just in case they left an observation satellite or something."

Stagar patted him on the shoulder. "Good thinking as always, Mister Epstine."

Stagar headed up to the bridge. The safeties needed to be turned off so the ship's systems could be re-engaged. Stagar didn't take a chance on a clumsy or stupid crewman giving them away. Near the end game he would not take any chances.

Lance would have to be taken care of soon as well. He wouldn't take charge, at least until Stagar had made delivery on Carlinium. Stagar kept the customer information in his head only. No matter how upset Lance might be, Stagar felt certain he wouldn't risk losing his payday. But just in case he'd take some precautions.

In less than fifteen minutes Stagar strode out into the bright sunshine, blinking tears from his eyes brought up by the brilliant glare.

The men stood before him. Obviously, Lance forced some military precision. Stagar took up position beside Lance and Harris and cleared his throat. "Good news men. The survey team is leaving the solar system." The men stood at attention and made no sound or action. Stagar expected at least some sign of relief. Perhaps Lance or the confinement had sapped their enthusiasm. He opened his mouth to encourage the men further, but was knocked to the ground. It took him a second to regain his bearings. As he came to himself he instinctively grabbed for his gun. The holster was empty.

Looking up he saw Harris moving away with the stun pistol spinning on his index finger.

He got his arm up just in time to block Lance's cane from striking his head. Pain shot through his arm as the cane made contact.

Stagar scrambled away from Lance, without getting up. That would be just the act of defiance Lance needed to really brutalize him.

Stagar looked to the men. Their eyes jumped back and forth between him and Lance. None moved to intercede. Stagar knew to expect no better from this low life scum.

"Lance, you can't end it like this. I've got the customers lined up. You need me. Don't waste your chance at a once in a lifetime payday."

"I'm not completely helpless," Lance sneered. "I've got contacts. I can make something without your pathetic assistance. But don't worry; I'm not going to finish you off quickly. We need to spend some more time together."

"Stagar!" a voice called from inside the ship.

All eyes turned to the hatch as Epstine fell out into the light. "Sta..," his voice trailed off as he froze in mid stride. He looked at Lance and then at Stagar.

"What is it, Pig Pen?" Lance growled.

Epstine took a few steps forward and steadied his gaze on Lance and swallowed. "They've locked down the whole planet!"

"What?" Lance said, raising his cane and stepping towards the technician.

"Sixty eight shield generators in orbit. The Planet's completely cut off. The shields cut off emissions so we couldn't pick them up with the passives."

"So," Lance said while stepping closer, "How do we get past them?"

"We can't. At least I don't know how. This is really powerful stuff."

Lance lifted his cane. As he reached striking distance Epstine called out. "I'm just telling you the situation. I have no control over it. I didn't put them there."

Lance froze in his tracks. "No, this isn't your fault." Lance said as he turned back to Stagar.

This time Stagar didn't try to get away. It would have been of no use and the beating would probably be less if he just took it. That would take some of the enjoyment out of it for Lance.

With the boot headed directly for his face, however, self-preservation kicked in and Stagar ducked. The blow made contact with the top of his head and sent him sprawling on the ground.

Chapter 11 War

At the Home-kind village Samuel spoke with the blurry shapes before him. "War?" Samuel asked.

"It is a shame that we are forced to do such a thing as this." Jawell responded.

"But, why are you going to war? Everything I've learned about your people indicates that you're kind, gentle, above all, helpful, and completely non-violent. When my people captured you, you considered it an honor. How can you go to war?"

"Unfortunately, the Eaters do not communicate. They are not intelligent as Your-kind are."

"Eaters?" Samuel relaxed his shoulders, releasing the tension projected from Jawell. With the long experience with Jahara he had developed the ability to block the emotion flowing from the Home-kind.

"Eaters are the kind that eat the outside of trees. They prefer the type of tree that the Home-kind taught to grow into our home. The Eaters also smash our crops into the ground as they cross over them to get to our home."

Samuel looked up to the mesh of gray and black lines that Jawell indicated was their home. Some blob like shapes darted in and around the branches. "So, if you don't stop them, they'll destroy your home?" Samuel sighed. It wasn't the worst cause to fight for.

"That is true. It takes many life times to teach the trees to grow into a place for this many Home-kind. If the eaters were to destroy this place we would of necessity separate into small groups and join to different places of the Home-kind.

"It would be the death of our group, the feeling we have built together here. This would become a black spot never visited again by any Home-kind."

Samuel felt tears well up. Closing his eyes, he sighed. If he weren't consciously blocking them, the feeling would still overwhelm him.

"Disruptive I imagine," he said after he regained composure. Samuel sat and stared intently at the native, striving to bring him into full focus.

"Especially it is for the young. Each place of the Home-kind has its very own feel. It is changing to the feel to have different Home-kind enter in. They bring their own feel to the place. It takes much time for the new feel to be created and all to settle with it."

"How many of these Eaters are there?"

"There are many more than the Home-kind. It is lucky that they all follow the ones that are in front. If the Home-kind can get those in front to change direction the others will be led away."

"So, you don't actually fight with them, to cause physical harm?"

The revulsion struck Samuel in the gut, like his body strained to wretch. He fought it down which seemed to calm Jawell also.

"No, absolutely not, Samuel Rochez," the native said after a minute. "We seek to save ourselves without bringing harm to others."

"I can feel how it affects you," Samuel said rubbing his stomach.

"What about accidents? How does that affect the Home-kind?"

"We strive to avoid them. On occasion an Eater is harmed and the Home-kind mark it as if one of our own had passed.

"There was only once, Samuel Rochez, a war that went terribly wrong."

"In what way?"

"The Eaters ran in the wrong direction and most of the poor things fell to their deaths."

"How did the Home-kind handle it?"

"They were taken by a great darkness. The Home-kind never heard from that group again and no Home-kind goes there. We do not know what has become of them. It is sadness for all Home-kind."

"Wow," Samuel responded. Jawell trembled emotionally. Samuel decided to change the subject. He lay back on the cool ground. "You lead the Eaters away, similar to diverting a stampede. How dangerous are they when you face them?"

"The Eaters have teeth that are strong. Some of the Home-kind are often lost in the attempt to turn the Eaters away."

An image flashed into Samuel's mind of large, glistening, buck teeth surrounded by charcoal gray fur.

Samuel felt the pride flow from Jawell. "They gave their lives in helping the Home-kind," he whispered.

Samuel broke the moment's reverent silence. "Jawell, I have some weapons that can be used in the war." Samuel patted his vest. "I'd like to help."

"But, Samuel Rochez, you damaged your sight in the eye storm."

"I can see well enough that I won't run into anything."

"Of course the Home-kind will be honored to accept you to help."

"Do you know when the battle will begin?"

"The Eaters will be out in the open in two or three more light times. It is then that we have the best chance to direct them away from the place of the Home-kind. The sentinels will let us know of the time for the Home-kind to move.

"Samuel Rochez, you will need to leave this light-time if you are to reach the place of war before the arrival of the Eaters. I will help by leading you there."

Samuel felt a rock form in the pit of his stomach. "Jawell, I don't want you to end up like Jahara."

"Between you and me, Samuel Rochez, we will be careful. It is but two light-times travel, so there is little risk."

Samuel thought of the limp rag Jahara was when the Home-kind took him. "How is Jahara doing? Can I see him?"

"It would not be helpful for Hara to be near you at this time. His unique feel is no longer with him. Hara must learn again who he is. The presence of you would set that work back."

Samuel scratched his head. "You called him Hara, isn't his name Jahara?"

Confusion came from Jawell. "He was called Jahara, but he is now Hara, as he was in his youth. Is this not so among Your-kind?"

It was Samuel's turn to be confused. "I'm sorry, what?"

Samuel felt Jawell's surprise.

"When young he was Hara. When Hara came to the time of serving, he became Jahara, a scout. He can never be a scout again and is Hara. When he is recovered he will serve the Home-kind in another way and will no longer be Hara."

"So," Samuel said slowly, "when you were young you were Well. Scouts get a Ja prefix to their names, making you Jawell."

"Yes, Samuel, that is the way of things."

"Jawell, there is another important matter we need to discuss, the Loscar."

###

Samuel leaned against a tree as he waited, listening to the stream bubbling nearby. Biting into a fruit, the feeling of resolution, peace, and apprehension floated through his mind. The feel of the place, Jawell called it.

Apprehension announced itself before he felt the tentacle wrap around his ankle.

"Samuel Rochez, it is my very great honor to meet one who is willing to help the Home-kind in many ways. I am the one called Gimert."

Samuel straightened instinctively. "Gimert, it is my honor to meet with one who helps to lead Home-kind. Jawell has told you of the Loscar?"

"Jawell has shared the feel that you have about this Other-kind."

"It is important that when they come none of your people try to communicate with them. They are not evil, but there may be misunderstandings that would imperil the Home-kind."

"I understand the urgency, Samuel Rochez. We will need to arrange a meeting of those who speak for all the Home-kind. We have sent two scouts with the warning that you bring. These two are all that can be spared at this time."

"Good, it may be more than a season before the Loscar arrive, but we need to be prepared."

"We will see to it once the war is over."

"Are you not leaving with Jawell soon?"

"Yes, and remember, when the battle begins, I'll use these." Samuel held out a grenade. "They make the sound of thunder, flash of fire, and will send parts of the ground into the air. We need to keep the Home-kind out of the area when this happens, or they may be injured or killed. And above all, do not panic. This is to dazzle and confuse the Eaters, not the Home-kind."

###

The greens and browns of the valley meadow were radiant in the morning sun. Samuel rubbed his eyes. They were the first real colors he'd seen since the eye-storm. The distance was blurry, but at least his near vision was beginning to come back. Lobbing grenades blindly was frowned upon in training, even more in action.

Arrayed on the hillside beside him, the Home-kind waited in uneven and meandering ranks. They were broken up into groups of four or five clustered together like a woven mat strewn between the shrubs.

Each group had a task in the coming battle, staging themselves in precision flight, bringing a wall of fluttering wings down into the leading pack of Eaters, wave after wave until the Eaters became enraged and started jumping and snapping at them in a frenzy. At that point the Home-kind would lead them on a different path that puts a mountain range between the Eaters and the village. In their frenzy they'd attack anything that moves. So Jawell had told him.

He'd use the grenades to slow the Eater's advance, giving the Home-kind enough time to do their job.

Samuel was woken from his thoughts by the presence of Jawell and another he didn't recognize. "Samuel Rochez, it is a very great joy to present to you my son Wellem.

"Son of Well?" Samuel guessed.

"Yes," Responded Jawell, "Tajanan, my mate, wanted it so."

"It's a good name," Samuel said laying a hand on Jawell's side.

"Wellem is just now of the age to help in the war. He will be at your side to tell the Home-kind of your intent so that in the fight we will all be working together."

Samuel placed his other hand on the smaller figure beside Jawell. "Wellem, it is an honor to meet the son of Jawell. I look forward to working together to divert this danger."

"Samuel Rochez, I too am pleased to meet a new friend so willing to help the Home-kind. My father has told us all of meeting Your-kind. I am most happy to..."

Wellem was cut short by a rush of anxiousness that blew over the company. The Eaters approached, Samuel understood without being told. The scouts flew over the advancing line of the enemy. Looking up, Samuel saw the scouts as specks to the east.

"The battle will begin soon, Samuel Rochez. It is time for you and Wellem to get into your place."

Samuel rose and began walking to the blind of bushes near the west end of the clearing, which sat on a small rise. It would give him a good field of view, and would allow a little greater lobbing distance.

As he marched, he took inventory of his vest: four grenades, two shock, two plasma, and a rifle set to projectile, utility knife, medic kit, assorted survival gear, and two food bars.

The rustling at his feet reminded him that Wellem followed.

As they reached the shrubs, Samuel un-shouldered the rifle and looked through the sighting system, found the Home-kind flying over the front ranks of Eaters. The readout on the sight read 1.23 kilometers.

"What are doing, Samuel Rochez?"

"Just gauging the distance."

"How does that device help in telling distances?"

"Here," Samuel said with a smile. "Climb up on my shoulder and see for yourself."

As the tentacle arms wrapped around his waist Samuel held steady against the pull. Not a difficult task, as Wellem was a fraction of a grown Home-kind's weight. Samuel spoke as the diminutive being moved up to his shoulder. "Now, I'm going to find the target and hold the gun as still as possible. You're going to want to look right here." Samuel pointed to the eyepiece of the scope.

After a couple of tries Jawell's son had the hovering Home-kind in site. "This is truly a unique experience. We must show this to my father and to the rest of the Home-kind. How does this work?"

"This particular style uses sensors on one end to project an image onto a small screen just behind the eye piece. There are controls on the side to adjust the view. I'll increase the magnification." Samuel pressed a button.

Wellem moved from behind the sight and back. "This is very strange and wonderful at the same time." His little body shook.

Samuel fought down the excitement that Wellem fed into him. "It's called a sight. There are more sophisticated ones with more advanced electronics and sensors, or even sound waves. This is about as simple as it gets. But it is durable and it doesn't need much of a power source. And, well, this is not a long range weapon, so there's no need for something more powerful."

"Thank you, Samuel Rochez, for sharing this information with me. I have enjoyed it very much! Can you tell me how the thunder-like devices you are going to use work? They sound as if they are very interesting as well."

"Rapid oxidation," Samuel said with a laugh.

Wellem didn't respond. Samuel jerked his head back in surprise. In the short time he had known the young Home-kind, Wellem had not stopped interrogating him.

Samuel summoned up an image of a grenade in his mind and took it apart showing each component to Wellem, along with a vivid image of an explosion. This left Samuel's young friend even more tongue-tied.

Turning back in the direction of the advancing enemy, Samuel looked through the sight again. About half a kilometer, they were making good time.

"You mean, such destructive power exists in the real world, not just made up stories?"

Samuel looked down at Wellem. "Yes, it does. It can be used for good purposes as well as bad. I feel fairly certain that the Eaters won't like it, but it will help the Home-kind."

A flourish of noise in the distance drew Samuel's attention. The first wave of Home-kind took to the air.

The tranquil woods on the far side of the meadow burst open in a shower of leaves. The dull roar of a moment ago elevated to a cacophony of snarling growls. The Eaters charged into the field.

The first wave of aerial assault descended upon the front line, creating a storm of action at ground level.

Pulling the pin, Samuel rested his thumb against the trigger button. He gauged the distance. Too close and he might distract them from the Home-kind's taunting, too far and the Eaters might not even notice.

"Is it time to explode now, Samuel Rochez?" Again Wellem shook with excitement.

The second wave fell on the advancing Eaters. The advance visibly slowed.

"At this rate, we may not have to. Your people's tactics seem to be working." Samuel fingered the pin. It wasn't quite time to reinsert it.

The line of battle snaked forward with pockets of Eaters surging forward only to be met with greater resistance. The Home-kind constantly shifted their forces to reinforce the weak spots in the line.

One of the advantages of telepathy, they reacted instantly to every situation, anywhere on the field of battle. Every commander Samuel ever knew would love to have this ability in their troops.

About twenty minutes after the emerging from the wood, the Eaters had managed to progress to about the middle of the field.

"Wellem," Samuel said, "They're making progress. If the Eaters don't turn soon, it'll be time for the fireworks."

Wellem's excited shaking began again.

"Can you tell if the Eaters are about to turn?" Samuel asked.

"No, it feels that they will need more time before the Eaters become angry enough to turn."

"Ok, tell them the big bang is coming." Samuel pictured in his mind the location of his target and the effect of the grenade.

He gave it just a second to sink in, pressed the button, and lobbed the grenade.

As he ducked, he caught a quick view of the Home-kind pulling away. Then there was a flash followed by thunder, shock wave, and tremors. Samuel rose to see dust and debris settling. The field was quiet, the Eaters in retreat. The Home-kind, however, were hovering as if frozen in the sky.

Samuel looked to Wellem. The little native trembled, but not with excitement. His eyes were fixed on the aftermath.

The battle had stopped. The blast had the desired effect on the Eaters, but also shut down the Home-kind.

Samuel dropped to his knees and grabbed Wellem. "Tell them to attack." The explosion had stunned the Home-kind to inactivity, and they fed on each other's shock. Samuel felt it building, more and more shock, confusion built upon confusion.

Shaking Wellem, he yelled, "Snap out of it!" He tried imprinting his desperation on Wellem, but the wall was too strong.

He rose and looked over the field. The Eaters had regrouped and advanced again towards Samuel's position. The snarling broke forth across the field.

"Attack," Samuel yelled at the top of his lungs.

The Eaters rushed forward, quickly approaching the blast site.

"Just great," Samuel muttered as he pulled out another grenade and sent it sailing.

After the blast the Home-kind remained stunned, and the Eaters retreated again. The way Samuel's day was going; they'd recover more quickly this time.

Samuel took aim at the line of Eaters. Jawell had said that they blindly followed the ones in front. It was time to see what they did when the leaders stopped moving.

Only a couple of minutes passed before the Eaters resumed their advance. Not knowing where the vital organs were, Samuel aimed for the center of the closest Eater's body.

Crack, the shot hit the target. The Eater doubled over and writhed on the ground. The line immediately behind it stopped.

Samuel chose his next targets along the line at intervals of every six to eight Eaters. Crack, crack, crack, the shots rang out. The advance halted. Every time an Eater took the initiative to move forward Samuel took him down. It was all he could do to keep up with them. He wondered how much ammunition he had left.

The feeling he got from Wellem changed. It was a small change, and he didn't have much concentration to spare to analyze it. The Home-kinds stupor may have been lifting.

Though the front line barely moved the Eaters growled louder and began snapping at the air.

Really, just great, he thought. When the ammo ran out, they'd be in the mood to tear him apart.

"Stop!" Wellem broke his silence. The rising tide of emotion flooding from the Home-kind filled Samuel with despair. What was he doing slaughtering these animals? He dropped the gun and fell to his knees. He stared in guilty disbelief at his blood stained hands. Tears came to his eyes.

Slowly, dimly, a sound broke through his consumed mind, a sound growing louder. Wiping his eyes on his sleeve, he stood up.

The Eaters advanced. His own fear fought down the induced emotions of the Home-kind. "Attack!" he yelled.

As if his call unlocked the chains that held the Home-kind back, they rained down on their enemy. The advance slowed, but continued.

Samuel shook off the last of the Home-kind influence and picked up the rifle. "When you all feel together it's overwhelming."

"Yes, Samuel Rochez, it is so with very strong feelings."

Wellem seemed colder in his response.

The battle advanced to within thirty meters of Samuel and Wellem. "We need to fall back, they'll overrun this position soon," Samuel said.

"The feeling is good that it will not take much more time to turn the Eaters."

"Good," said Samuel as he watched the battle. "Let's go."

Samuel broke the connection with Wellem as he turned for the woods. The burden of the Home-kind's emotions immediately withdrew. With so many present, he still felt it dully, like sounds underwater. His own emotions seemed foreign to him. He had wept for the Eaters he had killed in desperation. The Home-kind were willing to fight and die, but not kill. They must have evolved without predators.

The shade of the woods felt good as he entered. Turning, the front line was almost upon Samuel's previous position, about one hundred fifty meters distant.

Wellem entered his consciousness.

"Have we lost any one?" Samuel asked.

"Several have helped in giving their lives for the Home-kind." Again Samuel felt the pride at sacrifice.

They would undoubtedly have no pride in Samuel's actions that day. Samuel sighed. He had done the right thing once again.

Concentrating on the battle Samuel noted the bushes he was stationed behind were overrun.

After about ten minutes the front line had moved half the distance to the wood.

"Wellem, I only have stun grenades left. They're not as dramatic, but affect a larger area. If I'm going to use one, it's going to have to be soon. Are they turning?"

"It will be soon, Samuel Rochez, that they will turn."

"It had better be real soon, they're only twenty meters away," Samuel said lowering the rifle.

"Do we use another grenade?" Samuel asked.

"No, the Eaters are about to be turned away."

Samuel pulled out a grenade and ripped out the pin in one motion. "It's now or never."

The tentacle wrapped around Samuel's ankle tightened. "Wait, Samuel Rochez, there is still time..."

Wellem was cut short by loud growls accompanying a shock rippling through the Home-kind.

Samuel looked toward the south. A dozen or so Eaters had broken through the wall of defenders and were nearly to the woods. Pressing the activate button Samuel launched the grenade toward the band of Eaters. He grabbed Wellem and ducked behind a large tree.

The trunk trembled with the shock wave. Samuel looked up to see the wall of Home-kind still fighting. He breathed a sigh of relief. This time they weren't stunned. Neither were the Eaters, apparently, because a handful of them were bearing down on him.

"Fantastic," he muttered as he grabbed Wellem and threw him into the air. "Get out of here." Samuel sprinted into the wood with a pack of Eaters on his heels.

When enraged, they'll chase anything in front of them, Jawell had said. Glancing behind, he saw that he wasn't putting any distance between them. The only option he could see was to climb a tree and wait them out. A plan, he realized, that depended on his pursuers inability to climb, a hypothesis yet to be tested.

Ducking under branches and dodging trunks, Samuel looked for some way to escape. It was time to find out if the Eaters could climb.

Samuel picked out a sturdy looking tree with some branches about eye level. He hoisted himself up and climbed a couple of branches higher before the Eaters caught up.

They circled the tree snarling. Up close, he could see why the predominate image the Home-kind had of the Eaters was their teeth. They were the length of his finger but much broader. Every time one of these natives opened its mouth, its teeth seemed to flash.

The charcoal gray fir covered a sausage shaped body, similar to the Home-kind, but about twice as large, coming up to about Samuel's chest. Four tentacles supported their frame with two additional where the Home-kind had wings. They seemed to use these arms for support. Instead of flat heads, the Eaters faces came down at a nearly forty-five-degree angle and the four eyes were positioned on the top half of the face, a face that was dominated by their mammoth teeth.

Wellem swooped in over the Eater's heads and flapped up to perch on the branch next to Samuel.

"The Eaters have been turned! The Home-kind are leading them away now."

Samuel pointed to the growling figures at the base of the tree, "not quite all of them."

"It is true that several small groups of Eaters are in the woods and will continue on their way to the Home-kind village. It is good that small groups are easier to turn than large groups.

"Samuel Rochez, we must get away from these Eaters! They will hurt or kill you."

"I don't appear to be in any immediate danger. They can't climb, obviously. Eventually they'll get bored and move on."

"No, Samuel Rochez, you do not understand..."

Samuel felt the shiver through the seat of his pants and immediately looked down. The Eaters scraped their teeth across the trunk, tearing off the bark.

"No! It's past time to leave. Samuel Rochez, it is not my desire to see you die."

Samuel scratched at his temple. "I'm missing something, Wellem. How is their having a snack put me in danger?"

As if in response to his question, the tremor in the branch increased. The Eaters dug into the exposed wood, pulling out small hunks with each bite. "Giant beavers," Samuel said.

"What are these beavers?"

"An animal similar to the Eaters only much smaller," Samuel responded.

It only made sense; if they couldn't climb they had to take the trees down to get the bark above tooth level. Samuel thought back to the horde in the field. It wouldn't take much time for that many to take down every tree in the Home-kind's valley.

"I will help you, Samuel Rochez." Wellem said as he launched from the branch.

Samuel reached for the native just too late. "No!" He grabbed the branch to steady himself. "I've got the gun, Wellem"

Wellem swooped down just over the heads of the Eaters and circled about the tree. He let his tentacles thwack them in the back of the heads as he passed.

The rifle was at Samuel's shoulder before he realized it. Less than a minute later the Eaters responded to Wellem's harassment, by jumping and snapping at him.

The little native flapped away and up for a short distance and then circled back and dove at the Eaters. The first jumped, well off the mark. The second, the same, to no effect. Wellem darted under a branch and started a sweeping turn. An eater jumped out from behind the tree and caught one of Wellem's bat-like wings in his jaws. The helpless native flapped furiously about the Eater's face.

Crack, crack, Samuel squeezed off two shots, one high and one low to take down the beast. It fell face first onto Wellem. As the other Eaters moved in, Samuel took each down. Luckily there were no Home-kind present to stop him.

He lowered himself one branch and jumped to the forest floor. "Wellem," he said quietly as he extricated and cradled the diminutive Home-kind in his arms. Samuel held the limp frame to his face, and felt the gentle flow of air from the native's mouth. "Respiration, good." He gingerly ran his fingers over Wellem's body, looking for a pulse. After a moment he gave up. Maybe Jawell could give him an anatomy lesson later.

If Wellem were to survive, Samuel would have to get him to the Home-kind. Samuel looked around. The trees kept the Home-kind from spotting them. With Wellem unconscious, it seemed unlikely the Home-kind would feel him. The only hope he could see was to get back to the clearing. Samuel took his burden and headed for the field.

Chapter 12 Compassion

Samuel sat back, reviewing his work. The main tentacle that made the leading edge of Wellem's left wing had been severed. The splint and bandage Samuel used to bind up and immobilize the wing would have been good enough for a human's broken arm. But, the unknown regenerative properties of these natives meant his ministrations could possibly be useless.

The grass of the field lay flat, pressed into the ground by the hordes of Eaters. Spotted throughout the field, the lumps of Home-kind bodies lay motionless. Some could be alive, but unconscious, like Wellem.

Samuel leaned forward. Placing a finger between the cloth and native, he checked the bandages. They seemed tight enough to hold, and he hoped, not enough to cut off circulation.

While in physical contact he felt nothing from the native. Wellem's silence lent to the quietness of the field. Even the breeze was too gentle to rustle the vegetation.

Samuel stood and brought up the rifle. Searching the horizon with the rifle sight he saw no sign of the Home-kind, just trees, clouds, and mountains.

They would come back. Jawell would, at least. He would wonder about Wellem, besides, Jawell was his main contact with the Home-kind.

Samuel scanned the horizon one more time and shouldered the rifle. Wellem lay at his feet, still as death. Samuel watched him for any signs of respiration. The Home-kind obviously had something other than two big sacks for oxygen processing.

He sighed. Not knowing of anything else he could do for his small friend, he scanned the field. He picked out the closest body he could see and headed off for it. Maybe some of the others could be helped. .

It took over an hour to make his circuit back to Wellem. All seventeen of the bodies he'd found were dead. Most had multiple bite wounds and massive amount of dried blood. Several of them were torn apart, like the Eaters played tug of war with the carcasses. Two of the natives seemed to have been crushed by small boulders.

Samuel wondered on those two. The Eaters didn't seem to use tools, and he would have guessed an individual Eater wasn't strong enough to heft a small boulder by itself. Several could have teamed up to do it, but here again; they seemed too primal in their anger for such rational coordination.

Looking down, Wellem still lay motionless but breathing. Samuel decided to fetch fruit from the wood. Wellem would need it to help speed his recovery, if he were like every other life form Samuel had met.

###

A Home-kind stood next to Wellem's body. The mesh bag of fruit bumped against his leg as he walked. The feeling of Jawell hinted at his senses. As he spent more time with these people, he might learn to distinguish them all simply from telepathic emanations. As he arrived, a tentacle wrapped about his ankle.

"Jawell, I'm sorry. Wellem tried to save me from the Eaters..." Samuel trailed off. His sorrow at seeing his friend's son injured, maybe killed, had guided his words. His train of thought was stolen by feelings of joy emanating from Jawell.

"Jawell, Wellem is hurt, he may die. How can you be happy?" Samuel knelt to examine Wellem's splint again.

"Samuel Rochez, Wellem, my son, helped!"

That was it, a simple statement of fact that cut Samuel to the core. He couldn't help but feel pain for the suffering of Wellem. It was a waste. He didn't need Wellem's help. He could have and did handle the Eaters on his own.

"You will please stop, Samuel Rochez," said Jawell. "This is a moment of joy, a time for the Home-kind to celebrate and honor the help given by all in this day. This is especially true for those who gave the ultimate help."

Samuel turned to Jawell. "Can you help Wellem?"

"Yes, Samuel Rochez, the Ip are on their way to help Wellem. They should be here very soon."

"That's good." Samuel sat down on the tramped vegetation and stretched his neck. "How did it go with the Eaters?"

"They have been led away to where they will not harm the Home-kind. Most of the Home-kind are returning to our place. A few of the scouts have remained to watch the Eaters. They will bring word to the Home-kind if the Eaters turn in a direction that would lead them back to the Home-kind. It should only be one light-time or two before they will return as well."

"Jawell, how do you tell if one of your people is still alive?" Samuel held his hand in front in Wellem's mouth. "I can feel him breathing. Is there any other way?"

Jawell moved a tentacle towards Wellem's mouth, copying Samuel. "This is an amazing idea, Samuel Rochez. The Home-kind have not used a test of this nature before."

"Well, what do you do?"

"The home-kind can feel if another is alive. It is very, very rare that a Home-kind can be alive and not feel. It is sometimes just a faint hint of a feel, but it is there. Can you not feel Wellem, Samuel Rochez?"

Samuel gently laid a hand on the still form and concentrated.

"No, don't feel a thing. But, my kind are not as developed in this area as your people." Samuel removed his hand from the unconscious native.

"What other ways do you know, Samuel Rochez, to find if life is present?"

Samuel smiled. Some of Wellem's curiosity came out in his father. "Usually a pulse," he said.

Samuel held out his hand. "We place the tip of a finger here." He pressed at the pulse point on his wrist. "And we can feel the blood pumping through our system."

Moving his hand over to Jawell, he said, "Here, give it a try."

"Ah, yes, Samuel Rochez, I can indeed sense it," Jawell added after a moments hesitation. "I know nothing of anything that is similar in the Home-kind."

"Well, maybe the Ip will know," Samuel said.

"Samuel Rochez, if any of the Home-kind know, then all of the Home-kind know it as well. Is it not so with Your-kind?"

"Nope, I'm afraid not," Samuel retorted. "We're never of one mind."

"I cannot imagine what that must feel like. The feeling of aloneness would be too great to bear."

"We get used to it," Samuel said with a shrug.

"The Ip have come, Samuel Rochez."

Samuel turned his head to see.

Coming into view, just over the trees, a group of maybe thirty Home-kind flew. Each one held a cord that made up part of a net. The net held a gray uneven object that looked like a boulder.

Samuel stood up. "Jawell, what's going on here?"

"The Ip have come to make themselves helpful."

Samuel shot a glance back at the Home-kind bodies in the field. He tried to remember which had been crushed. "Just, how exactly are they going to help?"

"They are here to help Wellem; to save him from suffering a slow and painful death."

The Ip came close enough to make out the individuals. "But, Wellem could recover. He's unconscious, or in a coma or something, but he's still alive. You've felt it. There's still a chance for him."

"Samuel Rochez," Jawell spoke as to a child, "his wing is broken."

"So what?" The Ip cleared the trees and closed in on them. "He doesn't need wings to survive."

"Samuel Rochez, how can it be that you have such little knowledge? You have been with the Home-kind for some time now. Do you not feel?"

"I feel fine! But I don't see how you can be dismayed by the death of the Eaters, and joyous about killing your own son."

Jawell took what would have been a mental sigh. "If Wellem is unable to dance with the sky, he will become depressed."

"Depressed?"

"Yes, depressed," Jawell declared with finality

"But," Samuel started. The Ip with their boulder of death were directly over Wellem. A twang announced the first cord being released, followed by a second.

Samuel dove as a chorus of twanging cords broke. He scooped up the bundle that was Wellem and rolled out from under the falling stone. It landed with a thud a hand's breadth from his head. The reverberations in the ground echoed his pounding heart.

He lay there enjoying the simple pleasure of breathing, as visions of past encounters with death passed through his mind. Many of them he had brought upon himself, for what he deemed a good reason at the time. He quickly came to the conclusion that this was not the stupidest thing he'd ever done.

Samuel patted the stone. Maybe Jawell was right; this was there culture, their world. But, he wasn't going along with a senseless death unless he at least understood why.

After a few seconds, Jawell's presence arrived in his mind. "Samuel Rochez, I can feel your concern for my son, and that in your actions you are honestly striving to help. I do honor your desire for the life and health of Wellem. You do not understand what will happen to Wellem if he is allowed to survive with this wound."

"Yes, please tell me why depression is a capital offence." Samuel gently placed Wellem on the ground and sat up.

"With the damage to the wing of Wellem, as it is, he will no longer be able to get food for himself. Without food he will slowly wither away, in pain and die. This must be so with Your-kind as well as all-kind."

Samuel ran his fingers through his hair. "Wouldn't you or the others get food for him?"

"What is it you suggest, Samuel Rochez?" Jawell said aghast. "I have already told you that he will be depressed. It will not be possible for any of the Home-kind to have any contact again with Wellem."

"Okay, Jawell, we keep coming back to the same issue. Just relax and explain why depression is bad for you."

Samuel's calmer tone seemed to ease Jawell. "I would assume that any-kind would know. Perhaps your-kind have not the understanding because you do not talk or feel as deeply as the Home-kind."

"If Wellem were to have contact with the Home-kind the depression he feels would spread to the rest of the Home-kind."

Nodding his head, Samuel responded, "So the depression would spread like a disease. What effect would it have?"

"Soon all of the Home-kind would become depressed and stop working and in the end even to the last stop eating and eventually die. The Home-kind village would be no more forever."

"Oh," said Samuel. "It would be like when you all were frozen in the battle, feeding off from and reinforcing each other's shock.

"Okay, that's one big negative for your kind of telepathy. You must be constantly on guard against the wrong type of emotions."

"It is true that the Home-kind are prepared to act quickly when something like this can happen. You now have the understanding of this event, Samuel Rochez?"

"Yes, I got it."

"Then it will be that you will not interfere when the Ip return again?"

"Well, let's talk about that for a moment. Have any of your people ever recovered from depression?"

"No, Samuel Rochez. It is not possible for what you suggest to happen."

Samuel leaned forward and placed a hand on Jawell. "Could it be that no one was around long enough to recover?"

"I do not understand what you suggest, Samuel Rochez."

"Among many-kind hope and recovery can counteract depression." He pointed to Wellem. "He may be able to fly again. The splint and bandages work for many-kind. They may work for Wellem.

"If he knows that he may fly again, that hope may ward off depression. And, if he does recover, you son will have been saved and your village not endangered. Wellem would be able to help again.

"Isn't it worth a try?"

"You are certain, Samuel Rochez, that this will allow Wellem to be able to fly again?"

"No, I'm not. I don't know your physiology and I'm not a doctor. But, there is a chance, there is hope."

"Samuel Rochez, it may be as you say, but how long will this recovery of which you speak take to complete? Wellem could still suffer hunger to death. The Home-kind cannot risk contact with him until we know the depression has passed."

"Well, here again I don't know, but generally it would be six to eight weeks. Could your people leave a large quantity of food for him to survive on until then?"

Samuel felt Jawell's unease. "I must share this with the Home-kind. We will come to a decision soon for the sake of Wellem."

"Good, I'll wait with him. He'll need some one to tell him what's going on when he comes around."

"Thank you for your assistance with this matter, Samuel Rochez. It would be good if my son could help again." With that Jawell broke the link and took to the sky.

Just as contact broke Samuel felt something new in Jawell, hope.

###

Several hours passed before Wellem came to life. His initial thoughts were dedicated to processing the pain in his body. Samuel wished he knew more of their biochemistry. Several types of painkillers resided in his med-kit. Any one of which could ease the native's pain or kill him.

"Wellem, do the Home-kind use any kind of plant to lessen pain? I'll get some for you if there is."

Samuel's contact shook Wellem out of his self-absorption. "My wing! My wing! I can't move my wing! What is happening to me?"

"You were injured by the Eaters. I've bound up your wing so that it may heal."

"Heal? How is it possible for you to heal a wing?"

"Well, not me personally, but your body may be able to heal itself, if the wing is held immobile long enough."

"Where are the others of the Home-kind? There is no feel of them anywhere. Where is it that my father has gone to? Why am I here in this field alone? Where are the others?"

Samuel forced down the panic flooding into him and tried to force some calm onto Wellem. "Wellem, your father went to talk to the Home-kind about your wing. They are afraid that you will be depressed. We're hoping that by setting your wing that will not happen."

"Depressed? Then the Ip should come to help me. I must render help to the Home-kind, not endanger them."

"Wellem, you are not depressed. I can feel your confusion and panic, but you are not depressed. There is a good chance that you'll be able to fly again and not be depressed. Trust me on this. I've seen this technique work on many-kinds."

It was a risk, telling him everything would be okay, when he didn't know at all. But, Wellem needed hope more than any cure. Maybe if he learned to live without flight for six weeks, or so, he could learn to live without flight for the rest of his life without depression.

"So, the pain will go away, and my wing will become better?" Much of the stress had left him.

"Yes, but it will take time, forty-two light-times or so. You will be here in this field during that time. The Home-kind will leave food for you. At the end of that time, the Home-kind will come and check on you."

"Will you stay with me, Samuel Rochez?" Wellem's composure wavered.

"For a light-time or so. Just until Jawell comes back. There is a meeting of your-people I must attend, and we can't put it off for very long. The Home-kind will be in great danger if the Loscar arrive before we are prepared." Samuel rested his hand on Wellem's side. "Don't worry, it'll be hard, but you'll make it through. Just focus on being reunited with your family."

"Yes, I do understand your meaning. You will help the whole of the Home-kind by doing this thing. I will give my help by staying here and hoping to rejoin the Home-kind yet again."

Those brave words came from the young native, but he couldn't hide his true feelings. There were no secrets among the Home-kind.

"You're not alone yet, and won't be for days." Samuel got comfortable and pulled out a compass. "How'd you like to know how this works?"

Chapter 13: Carlinium

Blinking his eyes open, Stagar winced at the stabbing medical bay light. Voices beat against his ears, but his mind could only absorb the words like a stone. Slowly the pains in his body began to resolve and localize.

Bringing his hand up to rub at his burning right eye, he found an empty socket. He quickly checked the other. A moment later he realized that he wouldn't be seeing if he lost both.

Where could he have lost it, he wondered. He remembered having two eyes.

Something cold pressed against his neck. A voice grew loud in his ear as he felt breath on his face. "Wakey-Wakey, Stagar, time to die," it said in a singsong rhythm, but dripped with malice.

Stagar wondered with his slowly dawning consciousness, if this person knew where his other eye might be. Then, realization broke upon him with all the speed of a ripening melon. His life was being threatened. With all of his will he focused on the voice.

"Give it to him again," the voice said.

He quickly became uncomfortable and tried to pull his face away from something. He felt a biting pain in his nose. He took a quick sniff to try and clear the offence, but it burned the greater. The discomfort became lost in a fit of sneezing and coughing.

The room came into sharp relief. Lance stood over him with his favorite killing knife out. Williams drew his hand away from Stagar. He held a white capsule.

With the last sneeze he met Lance's gaze. "So, you're finally back." Lance said.

"What happened?" Stagar forced out.

Lance pulled up a chair and sat in one smooth motion. "What, you mean how you ended up here, missing an eye, with me in charge? I could show you, but you probably wouldn't survive. And, I'm willing to let you live a little longer, if you can prove yourself useful."

Stagar lay his weight back down on the table and caught his breath. Images flashed in his mind of the beating he had taken, and the mutiny of Lance.

Lance would probably keep him alive to conclude the business deals once they were off the planet. He always kept such details to himself for just such an eventuality.

But, something didn't feel right. He missed something, he knew. Just beyond his grasp an important detail lay hidden. Wanting to know all his cards before dealing with Lance, he stalled.

"Obviously you want something specific from me, or I wouldn't be alive to have this conversation." Stagar knew Lance well enough to realize that Lance wouldn't kill an unconscious man. He'd want to see fear and the life draining out of his victim's eyes.

"Do you remember what Epstine said just before your accident?" Stagar nodded.

Epstine, Stagar could see him in his mind standing outside the ship. He said something; something about the Loscar survey ships.

The memory came rushing into his mind, planetary lockdown. The survey ships placed satellites in orbit to form a shield around the planet. A virtually impregnable shield that kept others out and them in.

Of course it was the obvious move for the Loscar. So, they'd be trapped here, only to be discovered by the Loscar when they returned. Not exactly how he planned it.

Stagar kept his poker face on as the thoughts raced through his mind.

"So, Lance, you're hoping I can figure a way to break out of Lockdown?"

"Stagar," Lance drew out his words. "I have a nice, slow, agonizing death planned for you. Now, we can get started on that right here and now. If; however, you could come up with a way off this grub hole, I might be persuaded to put that off for a while.

"So," Lance smiled, "what you got?"

There was only one way to get past the satellites, they had to unlock them. The encryption would probably not be broken in his lifetime, if ever. This would be a bone to throw Lance while he tried to figure out another way.

"Epstine could start working on breaking the code lock."

Lance shook his head. "He's started, but doesn't think it can be done. I've given him three days, and then I start cutting off toes."

Lance absentmindedly fiddled with his knife. "I would prefer to start with the fingers, but he needs those to work on the code."

Stagar knew that no weapon in existence could break a lockdown, neither directed energy or explosives. The most powerful bomb ever built was used to try and break through a shielded planet and it failed miserably. They didn't have the materials to make anything even close to that yield. A group of anti-ship missiles and two laser cannons summed up their offensive capability.

"Wait a minute," Stagar said. "There may be a way." Stagar grinned. "Of course, it was impossible before, because no one ever had enough Carlinium."

Lance grabbed Stagar by the collar and drew him close, squinting into his one good eye. "What are you saying? Don't try and play me."

"Don't you see? We have vast quantities of Carlinium. If we can enhance a missile to harness that energy we may be able to generate enough of a blast to take out one of the satellites."

Lance slammed him back on the bed as he scratched his head. "Maybe. Possibly. That doesn't sound very reassuring, Stagar."

"Get me Epstine and Thompson and I can get it a lot closer to certain. Besides, Lance, this will be the biggest explosion you've ever seen. The largest since the big bang. Heck, it'll probably take a large chunk of the planet with it."

Lanced paused for a moment, obviously thinking. "Okay, I'll have Harris bring them to you.

"Now, between the two of us, I don't have to threaten you do I? You know what will happen if you try and cross me."

"Don't worry, Lance. I want to get off the rock as much as you do. Nothing else really matters, because if we don't get off, the Loscar will kill us all anyway."

As Lance reached the door, he turned. The corner of Lance's mouth turned up in a grin that lit up in his eyes. "Sorry about the eye, Stagar."

###

Stagar limped into the mess hall. Lance sat in the corner, back to the wall, finishing off the last of the eggs. The rest of the crew focused on their steaming bowls of food ration. In a by gone time it would have been called gruel.

Stagar sighed. If the plan hadn't been interrupted, he would be dining like a proverbial king at this moment. He brought excess rations, good stuff. The crew's feast, a reward and a distraction. With full bellies and promise of wealth, the jackals would be less likely to turn on him.

At least now, they were Lance's problem. If the crew got bloodthirsty, it wouldn't be his hide they'd come after.

Stagar sneered as he limped over to Lance. Lance didn't look up. "You know, breakfast is the most important part of the day," Lance said around the egg in his mouth. He sopped up the runny yolk with a crust of bread, and made a big deal of savoring it. Finally, licking his fingers, he stood up and dragged Stagar from the hall.

Once out of ear shot, he demanded, "What have you got, Stagar Inman?"

Stagar directed his eye at the floor. It was best to act submissive, until the right opportunity presented itself. Once they were off the planet. He would let Lance take the heat until then.

"Epstine and Thompson are running the numbers. But tentatively, the yield should be large enough to take out one of the satellites. We're not certain how big the shock wave will be, nor how much of it will escape into space and what will be trapped inside the shield. But..."

Stagar winced as Lance dug his fingers into the smaller mans shoulder. "I don't like buts."

"But," Stagar spoke through clinched teeth. "There may be a problem if the Carlinium has many imperfections in it. Something about shear forces and the crystal being broken and scattered instead of amplifying the explosion. And, well, naturally occurring crystals are never perfect, so we'll have to search for the best we can find."

"They're up in Epstein's sty now?"

"Yes," Stagar responded.

Lance slammed Stagar against the wall and headed down the hall. When out of sight, Stagar massaged his shoulder.

Looking around, Stagar found himself alone. Spoons in bowls made a dull tapping sound from the mess, while the ventilation system hummed.

Lance had forgotten to sick Harris on him. Without that bird dog, he had a couple of minutes free. And that would be all he needed for now. He limped down the hall in the opposite direction from Lance.

Chapter 14 Plans

Stagar stepped over the threshold into Epstine's hovel. The plump, harmless man looked up from a terminal with a wrinkled brow.

"Surprised to see me?"

"What are you doing here? Did Lance send you?" He pushed his chair back and stood up. "Does Lance know you're here?"

Softening his voice, Stagar closed the door behind him. "Mister Epstine, Lance doesn't need to know everything that is going on. He's much too busy trying to hold this crew of miscreants together to be worried about who talks to whom."

"But, Lance is in charge." Epstine crossed his arms over his chest. "He beat you blind. He doesn't like me. I mean, he really doesn't like me. He'll kill me if I cross him." His whole body began to shake.

"Lance won't kill you. He needs you, and he knows that. Besides, what harm can there be in two old friends talking?" The locking mechanism pinged into place as Stagar pressed the button.

Epstine put his hands on the display table in front of him, resting his bulk against it, shaking his head from side to side.

Stagar rubbed his hand along some of the equipment as he walked closer to the nervous tech. "I assume the security recording system is off in here."

Epstine straightened, paused for just a second, and shuffled to a corner and flicked a switch. The poor man trembled, leaning against the wall.

Reaching his side, Stagar put a hand on the tech's shoulder. "Everything will eventually be made right. Now, let's say we have a little chat about our mutual friend, Michael Lance.

"Now, Mister Epstine," Stagar ushered the man to a chair and sat him down. "We've had many profitable missions together, haven't we?"

Epstine didn't answer, nor look up. Moving around in front of the technician, Stagar rested against the edge of a control panel. "It's been several years and I've never let Lance harm you, or even bother you. Haven't I?"

Looking up Epstine said, "No," then resumed his examination of the floor.

Good, thought Stagar, the technician had largely capitulated to him. He didn't have much time to coax Epstine into his service.

"And I'd stop him now if I could."

Epstine looked up again, briefly.

"That's right, I'll be dead soon. Once Lance is finished demonstrating that I'm not needed, that he's better than me, I'll be expendable. Once I'm dead, who'll be there to look out for you, or the other men? Even though they are rabble, they don't deserve what Lance has planned for them. They may have let Lance take over, but they don't deserve to die."

"They're going to die?" Epstine asked with a quiver in his voice.

"You think that Lance is going to share any of the vast wealth we've collected? You think he'll let others survive that could point him out to the authorities, or the Loscar, or the business men who'll purchase our cargo only to see its value drop to almost nothing in a few weeks or months?

"No, he needs everyone to go away."

He put his hand on Epstine's shoulder and when the technician looked up, Stagar stared intently into his eyes. "And right now, the only one who can stop him, Mister Epstine, is you."

"But..." he began.

"Mister Epstine, don't think about yourself, don't think about me. Think about the rest of the men. Think of Mister Kim. He's just a boy. It's his very first mission. Does he deserve to die?"

Epstine shook his head.

"No he doesn't. Right now, we all need you to be strong, stronger than you've been in your life. You, Philip Epstine, need to become a hero. Will you do it for yourself, for the good of the men, and for me?"

"Well..." Epstine trailed off again.

Stagar noted the clock on the wall. He escaped Harris almost ten minutes before. Harris had to be searching the ship for him. If Lance found out he'd have teams sweeping the ship and surrounding area. He expected someone to bang on the door in just a few more minutes.

"It comes down to this. Do you want to live for years to come? To have a beautiful wife, a family, children who love you, or do you want to die on some unknown planet on the edge of the galaxy?"

"A beautiful wife?" He perked up a little.

"Yes, think of the wealth you'll receive out of this mission. You'll be rich beyond your dreams. You can afford to be made over, to appear handsome and young. You'll be rich. Now what woman can resist a handsome rich man? And on top of that you'll still be the sweet, lovable, person on the inside. The perfect package." Stagar patted the other man's shoulder.

"You can have it all; all your dreams come true. But for it to happen, you need to live through this mission. You're fighting for the future Mister Epstine, the men's, mine, and especially yours. Will you do it?"

Epstine looked down again. "What do I have to do?"

Putting on his most sympathetic voice, Stagar said, "That's right. You're doing the right thing.

"This will be very simple. Lance will want to push the button that launches the missile himself. He'll get a thrill out of it, of releasing destruction on an entire world. All you have to do is to wire a charge to the console, so that when he presses the launch button, it will also send a jolt of energy through his system that will shut down his heart and brain.

"Is that do-able, Mister Epstine?"

Looking up with a wrinkled brow, Epstine said, "Well... Yeah, there is enough power in the circuitry, but how will I get in there to wire it up?"

"You are the ship's technician. You are going to repair a minor component, and you want to check the equipment so that nothing goes wrong with the launch. No one will question you."

"Okay," he sighed, "I'll do it. But you can't tell anyone, ever."

"Trust me, Mister Epstine," Stagar smiled. "It'll be our secret to the grave."

Stagar cleared his throat, "There is one more issue we need to deal with."

"What else could there be?" Epstine asked wide-eyed.

"Lance is going to assume that I came to you for help in overthrowing him. He can be sadistic, but unfortunately for us, he's intelligent."

"What?" Epstine sat up and looked frantically around the room.

"Don't worry; there is a way to get you through it without revealing our plan. You cannot tell him what we are really going to do, or everything is lost, including your future. So when he comes to call, resist a little then tell him I asked you to sabotage the engine. That way when the ship won't take off, the men will lose faith in Lance. Then I can step in to save the day and get the men to rally around me."

"But what if he doesn't believe me?" Epstine stammered and his gaze dropped to the floor again.

"It's possible. I doubt these hooligans would rally around anyone they weren't afraid of, or who isn't buying them off."

"Stagar, I can't do it."

"Yes you can, and you will. Look, you'll be nervous, scared for your life, you don't have to fake any of it, don't try and be calm. Lance knows we're plotting against him, and he knows you can't hold your water when the pressure is on. Try to resist just a little bit, then let him have it."

"What if he doesn't believe me?" The technician trembled.

"You're repeating yourself, Mister Epstine. If he doesn't believe that story, tell him I asked you to put a nerve gas canister in his quarters with a timer. He'd expect something like that. And after you tell him this, don't look at him, stare at the ground, lean against the wall or sit down. You'll look more defeated that way."

Stagar looked at the clock again. Another three minutes had passed. He turned and headed for the door. "Just stick to the plan and I'll get you out of this, alive and wealthy"

"Stagar, I don't think..."

"Good," Stagar cut him off as the unbolted the door. "Do as I've..."

Stagar stopped just before opening the door. "Here's a good idea. As soon as I leave, go and get a canister of nerve gas and put it in Lance's quarters with a timer to go off in the middle of the night. Then you'll be telling the truth and Lance will have evidence to back it up."

Epstine's white-faced stare met his gaze. Stagar smiled the warmest, most reassuring he could muster, "Trust me, you can do it. Now, get to it as soon as I leave."

Stagar slid through the hatch without giving the technician time to respond. Despite his weaknesses, Epstine did have a moral center, which set him apart from the rest of the cutthroats on the mission. Stagar reassured himself before heading down the hall. The tech would whimper, cry, and complain about it, but he always ended up doing what he was told. He'd do the right thing. Stagar nodded to himself.

Seeing no sign of an all out search, he decided to make a detour to the weapons locker. Lance thought it secure, that only he could get in. Stagar patted the bulkhead as he passed through a hatch. He smiled to himself. Only he knew all the secrets of the ship. A few strategically hidden weapons on the ship would come in handy if Epstine failed.

Chapter 15: opportunity

The sun shone bright upon the field outside the ship. Lance had the men assembled, doing calisthenics. He drove the mercenaries out of bed every morning as the local sun came up. Their fear of him motivated them, as opposed to Stagar's coddling. Stagar allowed himself the slightest of grins. The forced workout would only turn them more against Lance.

Stagar leaned against the ship watching Epstine straining to keep up with Lance's vicious pace. A waste of talent. Epstine, the only good man among them, should have been working on calculations and designs with Thompson, instead of being beaten down.

As they finished, Epstine lay panting on the ground, all red in the face. Stagar looked to Lance whose breath came regular and slow. The brute wouldn't let his body move off from peak.

"Alright ladies, now that we've had a nice relaxing stretch out, we have real work to do. I have a plan to get us off this rock. To do it, we, and I mean you, have to find some pure Carlinium crystals, about the size of Epstein's head over there." Lance strutted in front of the disheveled men.

"Each and every one of you will go into the hold, uncrate the Carlinium and examine them. Thompson will teach you idiots what to look for. Find anything promising and bring it to him. If it's really promising, he'll bring it to me.

"Harris," he turned a pointing finger at him, "you'll supervise."

Standing with hands on hips he surveyed the group. Then with a guttural bark, "Get to it."

The men ran for the ship. All except for Kim, who stopped to help Epstine up.

Lance spun on him. "You let that overweight fat farm get itself up. He's a man, or should be. Nobody does his work for him." Kim bent backwards as Lance poked him in the chest.

Stagar turned from the scene and started for the hatch, when Lance's voice boomed over the field. "No Stagar, you're with me. Now!"

Stagar paused. He didn't know what Lance wanted now, but more than likely it would be unpleasant for him.

Turning, Stagar limped sheepishly towards the larger man. He nodded to Epstine as they passed each other. He would be the only ally he might trust.

"Yes, Lance."

Lance put his arm around Stagar's shoulder, as a friend might. No, this didn't look good at all.

"Yesterday," Lance started, "After I left you in the hall, where did you go?"

Stagar felt his pulse quicken with a slight jolt of adrenaline. "I went to the medical bay to get some more pain killers." He didn't really need the painkillers, but wanted someone to be able to verify his location in case questions arose.

"Yes, I know. I spoke with Green. But it should have only taken you a couple of minutes to get there. So, I had to ask myself why it took you over 15 minutes?"

Lance rested all of his weight on Stagar. The knee injury he'd suffered began to burn and send shooting pains up to his hip.

"I have a bum leg now. It took me so long because I waddle, not walk, and I stopped along the way to rest and massage the leg. Look, I was in no condition to run a marathon."

Lance shifted his hold to a headlock and dropped into a squat, bringing Stagar's full weight crashing down onto his knees. Stagar cried out.

"Now, I thought we weren't going to need this conversation. You must realize, that even if I'm not around, I know where you are and what you're doing. So, don't try anything, ever." Lance twisted and rolled over on top of Stagar resting his weight on his victim's chest.

"Lance," Stagar wheezed out, "there is a problem."

Lance lifted some of his weight off. "What kind of problem?"

Stagar sucked in a deep breath. Hopefully this distraction would earn him a reprieve. "All the Carlinium we have in the hold came from the same site."

"So?"

"Well, that was a generally contaminated site, it's likely none of the Carlinium will be suitable."

Lance squinted his eyes.

"Lance, you should send out a couple of teams to collect samples from other caches. If this one doesn't work out, well, there has to be some clean stuff on this planet."

Lance released him and stood up. "Good thinking," he said as he kicked the prone figure in the ribs. "I'll take it under advisement."

He left Stagar curled up on the ground. As Lance reached the hatch he called back. "You have five minutes to get to the hold, or I won't be so restrained."

###

As Lance entered the ship, he came upon John Harris, headed his way. Harris nodded his head in greeting and asked, "Where's Stagar?"

Lance answered him with a right cross to the face. Harris staggered back against the bulkhead. Before he could get a startled response out, Lance had him against the wall with is forearm crushing against his throat.

"Where's Stagar?" Lance repeated through clenched teeth. "You're supposed to be on him day and night. You were supposed to be on him yesterday when he had the run of the ship." Lance pressed in harder with each word, as Harris squirmed against the force.

"You wanted to talk to him alone!" Harris managed to squeak out.

"Oh, so you figured I'd do your job for you, while you digested your breakfast."

"No, no," Harris called as he grabbed at Lance's arm.

Lance pulled back and let Harris fall, holding his throat and gasping for breath.

"You see, my good and dear friend," Lance almost spat the words out. "Stagar is up to something. His passiveness is just an act. Given one minute to himself he can cause more mischief than the rest of the crew could pull off in a year.

"Stagar's not some bumbling fool. So from now on, you are with him every minute of every day." Lance raised his voice. "When he goes, you'll be there to wipe him."

Harris nodded his head in agreement.

"Good," Lance said as he helped Harris get up. "We have to stick together on this if we are to come out on top. Now go out there and get him."

###

It took three days to go through the Carlinium in the hold. None of it passed the test. The ten days that followed yielded no usable Carlinium either. Even small samples brought back by the expeditions had faults and inclusions. "Faults and inclusions," Stagar said to himself. Even these ruffians had grown familiar with the terms.

Harris's black eye had cleared up. The last visible testament of Lance's displeasure about the free time Stagar had gotten away with had faded; however, Stagar suspected the memory wouldn't. Stagar allowed himself a satisfied smile. The more of the mob Lance alienated, the easier it would be for him later. He simply needed to stand back and let Lance dig his own grave.

Stagar's smile quickly disappeared as he saw Lance out of the corner of his eye. Lance leaned against the hull, next to the pile of discarded Carlinium crystals. They meant nothing if they remained stranded on the planet. The only valuable Carlinium at this point would be the one special crystal that could get them off the planet.

Lance had taken to spending his time watching the men. He had grown quiet, like a hunting cat setting up to strike.

The men avoided him, not wanting to give Lance an excuse to come down on them. Only Epstine and Thompson spoke to him. They had to. And to most everyone's surprise, Lance didn't shoot the messenger.

Stagar knew Lance well enough to have predicted this. Behind his brutishness lay intelligence. Although he reveled in the beast, he could cage it when necessary.

"Lance! Lance!" Thompson came booming out of the ship.

Lance glared at him.

Thompson sprinted to Lance with something in his hand. Stagar couldn't make out what, so he got up and moved closer. Harris followed at his shoulder.

Thompson tossed the item to Lance, who caught it in one hand. It seemed like a fabric of some kind, with shiny objects knit in.

"What's this?" Lance asked.

"It's the sash we took off that grub we captured earlier." Thompson spoke quickly between gulps of air.

Lance moved it over in his hands, examining it in detail. He stood up straight. "This is Carlinium."

"Yes, and they are very clean. A few of them are perfect. They're small, but the best we've seen so far.

"Lance, this could very well be our escape."

The three of them were the only ones near enough to hear the exchange. They all froze as Lance contemplated. Stagar knew Lance wouldn't need his advice on the next course of action. It would take Lance just a little bit longer to reach his conclusion.

"Boys," Lance yelled. Those in earshot stopped and jogged up to the ship.

Lance held the sash aloft, and he spoke with a quietness that seemed to fill the whole field. "It's time that we look up our old comrade, Samuel Rochez." His smile broadened across his face.

Chapter 16 Hunted

Stagar watched the men's reactions. Confusion and blank looks covered their faces. Lance's joy at the thought of getting his hands on Rochez again broke across his face in an evil grin. Yes, they needed Samuel to find the grub's burrow, but if Lance approached this with the same blunt force he liked to use, Samuel could elude them.

"Lance," Stagar offered tentatively. "Could I talk with you for a moment, please?"

Lance turned, his happy face gone. "What is it?" he barked.

"I think you'll want to discuss this in private." Stagar nodded his head towards the men.

Lance snorted, clamped down on Stagar's arm, and hauled him toward the rear of the ship. With a shove from Lance, Stagar banged into the side of the ship, shoulder first.

"What is it?" Lance demanded crossing his arms over his chest.

"Well, we're going after Rochez. There are a few things you should know before planning this expedition."

Lance leaned in closer. "Get to the point."

Stagar did his best to look intimidated. "Rochez was a high ranking officer in the Human Forces."

Lance balled up his fist and examined it.

"All officers of that rank had transmitters hidden in their bodies. It's there in case they get lost or captured, a way of locating them."

Lance brought his gaze back to Stagar's eyes.

"He went straight to prison camp from the battle at Darnath. That, and since he's been avoiding human contact, it's probably still in him."

Lance nodded to himself. "And you can get the signal?"

"Epstine can get the signal. He's a pack rat of information with those systems of his."

"Good," Lance said and started to turn.

"But," Stagar's word stopped Lance. "It's not a very strong signal and with the Carlinium around, we'd have to be quite close to pick it up. Epstine can give you an estimate on distance."

"Okay," Lance started to turn again.

"And," Stagar waited for Lance to turn back his way. "Rochez will think we are long gone. If he sees the ship in a search pattern over head, he'll go to ground. If he hides among an outcropping of the crystals, we may never pick him up."

"What do you suggest, your eminence?" Lance slowed down the last words turning them into an insult.

"Use a couple of drones at tree top level. Once we know the general location we can bring the ship in close, but undetected, and then send out recon teams. Three men per team I'd imagine, with stun weapons. We need him alive."

Lance waited for a moment. "You got anything else to say?"

"No, that's it." Stagar shrugged.

"Good." Lance stormed off.

Leaning against the ship, Stagar relaxed and took a few deep breaths. He'd managed to give Lance the plan without adding to his injuries.

Stagar looked up to see Harris a few paces away. He'd obviously learned his lesson.

Sliding down the side of the hull, Stagar rested in a sitting position and began to ponder how he could use Samuel's return to his advantage.

###

The first rays of the morning sunshine felt good on Samuel's face. After two days of rain, he soaked in the warming light. He stood on the rock outcropping, stretching out and massaging bruised muscles. The rocky mountainside offered little for bedding besides boulders and gravel. Glancing up to the top of the ridge, he estimated they'd reach the top a little after noon. Once on the other side, Jawell promised him the ground would be gentler.

He hadn't had the opportunity to study the lay of the land from orbit. From this vantage point he could see the line of the river that almost took his and Jahara's lives. The Home-kind village lay behind some rolling hills. Samuel took a deep breath as he scanned the scenery.

A bright silvery spark of light caught his eye, but as he turned his focus it disappeared. The flash appeared for less than a second, only a visual snap of the fingers.

Surveying the area, he saw nothing out of the ordinary. Trees and grasses filled his view. The brown grass began to take on a greenish yellow hue as new shoots were coaxed out by the recent precipitation.

Bending down to pick up his vest, he paused to touch Jawell. "Let's get started, shall we?"

Several hours of scrambling over and trekking around rock formations brought them close to the peak. Samuel took a moment to share his canteen with Jawell. Mopping his forehead on his sleeve he said, "It's going to be a hot one today."

"Indeed as you say, Samuel Rochez, but it is none the less beautiful."

Samuel gazed out again. "It is that." A ridge of mountains to the northeast caught his eye. "Jawell, that line of mountains over there," he brought up an image of them in his mind. "Is that where you led the Eaters to?"

"Yes indeed it is, Samuel Rochez. They are on the far side. When the scouts last saw the herd, they were traveling down a valley directly away from the Home-kind.

"Where you come from does not have Eaters. It must be very nice for your-kind to not have to strive with this enemy."

"Jawell," Samuel said with a sigh, "There are many different types of Eaters. True, we usually don't have to deal with creatures eating our homes, but we have our enemies."

"Really," Jawell said with wonder. "What other type of hurt could you face besides the loss of home and family?"

Samuel shifted to a more comfortable position and took a swig of water. "My-kind are not alike," he paused and started again. "You, the Home-kind share your thoughts, so all know what each one is thinking. This is good for you. It keeps everyone honest."

"Honest?" Jawell asked.

"Jawell, you are better not knowing what it means. Basically we do have our threats from external forces, similar in some respects to the Eaters. But My-kind is often a greater threat to ourselves."

"How can this be, Samuel Rochez, are you not all of one kind to each other?"

Samuel reached out and petted the native. "No, we are not of one kind. There are those among My-kind that kill and destroy for the sake of destruction. At least the Eaters are just trying to survive."

"Samuel Rochez, I believe what you say because you say it, but it does not seem possible. Would you be destructive?"

"Well, you saw me kill many Eaters. I could kill and destroy if the cause were good enough or to stop a greater destruction."

"Your ways are not possible to understand. I will try to know what it is you teach, but it will be most difficult."

"Jawell, please don't try. You people don't need this type of knowledge. Besides we're on our way to do some good. Let's get started."

Samuel stood and turned around. Moving to his left he found an easy ascent. He tested the handholds a couple of times before pulling himself up.

A few minutes of climbing brought them to the last outcropping before the peak. Samuel wiped the dirt and sweat from his hands as he looked for the easiest path. Jawell sat near his feet. The native always waited for him to make the next level before flying up to join him. Samuel suspected that to the Home-kind it showed respect.

The ledges provided many hand and foot holds. "Another minute and we'll be at the top," he said as he started the climb.

His hand crested the ledge and he took a firm grip. Getting his feet to higher holds he pushed with his legs bringing his eyes just over the lip of rock.

He saw boots at first. Raising his gaze he recognized Kwanso Kim and two other mercenaries. One aimed a gun at his head.

Samuel let go with hands and feet; he just saw a flash as his head dropped. The ledge beat upon him as he slid down the jagged rock face. He covered his face with his arms, letting his elbows and forearms take the brunt of the buffeting. The shallow incline kept him from gaining much speed. He thudded to the lower ledge with a shout as the wind was knocked out of him.

As he lay there catching his breath, shouting bellowed from above.

"You missed him! Point blank and you missed him. I'm not taking the rap for this. If Lance is going to take this out on someone, it's not going to be me."

Recovering his breath, Samuel called out, "Kwanso, what are you doing here? You should have been gone weeks ago."

Why would Stagar choose to stay? He had the Carlinium, his future wealth secured; he had no reason to hunt Samuel down.

"We just couldn't go without you," came the response. One man's laughter rang out after the statement.

"What, does Stagar think I'll rat you out to the Loscar? None of you have to worry about that. I'd tell them the truth, that I was marooned here. But leave out the mining expedition. They'd believe me."

Pebbles tumbled and pinged off other rocks around him. The mercenaries had started to climb down after him, he realized.

Samuel pulled himself up and started towards the edge of the ledge. If he could get a little distance on them, he could lose them in the trees.

At the base of the mountain, in a small clearing a glint of what looked like metal caught his eye. Ripping the rifle from his back he brought its viewer up to his eye. The auto focus was instant. Three more of the men marched towards the base of the mountain. "Just perfectly wonderful," he mumbled.

"What is it, Samuel Rochez, that is going on?"

He stooped down to his little companion. "My-kind have come for me. I'm going to try and get away, but you need to get out of here now."

"Samuel Rochez," Jawell said with pride. "Their need for you is great. Is it not so, because they have come this far to seek you out. I am happy to the sky for you that you will again be able to help your kind."

"Jawell," Samuel said out loud, relaxing his clenched fists. "Remember what I said about the Eaters in My-kind. Well, that's what's going on here. I doubt my assistance will do much for them, but it will undoubtedly be bad for me."

A blast struck just to the right of his foot. Looking up he saw the muzzle of a gun and part of a face peeking over the rise above.

"Go!" he yelled and pushed Jawell away as he rolled in towards the mountain, out of the line of fire.

"Great, now what?" he said taking stock of his surroundings. They would be down in half a minute and the hunting party coming up would cut him off.

He rose to a crouching position, slung the rifle, and ran across the ledge. Slipping out of the vise seemed his only option.

He heard the thud of boots as one of the mercenaries landed behind him. The ledge arced along the side of the mountain. As long as it didn't switch back he'd be able to stay out of direct sight.

The ledge came to an abrupt stop at the edge of a cliff. Samuel looked down. The cliff fell straight down for twenty of thirty meters ending in jagged boulders.

The crunching sound of gravel beneath boots grew louder. Looking back, he couldn't see his pursuers. Only a few seconds remained to him. Reaching for the rifle he happened to look up. A small jut of rock overhung the ledge.

Letting the rifle fall against his back, he lunged to the ledge and frantically scrambled up. He pulled himself up and crouched into the rock as the scuffling of boots sounded below him.

"Where is he?" one of them said.

"He must have taken a cutoff somewhere back there that we missed."

Samuel heard the feet moving again. Then Kwanso's voice rang out from a distance. "No! He's over there, look around."

Samuel leaned forward, looking to catch sight of the men. How did Kim know where he was? Maybe he had seen him reach the edge of the ledge.

"Are you sure?" a booming voice asked.

"Yes, you're right on top of him."

It didn't matter how Kwanso could track him. They'd eventually find him. Samuel gingerly took out the rifle and stood up.

Inching towards the edge, he looked down upon two of the men who had been on the top of the mountain. "Don't move," he said with the business end of the gun aimed in on them.

They both looked up in frozen silence.

"Where's Kim?" Samuel demanded.

"Over here," came Kim's voice from his right.

From the corner of his eye he saw Kim prone on another small ledge. Just as he recognized the weapon in Kwanso's hands, he saw the muzzle flash.

Chapter 17: Reunion

Stagar checked the vital signs again. The read-out showed Samuel's health as normal, but it gave no indication as to when he would regain consciousness.

Pacing before the bed Stagar studied the still eyes, face and body for any sign of stirring. He needed to instruct Samuel, to plot the downfall of Lance. Between the two of them, they could take the ship back, and rid himself of the blight of Michael Lance.

Stagar clenched his fists, as Samuel's body lay limp on the procedure table.

He took an awful risk ditching Harris. His best hope would be if Harris didn't confess to losing his charge. They would both get away from punishment that way.

Harris's fear of Lance, however, might be too great. Confession would be less costly than having his failure uncovered by Lance. Lance appreciated weakness more in his enemies than in his allies.

Looking down at the motionless body he willed Samuel to wake up. Nothing happened. The status board read low but stable.

Stagar glanced at the monitor showing the hall outside the medical bay. It was empty. He couldn't count on it staying that way for long.

He walked back to Rochez, grabbed him by the shoulders and shook Samuel's limp body gently.

A light rumble reverberated through the floor. The monitor showed the hatch opening into the hall. Stagar shook more furiously, and patted Samuel's face.

The unconscious man let out a quiet sigh. Stagar patted his face with both hands. "Wake up, you fool! We only have a few seconds!"

Glancing back at the monitor he saw Lance approaching with several men in his wake. They were almost halfway down the hall. Stagar grabbed the Samuel's shoulders and violently shook his torso.

Samuel's eyes blinked open. Lance approached the door. Seconds remained. Stagar took Samuel's face in both hands and stared. "Look at me, focus."

Samuel's eyes locked onto Stagar's face. "Samuel, you must play along. That's the only way to get the slack we need. Don't challenge Lance; go along; be submissive. Lull them into thinking you are no threat."

Samuel's eyes drifted again.

Stagar stood straight up and stepped away from the table, just as the door slid open.

Lance strode in, leaning only lightly on his cane. "Stagar what are you doing here?" He quickly took in the room, "and where is Harris?"

Stagar folded his arms across his chest and rested against a desk. "I am not my keeper's keeper," he said looking down to the floor.

Four of the men filed in behind Lance, including Kim.

As Lance took a stride towards him, Stagar looked deliberately at Samuel. "He's coming around."

Lance turned his attention to the figure on the examination table. "Good," he said with a smile.

Both men moved to the side of the table as Samuel rolled his eyes around, not focusing on any one thing.

"So, you just thought you'd check up on him?" Lance asked.

Stagar shrugged. "It didn't do any good. He's barely conscious. I imagine it will be hours before he's able to think clearly."

The whooshing sound of the door announced another entry. "Lance, I swear, I only turned my back for a second."

Lance gripped Samuel's shoulder, and said to Harris, "We'll talk later."

Stagar noted the look of dread emerge on Harris's face. It served him right for throwing his lot in with Lance.

Turning his attention back to Lance he said, "from what I heard he took a nasty fall. Head trauma is a tricky thing. You can't coerce him back to full lucidity."

Lance's knuckles burned white on Samuel's shoulders. "No harm in trying," Lance responded. "He'll feel the effects when he wakes."

Scratching his chin, Stagar sighed. "Don't you think he has enough injuries? One more will not matter."

Lance released Samuel and turned on Stagar. Pressing his face close to the smaller man, "It matters to me," Lance said poking him in the chest.

Lance turned to Kim. "You caught him; now he's your responsibility." Lance stepped up to the four men. They pressed together and took a step back.

"Gentlemen," Lance said with a smile, "You've brought the lost sheep home; there's nothing to fear."

Lance placed a hand on each of the outer men's shoulders, as if taking the whole group as one. "At least two of you are to be with him at all times."

As Lance stormed towards the door, he called over his shoulder. "Tell me the instant he's conscious." Then he turned and made eye contact. "Don't underestimate him."

His gaze lingered on the men as if to burn his orders into each man's conscience.

With that he turned. "Harris, you're with me!" he ordered as he rushed out of the room.

Harris swallowed hard before following.

As they left Stagar made a mental note to turn the recorders back on. No doubt, Lance would be checking them.

Kim's crew remained silent for a moment, although the tension drained from the room. They spoke in hushed tones among themselves. Only Mixon looked his way, and that look burned with contempt.

Stagar took a moment to evaluate Samuel, and then the other men. He decided to leave. He would accomplish nothing in front of the riffraff.

With Samuel's return he had to modify the plan. Lance would be even more vigilant. The odds were against his being able to slip away again, that was, after Lance got through with Harris. He had to make the best use of the time. Lance would want both himself and Rochez on the bridge when the blast came. That would be his best chance, when Lance would be busy gloating.

With one last look back, Stagar slipped out of the medical bay, checked the hall, and headed off in the opposite direction Lance had taken.

Chapter 18: Revision

Stagar jogged down the halls, right at the first intersection then left, then two more down. His lungs struggled with the effort. If he'd been working out with Lance, he wouldn't be gasping for breath.

The antiseptic air burned in his nostrils. When not exercising, Lance kept the men busy cleaning the ship, rotating and restocking supplies, and whatever labor intensive project his little mind could come up with. Of course Stagar knew Lance was just keeping the men busy and tired. There would be less time and inclination for the crew to question Lance's ultimate plans for them.

Reaching the engineering room door, he took no time to catch his breath. Bursting in he called to the technician. "Mister Epstine, we've got Rochez, I need your help again."

"No!" Epstine stood up and rushed toward him. "You're not coming in here. We're not talking. I'm not listening. Just go!"

Stagar was taken aback by the speed with which the heavy man crossed the room, even more so when Epstine collided with him and pushed him towards the hall.

"But, you don't..."

"No!" Epstine cut him off and shoved him out the door.

"Epstine, please!" he called as the door slammed shut and the lock clicked into place.

Taking hold of the handle he pushed his weight against it, but it didn't budge. He banged several times on the door, for good measure. Checking his watch, he saw that one and a half minutes of freedom had already been used up. That was quicker than he hoped.

Stagar turned to his right and sprinted down the hall, taking his first left and stopping in front of an access panel. Opening the cover automatically turned off the security recording in the hall. He snaked a sweaty finger behind one of the cables and hit the hidden button freeing the fake panel to swing out on its hinge. He smiled. It was well worth the money to have these hidden access points scattered throughout the ship. Those and the old girl's other little secrets would all prove vital before the ordeal ended.

Tapping the terminal behind it brought a screen to life. Deftly working through the ship's schematic he located the tech room. Pressing the security icon he set the recording system to loop the last hour, then unlocked the door. It only took a few seconds to turn the system off, close it up and get back to Epstine's door. He stopped and took a deep breath before entering.

"No!" the tech roared, and launched from his seat. Sweat covered his red face and matted his hair. Stagar slammed the door and locked it before he could be assaulted. This time he dodged the onslaught.

"Mister Epstine, I've looped the recording, no one will be able to review this conversation." He moved around the central console keeping it between him and the enraged man.

"I'm not listening to you, Stagar. Lance will cut off my limbs. He'll cut them off in small pieces over a long period of time. And then, when he's done, he'll leave my torso on a carnivore-laden planet. I'll be eaten alive, unable to run or defend myself."

Stagar crossed his arms. "Lance told you that, did he?"

"He told me? Yes, he told me while cutting the tip of my little finger off." Epstine held up his left hand. The little finger squared off a centimeter short of where it should be.

Stagar had to admit that Lance knew how to motivate easily intimidated people. Others, like himself or Rochez, would take that as a challenge; the gauntlet being thrown down.

"The Medic sealed that up for you?" Stagar asked as they continued the dance around the console. "There isn't any more pain is there?"

"I don't care about the medic. I don't care about the pain. I care about Lance. What will he do this time?" Epstine, panting, stopped chasing Stagar and leaned against the bulkhead.

"That's all that has you worried?" Stagar smiled. "This time he'll give you a slap on your back hard enough to make you feel as though your eyes will pop out and say, good job."

"What... Why?"

"Because, my friend, he'll review the record and see that you very forcefully ejected me from the room without listening to anything I had to say. I'll make sure to be caught near the weapons locker. You'll be in the clear."

Epstine's breathing calmed a bit.

"That is, if I get out of here quickly," Stagar said, checking his watch. "You set up the charge through the launch key successfully?"

"Yes."

"Did anyone see you?"

"No, they were all outside."

"Good," Stagar let out a sigh. "You need to go and change it."

"What? No I won't. I'm not going back up there." Epstine stood away from the wall and began to move towards Stagar again.

"I think you'll want to. After all, you don't really desire to kill Rochez, do you?"

Epstine stopped. "Kill Rochez?"

"You're not a murderer. I mean, we've planned to kill Lance, but that's not murder. After all, he deserves it. But, Mister Rochez, that's something different. He may be a bit misguided, but he tries to do what he sees as right no matter what happens to him."

Epstine didn't respond.

"But, to the point: Lance will get much greater pleasure from forcing Rochez to launch the missile than from firing it off himself."

Epstine's face scrunched up and his mouth opened, but he didn't say anything.

"Remember, Mister Rochez threatened us all with a hand grenade over the life of a single grub. Imagine what he'd do to save a whole planet of them. Trust me; this is not lost on Lance. He'll want to look into Samuel's eyes as he presses the button that destroys his beloved grubs."

"Force him to push the button? How can he force him to do that? I mean, there is no way Samuel would do that."

Stagar glanced at his watch again. "I don't know, but Lance has certain creativity in getting people to do things that you and I can never hope to understand."

Epstine's gaze focused on the ground in front of his feet and fidgeted nervously.

"Phillip, no one really wants to destroy this planet. Well, no one except for Lance. We just don't have any other choice. You're doing the right thing working with Thompson."

Epstine shrugged.

"So you'll rewire the launch button?" Stagar moderated his voice to try and sound supportive and concerned.

Epstine nodded.

"What we need is a distraction. Can you rig it so that the fire suppression system and the collision alarm go off when the button is pressed? Oh, and add in the reactor overload alarm for good measure."

"And the missile?" Epstine asked still focused on the floor.

"Of course," Stagar stifled a laugh, "launch the missile. We need to get off this rock."

Epstine nodded his head.

"How much time will it be from launch to detonation?"

"A little over twelve minutes."

Stagar stood up straight. It should only take a couple of minutes at most; missiles are fast. "Twelve minutes, why so long?"

"Thermal coefficient of expansion."

"Yeah, so?"

"Traveling through the atmosphere, the friction will heat up the missile. The Carlinium is nice but not nearly refined quality. If it heats too much the inner surfaces may warp. Those surfaces are critical to the chain reaction. If they're not lined up correctly, it will just blow apart. That's what's been taking so long."

"Twelve minutes," Stagar let out a low whistle. "That's a lot of time for Lance to raise havoc.

"You'll have to go into hiding immediately after the launch. There's no way to tell how soon Lance will come looking for you."

Epstine took a deep breath, but otherwise didn't react.

"Hide in Lance's quarters. It'll be the last place they'll look. I'll find a way to get you to safety before it's too late."

Stagar needed to do something to build up the faltering man, so he crossed the room and gave the technician a hug. "You're a good man, Mister Epstine." He released the hug and stepped back, looking intently into the other mans eyes. "Are you alright?"

Epstine stood up straight and cleared his throat. "I can do it."

With a nod Stagar exited the room and sauntered down the hall. He'd give Epstine a bonus once they got out of this. If the fat man had the courage, Stagar might even let him pull the trigger on Lance. With his first design subverted by the capture of Samuel Rochez, he needed to come up with another plan for the final demise of Michael Lance.

Chapter 19: Options

Samuel recognized the antiseptic ceiling and walls; it took a moment to realize where he had seen them before. He raised a hand to gentle his throbbing skull. Groaning through the arduous ordeal of sitting up, he put the jigsaw puzzle of his memories together.

"Hey, he's up," a voice said. Turning towards the sound caused the room to spin and Samuel flopped back on the table.

Stagar must have decided to take him alive in order to keep him from informing the Loscar of their activities.

Samuel rubbed his temples.

He heard voices, but didn't focus on them.

But why take him alive? It would be easier to silence him permanently.

The door swooshed open and Lance entered, followed by Clancy the medic, Stagar and Harris. Samuel's attention turned to Lance's sidearm, a white handled stun gun, the kind Stagar always wore. But, he noted, Stagar was unarmed.

He met Stagar's one eye, the other hidden behind a black patch. He then sized up Lance. Except for the limp and cane he still appeared as immaculate as ever.

"I see things have changed," Samuel said, raising his head off the pillow.

"For the better," said Lance with a crooked smile.

"What do you want with me? You should have been gone weeks ago."

"Lockdown, Planetary lockdown," Stagar said.

Lance's smile faded for a moment, but returned quickly. "Yes, planetary lockdown; and you, Roach, are the key to opening it."

Samuel's mind raced. He didn't know how to break a lockdown. Key codes, commands, protocols, assault; they all had been tried by experts, who had failed.

Samuel laid his head back down. "Sorry, you're talking to the wrong guy. If anyone on this planet can figure it out, it's Epstine."

Lance's smile broadened as he sat down in one of the chairs. "We already know how."

"Then why do you need me?" He looked to Stagar for some clue, but the expressionless stare that came back revealed nothing.

"Let's see," Lance swiveled a bit in the chair, but kept his eyes on Samuel. The Cheshire cat smile never falling from his face. "You can't think of any way to break out of lockdown. Really? And I'd heard that you were a bright guy.

"Come on, try and figure it out. I'll even give you a hint." Lance's eyes opened wide as he said, "Boom." He let out a little chuckle.

Samuel looked to each of the others in the room, but none gave anything away. "You can't blast your way out. That would take more explosives than has been assembled in any one place. The only thing that could yield that much energy at once is..."

Samuel paused as he realized what they had planned. "Carlinium, you're going to start a chain reaction with Carlinium."

Lance applauded in a very slow rhythm. "You see, Harris, the Roach isn't stupid."

Samuel nearly lost his balance. "But...but a blast of," Samuel paused and swallowed, "that would be enormous."

"Yes, it would," Stagar confirmed, nodding his head.

Samuel could barely take in the extent of the explosive force that would be unleashed upon the planet. "Wait, wait," he said holding up his hand. "That much energy, what would it do to the planet?"

Lance moved his hands away from each other while exaggerating the words. "Again, boom."

Stagar cleared his throat. "Somewhere between twelve and eighteen percent of the planet will be vaporized, and a large part of the atmosphere will be ejected into space.

"Epstine's in uncharted territory here. He doesn't know how much the lockdown shield will inhibit the escaping gas and debris." Stagar shrugged.

"Yeah," Lance added, "and we'll use the planet as a shield to protect us from the shock wave."

Lance smiled like a delighted child. Samuel had never seen the brute express real joy before.

Lance leaned forward and stared Samuel in the eyes. "We all know what that means for the grubs." He sat back and spun around in the chair once.

"No, you can't, you just can't. There are millions, if not billions of intelligent people on this planet. Not even you, Lance..."

The words caught in his throat. The mercenary beamed with mirth. Samuel looked to Stagar.

Stagar shrugged and looked down, "Prices must be paid."

"No!" Samuel yelled, as he rose from the table and hopped to the floor in one fluid motion. Pain in his left hip exploded into his being. He flopped to the floor, hitting a table and scattering its contents.

Lance stood. "Pick up the trash and lash him to the table."

Samuel felt hands hoist him to the examination table. Tight bands wrapped quickly about his arms, legs and torso.

Lance leaned in close, his mirth tempered. "Now, what we need from you is the location of your little friends."

Samuel stared defiantly back.

"You see not just any carlinium will do. We need something very, very, pure." Lance snapped his fingers and held out his hand. Harris handed him something.

Lance held the object before Samuel. "Do you recognize this?"

Shiny bits sparkled in a woven, narrow piece of fabric. Samuel recognized Jawell's sash. He pulled up his hands to take Lance by the throat, but the restraints held. Rocking his shoulders side to side he tore at the restraints with all his might. Nostrils flaring with the effort, he searched the room for anything, anyone that would help.

"Ah, yes," Lance continued. "You are going is to lead us to the grubs."

"No, I am not!" Samuel stared directly into Lance's eyes.

Lance placed his forearm on Samuels's chest, crossed his legs and rested his weight on his victim.

"Of course you won't, at least not willingly. Now, I could take the next couple of days and beat it out of you in a variety of artistic ways."

"I won't tell you anything."

"No, I imagine you wouldn't." Lance cocked his head to one side. "But that doesn't mean it wouldn't be worth it. Unfortunately, we do not have that kind of time. So, we're just going to have to rely on modern medicine. Clancy," he called. "Give it to him."

The medic came around Lance with an injector. Samuel pulled against the restraints as the cold metal pressed against his shoulder. He couldn't even feel the hundreds of microscopic needles as they penetrated his skin.

Almost immediately the room began to spin and darken.

"And while you're at it," he heard Lance's voice, "fix his hip. We'll probably have to take a bit of a hike."

Chapter 20: Village

Everyone remained silent on the bridge as Kim and Stevens led Samuel in. Stagar noted the matted hair and flakes of dried sweat about Samuel's face.

It had not been a good night. The reactions to the inhibitors could push a heart patient over the edge, and a sizable percentage of survivors suffered strokes.. Samuel appeared to be one of the lucky ones.

"Prop him up at navigation," Lance barked.

Once they maneuvered him behind Espizito, Lance said in a relaxed tone, "Let's get this done." Nodding to Phillips, he added, "Take her up."

Stagar felt the rumbling of the atmospheric engines through his boots. The central view screen showed the ground slowly falling away.

"Hover at three hundred meters."

It only took a few seconds to reach the designated altitude.

Lance rose from the command chair and took two steps over to Samuel. Grabbing the drugged man's chin, he pointed his face towards the screen. "Now, tell me," he said almost sweetly, "where are your friends?"

The screen reflected in his glazed eyes. Raising a trembling hand he pointed to the screen. "Beyond those mountains and across the river," he slurred.

Lance's face tightened in a smirk. "And then?"

"To the west of those mountains in a valley. I... I can't tell from here," he stammered.

Lance patted him on the head. "Good boy. We'll get you closer and it'll come back."

Lance turned. "Let's go."

Philip's hands danced over the navigation console. The landscape raced down the screen for the few seconds it took to reach the river.

Lance stood erect watching the terrain on the screen. Without taking his eyes from the screen he asked Samuel, "Does this look familiar?"

"I'm not sure." Samuel winced as if the failure to give a definitive answer hurt. "I was mostly blind at the time."

Lance looked to the medic.

The medic shrugged. "The diag reported some optical trauma, and right now he can't lie, so yeah."

Lance placed a hand on Samuel' shoulder. "Now Roach, you're a bright boy. You can figure it out. Which way should we go?"

Staring intently at the screen Samuel pointed again. "It should be in those hills to the northwest. It's in a valley with a stream. On the north side of a ridge."

"Very good."

Lance stood and pointed to the screen. "Bring us up over those hills and scan for grubs."

Again the landscape scrolled down the screen for a few seconds, until the ridgeline rested at the bottom of the display.

"Got 'em, Lance!" a voice called out. "Two valleys over to the East."

"Good, take us down on the opposite side of the ridge from them. Move in low, surprise attack."

Lance patted Samuel on the head again. "Good Roach," he said with a broad smile.

He took the command chair maintaining his jovial expression, and flicked on the intercom.

"Gentlemen, load up. We're going in for a grub hunt, points for all confirmed kills."

Turning off the switch, he said to the men flanking Samuel. "Kimmy, bring the Roach's translation equipment and make certain the medic's got the recovery drug."

Kim nodded and went out the hatch.

Lance stepped over to Samuel and grabbed him by the hair. Yanking his head back, he looked into the distant eyes. "Your work for me isn't done yet."

Looking toward the two men flanking Samuel he said, "Take him down to the hold, we'll disembark from the main hatch." As they grabbed Samuel, Lance added, "And, let everyone else know."

The ridge's gentle grade made for an easy ascent. Kim and company took turns shepherding Samuel on the trek. Stagar watched as they supported Samuel on the steeper grades.

They crested the ridge right where a spring gushed from the ground. It disappeared under the trees just below them and appeared again on the valley floor.

At the base of the hills a lattice of black tendrils grew over the stream.

"The grubs are busy little vermin," Stagar said.

"What?" shot back Kim.

"Well," Stagar pointed, "look at it. The trees are woven together. You don't believe that is normal growth, do you? I'd call it a city."

Kim gazed for a second, shrugged and jogged a few steps to catch up with Samuel's minders.

"Keep moving." The butt of a gun jabbed meaningfully into his back. Stumbling forward he recovered his footing with a splash. Pulling his foot from the stream he shook off most of the water and trudged on after the others.

The descent took about fifteen minutes of disciplined silence. The dense forest covered their advance.

They stopped a few steps within the cover of the trees. Lance drew his rifle and signaled the others to do the same. He stared each man in the eye before turning his back and sprinted out of the woods with a shout, "Yah!"

The rest of the attackers charged after him. Stagar with his minder and Samuel with his, followed slowly behind.

Stagar blinked in the bright sun as he stepped out of the trees.

The closest of the grub trained trees burned with a dark blue flame. Lance took timed single shots counting off as the critters fell from the sky. The others shot at random grubs and areas of the trees that might contain life.

Stagar leaned over to Kim. "I'm no grub lover, but senseless slaughter is by definition, senseless."

Kim glanced at him through the corner of his eye but said nothing.

Stagar sat in the grass and watched as the carnage ended with a call from Lance. They regrouped around Stagar and Samuel.

"Ok medic, bring him round," Lance said to Emery.

The medic took out an injector and headed toward Samuel.

"Kimmy, equip the Roach. He's got a job."

Kim and the other minders set the translation equipment beside Samuel.

A moment after the injection, Samuel fell limp on the ground, his breathing fast and shallow. His torso shook with each breath.

Stagar looked on with the rest of the men forming a semi-circle around the prone form.

"How long?" Lance asked, squinting at Samuel.

"Couple of minutes, eight to ten at most." Clancy shrugged.

The nearest blazing tree heated Stagar's back. He turned to see it totally engulfed, flames arching high into the sky. If it weren't for the still air, the flames would have engulfed the entire structure. As it was, only the one tree burned.

The grubs flew from the stream to the fire, four to a woven basket, dribbling splashes of water as they hauled it up. They doused the trees next to the fires. It seemed they had dealt with fire before.

Stagar watched the coordinated efforts to save their home and realized that the grubs were more resourceful than he had expected. He filed this information with the rest of the random data floating around his consciousness. Any tidbit of information could become critical down the road.

"Bang," a single shot rang out. Stagar saw Lance from the corner of his eye with rifle raised to his shoulder. Following the line of fire, he saw three grubs struggling to keep a half empty basket aloft. Three of the four cords were attached. A grub flying a bit higher held the remnant of the fourth cord.

"Good shot," someone said. "Why not put holes in their buckets? Make 'em work for it."

Lance snorted. "Target's too big. Where's the challenge?"

Stagar stepped back as a hefty branch crashed a dozen meters away. Wiping the sweat from his brow, he took in the whole scene. The vermin held back the blaze like a machine, while the human rabble took occasional pot shots. He moved further away from the heat of the blaze and sat in the grass not far from Samuel.

His drugged up body had begun to relax, breathing more regular.

He leaned back on his elbows and watched puffy clouds drift across the deep blue sky. In the distance, rugged mountains rose up from the plain.

All in all, he thought it was a very nice day.

###

Samuel came to life with a shriek. His swollen red eyes blinked several times and he gasped for breath. Rolling to the side he retched out the contents of his stomach. Stagar reminded himself that every drug has its side effect.

Stagar rose and walked over. The burned trees smoldered in the background as acrid smoke scented the air. The bucket brigade slowed to douse the few spot fires about the area. The rest of the grubs roosted on the remaining trees and watched.

Samuel dry heaved a few times before sitting up. It took all his strength, Stagar noted. Although life lit in his eyes, his body trembled with the effort of being alive.

Motion from the branches drew Stagar's attention. The grubs parted as one of the creatures moved to the forefront. It stopped there for a second before launching into the air.

A chorus of activating weapons harmonized around him as the grub glided towards them.

"They got the message," Stagar said. "Let it approach."

"Get that equipment on the Roach," Lance ordered. "Stagar, pitch in."

Stagar and Kim sorted through the equipment. The headset configuration proved obvious enough. The rack of connectors, pads, and probes on the other end of the box defied the two men's understanding.

"Red and blue," Samuel waved faintly with his hand.

Taking the cables, he struggled to work the pad through the fur to the skin.

"Kimmy, speed this up!" Lance barked.

Taking over, Kim deftly attached the pad. Stagar noted the smile on the young man's face. As he attached a clip on the opposite side he joined Kim. Maybe it was the nice day, the gentle fur, or the tactile detail work, that satisfied him. He just couldn't keep it in. His smile broadened

"You ladies having fun?" Lance mocked.

Stagar dropped his hands and shook his head. The smile left his face. He still felt the happiness, but duller, like from a distance.

"That's enough," Samuel whispered.

Stagar and Kim stood up and stepped back.

Lance threw the sash in Samuel's lap and grabbed him by the scruff of the neck. "Find out where they get these crystals!"

###

"Samuel Rochez, It is a pleasure to the sky to find you are well. Your-kind have the most desperate need for help, as we can tell by the efforts they have gone through.

"We do not understand the Your-kind's actions, but the desperation is clear."

Samuel's weakness kept him from resisting the native's effervesant effects. "Yeah, they're not subtle. I'm sorry for the devastation.

"Look, we will go and leave your people alone. All they want is to find the source of the crystals in this sash."

"Samuel Rochez, there is something dark and heavy that you are holding in your thoughts. Is it a problem that I may be of some help with?"

"Their weapons are far too effective for the Home-kind." Samuel squared his shoulders. "No, there is nothing you can do. I'll take care of it."

"But, surely, would it not be much easier if the Home-kind were to help you in this?"

"Look, they are going to destroy all the Home-kind everywhere, all things alive, the Eaters, the trees, everything will be gone."

"But how is this thing to be possible?"

"Remember the grenade I used on the Eaters?" Samuel brought the image of the explosion up into his mind.

Visualizing the clearing of the planet, Samuel continued. "There are devices with much more power."

Jawell didn't respond. The shock flowed into Samuel from the collective understanding of the native community. A couple of the mercenaries gasped. They obviously felt it too.

"I'll find a way to deal with these guys. But first, to stop them from slaughtering your people, we need to show them where you got these crystals." Samuel held out the sash.

Jawell responded, "Ah, yes,"

Samuel felt a tingling of pride.

"These are of the most clear type. They come from a cave that is close to here. I would be most pleased to help by leading you to it."

"Of course you would, but there is no need to subject you to that. Just show me where it is in your mind."

Samuel felt the hurt feelings, instantly, and added, "This will help you and the Home-kind in ways that I can't explain."

The native's spirits picked up. "Here it is as you have asked, Samuel Rochez."

Samuel's mind filled with an aerial view of the village. He sped off to the west along the ridge, until he came to a long thin ribbon of a waterfall. Soaring over the top, he flew up into the foothills. A meadow spread out before him, beside the stream that fed the waterfall, a line of trees marking its path. He approached the source of the water where it emerged from the mountainside. A meter or so of open space gaped above the water level, making it look like a mouth belching forth the stream. He swooped in and blinked at the brightness. Sunlight reflected off the water raining down from an opening above. It seemed to be caught and amplified in the crystal-encrusted walls. A glass sand beach opened up on one side. He settled on it.

All at once, Samuel sat back at the village, staring at Jawell, with a light smile on his face. Coming to himself, he blanked his expression.

"Thank you Jawell. I'll take it from here."

"What will you do, Samuel Rochez?"

"First, I'll lead them to the Crystals, so that they don't come back and slaughter the rest of the Home-kind. It will take some time for them to make the device. I will find a way to sabotage it."

"But there are many of Your-kind. How can you do this without help?"

"I've got it."

Before the native could reply, he pulled away from contact and unplugged the translation equipment. Some strength returned to his body.

Looking around he saw Lance. He held his rifle up to his shoulder. The crack of the rail gun went off. Samuel heard a rumbling in the trees before he saw a section of branches falling. The jerk was taking pot shots at the tree weaving, trying to cut out critical support branches.

"Lance!" Samuel yelled.

"I'm busy," came the matter of fact reply.

"I have the location of the crystals." Samuel saw Lance's shoulders drop a bit. He couldn't hear, but felt certain the mercenary sighed.

Resting the gun on his shoulder, Lance called out, "All right, ladies, let's get this show on the road." Then, turning to Samuel, "where is it?"

Samuel pointed to the mountains in the distance. "On the side of a mountain, over there. We don't need the native; I've been in the area before."

Perhaps the after effect of the drugs dulled his mind, but Samuel just blurted out the phrase without thinking. The smirk on Lance's face gave away his mistake.

"Well, if we don't need him." Lance swung his weapon into firing position, and aimed.

Samuel flopped down in front of Jawell, blocking out his whole body. The crack of the gun and the thud of the projectile came at the same time. The impact, a couple of centimeters in front of Samuel, kicked dirt into his face and eyes.

He rolled over and touched Jawell, "Get out of here now! Stay low until you get into the trees."

Struggling to stand up, Samuel wiped the dirt from his eyes, as best he could, blinking hard to get the last of it out.

Lance's laughter came from the distance. "Emery, help the roach.

"Kimmy, you take point. Let's go, everyone, back to the ship. We've got one more little hop, then we can get out of grubsville."

Chapter 21: Harris

Samuel sat in the shade of a lone tree, sweat stinging the corners of his eyes. He squinted through bright sunlight at the hull of the ship. He could damage little that could not be repaired given time and determination.

"Forty-six, forty-seven," Harris counted in the background. Lance continued the relentless calisthenics. Glancing their way, Samuel noticed Harris struggling with the sit-ups, his face red and his body trembling. His voice came raspy and strained. Lance pushed the men harder and harder. Each day there were more reps and longer sessions.

Returning his attention to the ship, he saw three options: one, keep them from building the device long enough for the Loscar to arrive; two, destroy the device and hope they couldn't build another before the Loscar got there, or three, sabotage the ship. While mulling the options over, a new thought came to him. If the other options failed he would have to disable or kill one or more key people. They wouldn't be able to complete the weapon without Epstine or Thompson. The fact that he thought it shocked him. Would he trade the lives of a small group of men for all life on an entire planet?

He envisioned the planet a ruined hulk hung in space. All the Home-kind, Eaters, all life, even the rivers and plants, all reduced to rock and dirt. Those that survived the blast would suffocate in the reduced atmosphere. The ejected matter would fill the atmosphere blocking out the local sun for months. The surface would be frozen.

Samuel sighed. He hoped it wouldn't come to killing.

The problem was that all of the options had their faults. The odds of outwitting a well-armed group of mercenaries by himself were slim at best. Unfortunately, space ships were designed with redundant safety systems on board to keep anything catastrophic from happening. Bypassing enough of them and rigging an overload would take many hours, perhaps even days. Even if he succeeded in disabling the ship, it would be for naught. Lance would refuse to lose to Samuel. If the Loscar came there would be no chance for escape, and Lance might set off the device out of spite.

Killing Thompson and Epstein would be problematic. The thought turned his stomach. He stopped in shock. They were the two men who could make Armageddon for this planet and its inhabitants. Without them, it wouldn't work. He didn't know Thompson but Epstein didn't seem worthy of death. As the key to saving all life on this planet, he reminded himself, he had to consider all options.

To kill anyone he would have to get away, acquire a weapon, and hunt them down. He couldn't be certain to get to them before being recaptured or killed himself.

Destroying the weapons could be done with a stealth mine. He'd have to be free long enough to get to the armory, break in, set the device, and hide a remote where he could get to it easily. If he had enough time he could even set some on critical systems as well. He needed a distraction to lose his bodyguards.

As he looked over at the men, his eyes made contact with Lance. A thin smile spread across the sadist's face. He would probably have to kill Lance in the process.

The thought struck him. He'd never actually planned to kill anyone in his life before. In military service he had to kill a number of times. He had not felt guilty about the Eaters. But never had he premeditated the demise of any one single individual. Stagar might even help. The men would probably be cheerful to see the end of Lance, but not very likely to follow him and give up their plans to escape. They wouldn't follow Stagar again, either.

And the resulting power vacuum could provide him with opportunities, or get him killed really fast.

At any rate, Stagar couldn't be trusted. His only goal was to escape the planet with his treasure and leave a fireball in his wake. He stored the thought away for later consideration.

A commotion interrupted Samuel's thoughts. He looked over, and saw the men gathering around Harris, who lay violently convulsing on the ground; the men formed a semicircle around him. Samuel looked for a moment to ascertain the situation. Then he checked his guard. The mercenary kept most of his attention on Samuel. He would need a grander distraction to get into the ship unsupervised.

"Clancy!" a voice called out, "Clancy, get your stuff!"

The medic ran for the ship.

After a moment Samuel felt a muzzle pressed against his shoulder. He looked up into the eyes of his guard, Rod Intempe.

"Get up. Let's see what's happening."

Samuel rose to his feet, dusting off his pants and strolled over to the semicircle of men, Rod prompting him onward. They arrived about the same time as Clancy.

"I need a couple of men to hold him down," Clancy called as he rifled through his bag.

No one moved.

Lance called out, "Stagar, Roach, you take him."

Samuel examined the quivering form. The body glistened with sweat and his eyes rolled back as he shook on the ground.

"Medic," Samuel said, "give me some gloves." He wouldn't take any chances that this might be contagious. The medic took out a couple of sets of gloves, passed one to Samuel and the other to Stagar.

Both men came down to their knees and rested their weight on Harris's arms and chest. Their efforts only dampened the movement but it proved enough for the medic to work.

Clancy took a rectangular device, about the size of a thumb, and placed it on Harris's forehead. Pressing buttons on the sides, the medic scrolled through a number of displays.

"The problem is not in the brain," Clancy said.

The medic deftly took an inserter and pressed it against Harris's forearm. Drawing the viewers over his eyes, he grabbed the control pad out of the medic kit. It only took a few seconds before he spoke again. "Man! Oh yeah, there's definitely something in his bloodstream. I'm trying to recalibrate now."

The circle of men moved away from the quivering body.

"What is it?" asked Lance.

"His system is completely overrun," the medic said without looking up. "There is some kind of micro-parasite in there. But it may be too late. There are just too many of them for the Bio bots.

"Oh no!" Clancy said. "We've got organ failure here, massive organ failure."

Harris's body calmed as the seizure subsided. He laid there, eyes staring upwards unfocused.

"Can you do anything?" Lance asked calmly.

"No," the medic said incredulously. "We don't have the facilities to deal with this and I don't have the skills to do transplants, even if we had time to grow some. We're going to have to freeze him until we can get him to a full medical facility.

"I need a couple more men to carry him into the freezer units," the medic called, removing the goggles and tossing down the pad. He stood up looking at the stationary men.

"Wait," Lance said.

"He may only have minutes, Lance."

Lance sneered. "No one ever comes out as good as they go in. They lose their muscle; lose body mass, their tone. They become weak and frail."

"Yeah, but if we don't, he'll die."

Lance took a step closer. "Harris wouldn't want that."

"Lance, you do get the point? It's the freezer or death. Given that choice any sane person would choose the freezer." Clancy looked to the men holding the body. "Come on, Stagar, Rochez, you're already gloved up."

Lance nudged Harris's shoulder with his boot and said, "Harris, you hear me. Harris, you want to die like a man or live as a washed out wrung out dish rag?"

Harris seemed to respond to the voice, moving his eyes slightly in Lance's direction his lips trembled struggling, it seemed, to form words.

After several tries a quivering and faint voice said, "Freeze me."

Lance's eyes tightened. Samuel thought he saw the corner of Lance's mouth turn up slightly as he raised a gun to Harris's head. "Nah, you don't want that." The crack of the gun ended the shallow rapid breathing, the tremors and everything that was John Harris.

Lance turned and called over his shoulder, "Medic, incinerate the body. Roach, clean up the mess."

The men remained as still as Harris.

Stagar seemed stiff, his eyes moving left to right. "I wonder who else is infected?" he asked quietly.

Clancy came to life first. "All right, form a line!" He ripped off his gloves, tossed them in a bio-bag and pulled out a new pair. "Be calm and we'll get through this pretty quickly."

"No." Lance didn't yell, but his voice carried over everything. "If you're infected, you're infected. Knowing about it isn't going to change the fact that you're dead."

"But, the infection didn't kill Harris, you did." Intempe spoke boldly enough that everyone turned towards him.

"Yes," another added. "I choose the freezer, if I'm infected."

"Do we have enough freezers?" another voice asked.

Lance stared, frozen-jawed at the group for several seconds as questions built up.

"I'm sorry I had to do that. Harris and I had an agreement not to let each other suffer, to put us out of our misery. I would want any of you to do the same for me."

Samuel and Stagar still knelt at Harris' side. So Samuel was the only one that could see the smirk on Stagar's down turned face.

"Go ahead; play your games," Samuel whispered, "just leave me out of it."

Stagar looked up, and where their eyes met, he winked. "Harris jumped in the water. You kept everyone else out. He's the only one infected."

Stagar's plans fell far short of Samuel's goals. He had to stay focused on saving the planet and the Home-kind, and let the mercenaries deal with themselves. Shaking his head, he looked away.

"All right," Lance said, "get yourselves tested, but then it's back to work." After scanning the men, he turned and headed for the ship.

It took over an hour for all the men to be checked out. None were infected. They sat in small groups, engaged in hushed conversation. Two men shoveled dirt over Harris' ashes in a far corner of the meadow.

Lance's voice broke the quiet, "Everyone not involved in cleanup, 150 push-ups now." His hardened metal face glared at the group.

The men, bludgeoned into submission, hit the ground and continued their work out.

"Kwanso," Lance called.

Kim rose and trotted over. Lance rested his hand on the young man's shoulder. "With Harris gone, you're in charge of Stagar as well as the Roach. Organize the men so they are never alone and keep two men on the Roach." Samuel saw Kwanso swallow hard, but the young man nodded

"Very good," Lance beamed. "Now, lead the drill!" Lance said spinning the slim man around.

"Me?" Asked Kwanso, a tremble in his voice.

"Lead the drill," Lance repeated with a laugh as he sauntered towards the men.

Kim called the count, "Fourteen, fifteen..."

Lance wandered among the men. Those not working hard enough for him got his cane in the back.

Samuel thought that he could come to grips with killing Lance.

Chapter 22: Diversion

Samuel kicked at a dirt clod and stumbled forward, wincing at the pain. The previous night's attempt at losing his guard had ended in a tackle that twisted his ankle. He walked in circles putting weight square on the foot, until the pain subsided. No sprinting over uneven terrain any time soon.

The early light of dawn lit up the horizon with purple and green. Samuel watched as the men stumbled out of the ship, stretching and yawning. Lance never allowed them a good night's sleep. No wonder they milled about zombie-like, dark wraiths in the dim morning light.

Lance came off the ship and set himself among them, a firework in the dark of a night sky. Clapping everyone on the back, he pronouncing a good morning onto each and every one of them. He seemed mirthful. Samuel walked towards the company. A happy Lance indicated that something bad was about to unfold.

"Men, gather round," he called from atop a small mound.

The group, like Samuel, seemed drawn to this new incarnation of Michael Lance.

"Good news, men. We're getting off this rock. Thompson and Epstine are finally done! I know it's been hard on you these weeks, stuck on this uncivilized backwater. But, we've survived Stagar's bungling and we're about to be free and rich. Thompson's going to get some shut eye and give it one last check out with a clear head. And that will be the end of grubville for all of us.

"You've all worked hard and done your part. And so you've earned this reward." Lance pointed to the ship.

A rumbling sound came from the hatch as the meal cart rolled out.

"Hot breakfast for everyone!"

The Zombies came to life as they ran to the device of gastronomic delights.

Lance looked to Samuel's guard, who dutifully waited near his charge. "Go ahead, eat. I'll watch the Roach for a while."

Samuel looked sidelong at Lance. "What are you playing at today?"

"What's it going to hurt?" Lance said with a broad smile and a shrug. "You can eat too."

Lance looked over the men. "Kimmy," he called, "Bring a plate over for the Roach. Everyone eats well today."

"For tomorrow we all die," Samuel added.

"You've got a very sad view of the universe and the wrong idea about me." Lance used his cane to lower his weight to the ground and sat on the mound. "I'm not above rewarding hard work, dedication, and loyalty."

"Like Harris?"

"Well... everyone serves in a different way." Lance's smile didn't break at all.

"So, everyone gets a last meal?" Samuel glanced at the jovial body of men. "I note you're not eating."

Lance let out a blaring belch. "Oh, I ate first. It allows me to keep an eye on things. And, no, this isn't everyone's last meal."

Samuel shook his head.

"Take your friend Kimmy for instance," Lance gestured towards the cart. "He's been obedient to a fault. He even brought you in. No small task." Lance tapped his bad ankle with the cane.

"I'd take him on future missions. He knows his place and doesn't have a problem with it."

"As opposed to me and who else?" Samuel squatted on the ground. At most he had 5 or 6 hours to thwart the plan.

"Here's the difference. You know your place, but won't stay there. Always trying to change the game and do things your way. Stagar," Lance laughed, "Stagar doesn't know his place at all. I've needed to direct him since the day we met. It's like being a mother, I suppose."

"Why are you telling me all this? You're talking as if we are old friends."

Lance's smile shrunk a little as he shrugged. "Why not? For starters, you don't really care, and there's the fact that the information is useless to you, and finally I just wanted to spend a few minutes relishing your impotence."

His smile grew broad again.

Samuel started to reply but a prickling at the back of his brain caused him to turn just as a massive flock of Home-kind burst into the clearing, filling the air around them with empathic energy. Their bodies and wings ripped through the air in a roar that seemed to push him back. Samuel fought back the urge to run. Being on the receiving end he wondered how the Eaters endured it for as long as they had.

The men scattered, some fired blindly into the sky. Lance struggled to his feet and started firing with the only weapon he had on him, the stun gun. He yelled "My rifle, get me my rifle, you lard butted slimes!" as he worked his way towards the ship.

This distraction might have been just what Samuel needed. But, when he started for the ship, a knot of men gathered around the entry port. Lance pulled them together through sheer force of will. The men feared him more than the mental onslaught about them.

Home-kind bodies fell from the sky and plopped nearby. According to their moral code, they died in the act of service, helping. Samuel shook his head. That terribly misguided endeavor wasted their innocent lives.

He nudged a carcass with his foot. No sign of life. The cold, efficient, advanced human weapons cut through the simple natives with uncaring precision.

Looking up, he saw Lance urging the men on, his rifle blaring with the rest. The man had no conscience, none of them did.

A familiar presence interrupted his thoughts.

"Samuel Rochez, it is a pleasure to see that you are well. We came to help you get away from Your-kind. This is now a good time for you to come with us."

He knelt down and placed a hand on the simple native. "Get out of here! Jawell, your people are dying for nothing. I have to stay with My-kind to save you and your people. You have to leave now. I'll think of something. Go now, quickly!"

Jawell sent waves of disappointment through Samuel, which he managed to hold back. "Is there not anything we can do to help in this situation? We would be pleased to the sky to help you and the Home-kind."

"Not unless you can set a bomb."

"We can do many things, Samuel Rochez."

"Yes, you are quite capable," Samuel said half to himself. "You've woven fabric, trained trees and planted and harvested crops. You might just be able to help.

Jawell, get your people out of here and then meet me by the stern of the ship." Samuel formed an image in his mind of where to meet and how Jawell should touch him to communicate, without being detected.

Looking up from Jawell, he saw the Home-kind bodies building up on the ground. The men, spurred on by Lance, shot wildly into the flock of Home-kind. With the density of flying forms the men couldn't miss.

Samuel ran at them yelling for them to stop. Before he covered ten meters the cloud of Home-kind vanished. The men, dazed and panting lowered their weapons.

"What was that all about!?" Lance roared, marching toward Samuel, who stepped back.

"I don't know, maybe it was some ritual goodbye." Samuel stepped back again as Lance got close to striking distance. "Without the translation equipment we can't possibly know."

Lance slowed a bit. "It felt like an attack."

"Their culture is foreign to us," Samuel lowered his tone of voice and switched into lecture mode as the most calming thing he could think of. "This sort of thing may elicit joy in others of their kind. We are foreign to this planet. There are a great many examples, through history, of the difficulties in understanding different life forms. When humans first landed on Ternec 4, the commander..."

"Shut up!" Lance paused, then turned away from Samuel, but threw a curse over his shoulder, "Grubs."

Striding up to the men he bellowed, "Alright girls, time to clean up the place. Finish your mess and then pack everything on board. We're leaving, and soon." He spat as if to put an exclamation point on his statement.

Samuel looked around. For the moment, no one watched over him. A general bustling noise came from all around him. Some men were getting food; others cleared the area of Home-kind bodies.

"Hey, Roach, what do you suppose one of these tastes like?" The limp body hung from a man's hand. Samuel turned without taking further note and walked towards the stern of the ship, forcing himself to take it slow, in an attempt to look casual.

"Wait there!" Kim's voice called.

Samuel turned. The young man strode up and shoved a plate of food at him. "Here, eat."

"So, the condemned man gets a last meal?" Samuel said. Kim did not meet his gaze.

Samuel resumed his route to his rendezvous. "What to you think is going to happen next?"

"Next? Next, we get off this rock, and we all go our separate ways."

"And what about this planet and its inhabitants?"

They drew near Samuel's destination. "Are you going to eat that or talk?"

"I can do both." He slumped against the ship just at the corner. Not knowing how long Jawell would take, he needed a reason to stay where he was. "So, get away and forget about it. That's your plan?"

"What, you think crossing Lance and waiting for the Loscar is a plan with any kind of future to it?" Kim's voice went up in pitch.

Jawell grew near. Samuel shrugged towards Kim and delved into his food. While eating with his left, he placed his right hand on the ground just beyond the end of the ship. His body and the ship blocked anyone's view of Jawell. As long as Kim didn't take to wandering about, but kept to Samuel's left, no one would see the conspiracy unfold. With his peripheral vision he noted Kim lean against the ship.

The mining charges could be used to blow the missile up. They were not kept in the armory, like the traditional weapons. Being completely inert unless activated, less care was taken in storage of the devices. Hopefully Lance had forgotten about them, or left them out intentionally to hold out hope for Samuel that would never be fulfilled.

###

Jawell swooped into the smooth cavern and landed a short way inside. The ground beneath his body chilled his limbs. It felt smoother than a streambed rock, and flat. Looking all around, everything he saw was flat. What could cause such flatness? This other-kind had very strange yet wonderful ways. Light glowed from small suns along the wall. He moved in front of one. They stuck out and were in some strange way darker than light is.

Thump, thump, thump, he heard a sound growing louder. He turned his attention towards the sound. A dull half awake feeling came with a sound. He wasn't to be seen, he remembered. Casting about for more other-kind he found none.

Springing to the air he flapped twice and leaned into the first turn Samuel Rochez showed him.

The tight space made soaring easier, the air held firm under his wings. He touched down on the next corner and leapt into the air feeling the rush of air flow down his body. Too soon he came to the last opening. Pulling in his wings, he dropped through it and flared out into the large cavern beyond. He circled twice enjoying the strange light and the look of the place. Finally, he settled on the box Samuel showed him.

Hopping down on the side as told, he slid a silver latch to the side. The box clicked and hissed and then the cover rose up. Jawell pulled out one of the packages containing a small smooth stick. It took all four limbs to open the package. He pulled out the stick and found it heaver than a stick of its size is. Looking at it from all angles, he rubbed it in his arms, again the strange smoothness. Only the lever Samuel Rochez pointed out interrupted the smoothness. Setting the stick on the ground he returned the empty pouch to the box.

The lid held a group of small oval items. He took one as Samuel Rochez instructed. Lifting it several times, he marveled at the lightness. Samuel Rochez called it a controller.

Holding both items, he flapped hard, beating against the air dragging the extra weight up to the opening. Passing through, he landed breathing heavily. He was Ja, adept at long flight, thanks to the sky he was born with long and slim wings. Carrying items needed the broad wing of the El.

When his breathing returned to normal, he leapt into the air and followed the path Samuel Rochez set for him. Very soon he swept into the cavern with the target. The long, thick stick with bumps and shapes lay on a table. Several openings darkened the smooth skin.

Samuel Rochez told him there could be five. The one in the middle would be best if it were open. Jawell didn't understand much of what Samuel Rochez said about the item, but understanding was not necessary for helping.

He hopped up to the table and compared the openings with the image from Samuel Rochez. He found the middle closed, but the second option lay open. He flipped the switch and worked the stick up into the body as instructed. He pushed until it would go no further.

Rising up to his full height he spread his wings and spun his eyes in a circle. After celebrating the completed task he leapt from the table and flew back to give Samuel Rochez the small oval.

###

Samuel sat watching the sun move higher into the sky for half an hour, maybe more. He struggled to avoid looking directly at the hatch but keep it in his peripheral view.

The men, mostly sitting in small groups, lazed about. Lance spoke quietly with Kim.

The plan was simple. After setting the charge, Jawell would fly out and drop the control behind the stern of the ship. He would then pick it up and press the button. The resulting explosion would destroy the missile and much of the equipment in the room. With luck, it would take quite a while to reconstruct a bomb and a new delivery system.

Looking over to the men, Lance still spoke to Kim, who kept his eyes down, but nodded.

Lance would kill him on the spot if he knew. But this would almost certainly give the Loscar time to arrive before some other doomsday plan could be implemented.

Taking a deep breath he steeled himself. If this were to be his last act, it would be a good one.

"It's one of those grubs!" a voice called out, immediately followed by drawing of weapons. Jawell had just emerged from the hatch and seemed to stop in the air for an instant and then beat his wings to hover.

Samuel gasped. Without the many minds of the Home-kind to combine with his, Jawell would be overwhelmed by the emotions of the men; which at that moment screamed surprise and confusion. Samuel yelled, "Fly away!" and strove with all his will to send it as a command, like he had done with Jahara at the river.

A shot rang out at the exact instant that Jawell dove. He swooped up into the air with more weapons ringing out. They died out as the figure grew small in the distance.

Samuel caught his breath. Trying to save Jawell distracted him from the mission. He started to walk over to the stern of the ship to see if Jawell dropped the control. He hadn't noticed it fall, but could have missed it. If not, Jawell would return to complete the task, he felt certain. He could sit there and wait, appearing dejected to the men and Lance.

"Bang," a shot fired. Samuel looked up in time to see the speck that was Jawell, fall from the sky. He turned.

Lance lowered his rifle with a smug grin. "That's how you shoot a moving target at a distance."

Samuel ran at the grinning demon, hands prepared to squeeze the life out of it. The pain of his ankle was swallowed up in his rage. Their eyes met, and Lance's smile changed to one of amusement.

Samuel barely noticed Lance put a hand in his pocket and pull out a small metal device. Lance winked and pressed down on it.

Samuel fell to the ground with a thump. Pulling and pushing on muscles that always worked did nothing. He lay there, immobile as a clump of dirt. Breathing continued and his pulse boomed in his ears, so he knew he lived.

Boots crunched in the dirt near by.

Chapter 23: Launch

Samuel's mind raced. It wasn't a stun gun Lance had pulled out, and he wasn't unconscious, just immobilized. They must have implanted a blocker, a shunt, to stop all voluntary muscle movement at the brain stem.

"By now you've probably figured out that we put a blocker into your neural system." Lance said. "While the medic patched you up from your nasty fall I had him install a little insurance."

Samuel tried to turn his head to look up, but nothing happened.

"I'll let you cool off a bit before returning the use of your limbs." Dirt crunched near his head. "Kimmy, take a couple of men and bring the Roach to the bridge. Prop him up in a corner while we finish."

Hands gripped his shoulders and lifted him from the ground. He couldn't get the control in this condition even if Jawell had dropped it at the right spot. At some point Lance would release the blocker and he'd have to get to the cargo hold for another control.

They turned him around and hauled him by the shoulders. For a moment his eyes fell on the patch of sky he last saw Jawell in. He wondered if the native were dead or just wounded. If injured, would the Home-kind kill him? If he didn't stop the mercenaries, it wouldn't matter; Jawell, Wellem, Jahara and all the Home-kind would share the same fate.

The metal echoes announced their entry into the ship. Samuel could do nothing until Lance allowed him to. The brute undoubtedly enjoyed the situation.

Left sitting against a wall he reviewed the path to the hold. When he got his chance he wanted to have every turn memorized. He wished more than anything that he could close his eyelids. Incessantly looking out into the bridge made it harder for him to concentrate and his eyes burned dry.

The bridge buzzed with the noise of preparation, reciting checklists, and communications with engineering. Although the focus of his gaze remained fixed, he took in all the motion through peripheral vision. Each of the men ran through his tasks with practiced ease. Years of repetition choreographed the dance they went through.

Lance's entry deadened the commotion. He took the captain's chair. "Is she ready to fly?"

"Yes," came the simple response from the pilot.

"Good, take her up."

The ship shuddered slightly as it rose into the air.

Stagar entered the bridge with two armed guards at his back. He took up a position between the door and the captain's chair, and gave a slight nod to Samuel.

Stagar had some sort of plot Samuel knew, he only hoped it would give him the opportunity to act on his own.

"We're in position, Lance."

"Excellent! Time to reanimate the Roach." He gestured to Kwanso Kim. "Kimmy, be ready in case he tries something."

Kim drew a handgun and stepped back.

Lance squatted in front of Samuel. "Now, you're going to behave yourself, aren't you? If not you'll be going right back to suspended animation. A sheathed blade doesn't draw blood, if you get my point."

If he were to have any hope of saving the Home-Kind he had to be mobile. He took a deep breath, one of the few things he could control.

Lance took out the small control. In one smooth motion he pressed the button, stood, and turned his back on the now able bodied man. Samuel recognized the taunt. Lance obviously trusted he had nothing to fear from him.

Closing his eyes, Samuel rubbed liquid back into them. Slowly he rose, staring at the back of the callous monstrosity of a man. A lot of satisfaction would be gained from tackling and bashing his brains in. However, against a man half his age and twice his muscle he would fail and that would do no good for the fate of the planet.

He followed with head down, constantly scanning the room for any chance of escape. Stagar stood, expressionless, arms crossed against his chest.

Lance led him to the weapons console. "I've had them reorganize things a bit."

A sheet of metal covered the table of a console, with a single large, red button off center to the right from where Samuel stood. A chair sat on either side.

"Have a seat," Lance said.

Two men forced Samuel down when he didn't react immediately. Lance sat across from him.

"I've given this moment a lot of thought." Lance's smile vanished. "This button launches the missile that will rain destruction on your favorite little planet. I want you to push this button. Will you press it now, please?" The question reeked with sarcasm.

"No." Samuel folded his arms over his chest and sat back in the chair.

Lance sat back as well. "I figure there is no way that I can get you to push the button willingly. But then, there is no harm in trying. Besides, it's better this way."

Samuel looked to the door and counted the men in the room; way too many.

"You could be drugged again, or I could cut off your arm and use that to press it. I admit the second option has a certain appeal. Having you watch your disembodied arm doing the destruction. None of those options were all that satisfying, really. Yesterday, however, it came to me. And, so, here we are."

"No matter what you do to me, it will still be you that is actually launching the missile." Samuel gritted his teeth doing his best to sneer at the man opposite. "There is no point in my resisting. The button will be pushed one way or another."

"True, but I really don't think you'll be able to stop yourself." Lance leaned forward with a gleaming smile that filled his eyes. "Just to make things interesting, if you win I'll let you live."

Samuel snorted.

"Not that you'll appreciate it any, but I'll lose some satisfaction on the deal."

Samuel's gaze darted from man to man. Some looked away; others stared back but none smiled except for Lance. At least none of the others seemed to take joy in the act of terracide. When his eyes fell back to Lance, the sociopath roared a full belly laugh.

"There is no hope for you here, Roach. No last minute rescue. You're alone and defeated. All that is left is for you to realize it."

Lance spoke to the men holding Samuel. "Hold him, so he doesn't try anything crazy, but let him have enough leeway to put his whole body into it."

Lance bellied up to the table resting his elbow on the center, forearm vertical and hand open.

Samuel recognized the position. "You want to arm wrestle for the planet? Lance, you're insane!"

Samuel's seat scraped the metal deck while being pushed into position. He sat firm of back with arms folded tight.

"Good! Good," Lance said, "you're getting into the spirit of it already."

"Gentlemen," Lance said looking to the men behind Samuel. "I need an arm to wrestle."

Strong arms pulled at his wrists, striving to pull apart the vice of his appendages, his breath came heavier as he drew his arms in tighter.

A hammer punch thudded against the side of his abdomen. The jarring pain startled him enough for his arms to be pulled off his chest. One man held his shoulders while the other manipulated his right arm into position.

Lance clamped down in the proper grip. "Ready, set, go!" He said and slammed Samuel's hand down so that it rested on the button, but didn't push it.

"Ah, come now, Roach, you're not even trying."

Samuel responded by imagining Lance burning alive. He stared Lance dead in the eyes.

"You can't muster an ounce of strength for your precious grubs who are about to be burned up, asphyxiated, or frozen on the barren hulk this world will be in just a very few minutes?"

Samuel looked away.

"Can we just get this over with, Lance?" Kim asked.

"All the plants? Animals? Don't you have anything to give for any of them?"

Samuel scanned the men again, this time they all looked away. Except for Stagar, who nodded his head and raised his eyebrows. Samuel shook his head at the sad little man, and whatever he intended.

"You disappoint me, Roach," Lance continued. His smile contorted into a carnivore's bite. "You're just as soft and weak as those pathetic little grubs you pretend to care about. It will now end for both of you." He spat out the last few words from a stone-hardened face.

The pressure grew on the back of Samuel's hand. The button responded. It moved ever so slightly. Samuel arm muscles rippled and strained as he pushed up the gripped hands so that a space opened between his hand and the button.

The tightness relaxed out of Lance's face. "Now that's more like it."

He continued his straining until he moved them about a quarter of the arc.

With a snorted laugh, Lance slammed their hands back to within a millimeter of the button. Grunting with the effort, Samuel forced back to about the same point. He knew Lance was toying with him, and at any time he could slam the button. He should just give up; his efforts only satisfied Lance's warped desires, and nothing else.

Again his hand rushed to within a hair's breadth of the button.

"Lance," Kim chimed in again, "please, just do it."

Lance looked over as if he only then realized that there were others in the room. "Since you said please."

Lance stared intently into Samuel's eyes and pushed their hands down, relentlessly, millimeter by millimeter.

Shifting his weight, Samuel pulled harder. Two seconds, three seconds, he counted. His hand came into contact with the button. Then in one final surge, his hand crushed down on the button.

Click, Samuel thought. He expected a click, followed by a distant whoosh. But at the instant the click should have come, a cascade of white gas filled the room, cutting visibility in half. At the same time a dizzying array of alarms and klaxons went off.

Men murmured as Lance called out orders. Before Samuel could process what happened someone pulled him to his feet and dragged him away from the table. He pulled back and heard Stagar whisper, "Come."

They fell out into the hall and Stagar closed the hatch. It took another second of Stagar leading him before Samuel came to himself. He shook his arm free and bolted for the cargo hold.

"Samuel," Stagar called chasing after him. "You still have the implant. Any second now Lance will realize you're gone and press the button. You'll be dead on the floor waiting for them to pick you up."

"Then I have to hurry!" Samuel shouted.

"This will all have been for nothing."

Samuel kept running.

"I'm sorry," came the voice from behind.

Samuel's legs and body failed and he slammed into a bulkhead flopping to the floor.

The pain burned through his left shoulder and chest, which took the brunt of the impact.

"Sorry," Stagar said panting, "but you weren't listening to reason."

Again his frozen open eyes fixed on a single point, staring up at the ceiling. He saw the ceiling move as Stagar dragged him down the hall and to one side.

"It's lucky you chose this route. If you had turned right back there I'd have to drag you a lot further and we might have been caught."

Stagar released him and Samuel heard tapping and a click. In just another few seconds Stagar pulled him into a long narrow room off the side of the hall. He didn't recognize it. Another clicking sound and Stagar stood over him in his field of view.

"Now, this is a jammer." Stagar held up a pen-sized device. "It is programmed to block your transmitter, so they can't find you, and also the signal that controls your blocker." Stagar sighed. "I'm going to turn this on. Just remain calm and we'll get through this."

Stagar pressed the only button on the device and a small green light came on.

Samuel jumped up and took the other man by the throat and began the work of strangling the life out of him. "You've killed them all!"

A shrill ringing sound shot into Samuel's ears. So harsh and shrill that he had to cover them.

Stagar held up another small device, "Auditory assault is a great defensive tool." He placed a hand on Samuel's shoulder.

"As I said, just be calm and we'll get through this." Stagar rubbed his throat. "We're in a hidden chamber. Lance will never find us. I can even control most of the ships functions from in here. All the security feeds are off. Now, in a few minutes the missile will reach its target. Lance will focus on getting the ship out of here before mounting a full scale..."

"A few minutes?" Samuel cut him off, "how many?"

"Nine or ten. Epstine explained that the friction of the atmosphere..."

"Stop!" Samuel ordered. "That's enough time. How do I get out of here?" He pushed past Stagar to examine the wall.

"Time for what?"

"To blow up the missile."

"Wait, how can you..." Stagar paused for a second. "What, are you crazy? After all we've gone though to get off this rock?"

Turning to Stagar, Samuel saw the man eying the jammer in his hand.

Bam! Samuel threw a left jab to Stagar's face and wrenched the jammer free with the other. "Thanks," he said to the reeling Stagar.

It took a few more seconds to find the latch, and Samuel sprinted out the hidden door and down the hall.

Chapter 24: Plan

Samuel shot from the compartment and sprinted down the hall. Skidding around a corner he came up short facing Kwanso Kim.

The young man's face lit up with surprise, followed instantly with recognition and then the barrel of his gun trained on Samuel.

"Where did you come from?" asked Kim.

“Kwanso, you have to let me go."

Samuel rushed the words out feeling the seconds burn away.

The young man broke eye contact as he spoke. "Why? The missile is away, there is nothing that can be done now." Kim shook his head slightly.

Samuel started forward, but Kim’s focus hardened on him and his grip tightened on his weapon.

"There is still time, but only a few minutes. Let me go Kwanso, please? We can still save the planet."

"And then what?” Kim stood erect. “You still have no plan. Look, if I help you and we succeed, what will Lance do? What will the Loscar do when they arrive?”

"So," Samuel crossed his arms across his chest, “you're willing to let a whole planet die to save yourself?"

Kim shook his head. "I'm tired of talking about it. We're under lockdown. This is the only way out, unless you can convince the Loscar to let us go."

Samuel latched on to that phrase. The Loscar held the only key to the lockdown.

“Wait a moment.” Samuel raised his hand, pointing a finger at Kim and shaking it slightly. “You’re right, the Loscar have to open a hole in the shield to get in. We can use the same hole to get out!”

“Right,” Kim snorted, “and they’ll just let us pass? Thank you very much and have a nice day.”

“Of course not, but they don’t have to know.”

Kim opened his mouth to object but Samuel cut him off.

“The satellite formation that makes up a lockdown puts out incredible amounts of energy. If we fly close to the shield, we’ll be undetectable. Epstine can figure from their orbit and rich deposits where they’ll open a hole.”

“It will only be open for a few minutes. Even if you are correct and the lockdown will hide us, as soon as we enter the gap we’ll be visible.”

Samuel took a step closer. “When landing, all attention and most sensors are directed forward and down. There is a chance someone will notice, but we can minimize that by slipping out near the edge and maneuvering to keep a satellite directly between them and us.”

Kim lowered the gun barrel slightly and creased his forehead. “We can’t get very far on that, we won’t be eclipsed by a small body like that for long. As we move away from it...”

Samuel cut him off again. With each second he wasted in chatter, the missile drew closer to its target. “We blast the engines once for escape velocity and go dark. This planet has several moons; we can coast to one of them and get in close behind it. No passive system would pick us up.”

“And stay in its shadow until we are on the far side of the planet.” Kim added.

“And use the same burst and coast technique to get the local sun between us and the planet, and then out of the solar system.”

“Home free?” asked Kim.

“Home free.”

They paused for just a second both looking at each other.

“Will it work?” asked Kim.

"We'll need Epstine to know for sure." Samuel trotted past Kim. "Find him and bring him to the hold." As he reached the corner he threw back over his shoulder, "If you see anyone else, tell them you've already checked the hold."

"What are you going to do?" Kim called.

Samuel ignored it and broke into a full out run.

The hold door loomed in sight in just under a minute. Samuel burst through, slid down the railing and clambered over the crates. Sweat ran down into his eyes and breathing came heavily.

Slipping down the back of the crates he came to the mining charges box. He threw it open. The lid banged against the wall, and he ripped out a control unit and hit the on button.

A red light indicated its activation, but not in range of any charges. He pressed the scan button. The red light blinked along with the word: Scanning.

The missile could have flown out of range. In which case, he had failed. How many minutes had gone by? He refused to believe that the missile exploded already. Every fiber of his being focused on the word, Scanning, and the red light. His finger rested on the detonate button.

Not being a miner he could only guess the range of the control.

The sounds of movement out in the hall beyond the hold drifted in through the open door. Kim couldn't be back with Epstine this soon. Therefore it had to be someone searching for him. He closed the lid gently, and backed against the crates, never taking his eye from the control.

"Did anyone search in here?" A voice echoed in the large hold. "Lots of places to hide."

Tap, tap, the sound of boots on the stair made the hair on Samuel's neck stand up. Still the control read: Scanning.

Samuel opened his mouth and breathed slow, steady, and quiet. The thud of footfalls on the deck replaced the high tapping sound of the stairs.

"Should we start climbing?"

"Nah, not yet. Check the corners, the office and behind stuff first."

The footsteps grew a bit more distant. Samuel couldn't tell if there were two or three. He doubted there were more than three.

A light pinging chime came on as the light turned from red to green and Samuel pressed the button. Nothing seemed to happen. The sound continued. He read the display. It said: Select target to activate connection. Below it shown an item number he assumed was the ID number of the charge in the missile. Scanning the control front and back he didn't find a select button.

"Do you hear something?" The footsteps stopped.

Samuel pressed his finger down on the display over the item number. The display changed to: Selected. Then when Samuel pressed the detonate button the screen went blank and the sound stopped.

"No, what'd you hear?"

"Don't know, could have been nothing."

"So, what does nothing sound like?" asked one of the men with a laugh.

"Shut up and search," the main voice responded.

Samuel shook the device and tried the power button again. Slumping against the crates he gazed at the dead device. "What could have gone wrong?" he wondered when the device came back to life with the words: Confirmed detonation.

"Yes!" he muttered under his breath and chuckled for an instant. The Home-kind and their planet would be safe. Next he had to get Stagar's brood off the planet before they came up with another destructive plan. He gently slid to the floor and waited to be discovered.

The footsteps continued in the background with occasional muttered conversation.

It would be nice to make it back to the planet to ensure the Home-kind's and Loscar's first meeting went well, but he could live with this. It would be best to get the crew and ship off the planet on the off chance they could make another Carlinium warhead.

He didn't know who were on the other side of the crates or if they would be as easy to convince as Kim.

"Well, nothing here, I guess we'll have to climb the crates and search every crevasse."

The tap, tap of footsteps on the stairs announced the arrival of others.

"What are you doing here?" asked the dominant voice from the hold.

"The hold's already been searched," came Kim's voice.

"And what are you doing with him?"

"Lance wants him tied up down here so he can't play with the ship's systems any more. I'll take care of it, you continue the search."

"Ok." A simple response as footsteps shuffled in and out. Finally Samuel heard the door close and the bolt set.

"Samuel, where are you?"

"Coming." He pocketed the control and pulled a couple of charges and climbed the boxes. If he could set them off in the missile bay it would eliminate the possibility of building another weapon of mass destruction. Once his head crested the pile of crates he said, "Here."

On the other side he approached the trembling engineer.

"What, what, are you doing here? Kim, what's going on?"

"Relax," Samuel put his hand on Epstine's shoulder. "We just want to talk."

"We? Does Lance know about this?"

Kim and Samuel looked at each other briefly and then back to Epstine, who backed towards a wall.

"No, of course not." Epstine pointed a finger at Samuel. "He wants you dead." He wiped his hands on his pants and jumped slightly as he hit the wall.

"No," Samuel shook his head. "We need your help to leave this planet, and leave it in one piece."

"The missile didn't detonate; it disintegrated in flight." Epstine drew a deep breath and widened his eyes. "That was you! But, how?"

"Yeah," Kim added, "how did you pull that off?"

"That's the past." Samuel didn't take his eyes off of Epstine. "Although it can come back to haunt, it's not our problem at the moment. We have another way off this planet."

"It's Stagar; Stagar put you up to this, didn't he? He wants to see if I'm loyal to him. It's a test."

"No, this isn't one of Stagar's little plots. It's a real chance to save ourselves and an innocent planet from destruction."

"This couldn't be a setup by Lance, could it?" The engineer mumbled. "How could he get you in on it?"

"Epstine, Kim is Lance's right hand man of the moment, and I'm his nemesis in this. Would we be working together on this if either of them were setting you up?"

Epstine froze. "I, I can't be talking to you. If either of them find out, they'll kill me. Especially Lance."

"We can protect you from Lance, and Stagar won't interfere." Samuel raised his voice, "Will you, Stagar?"

The intercom crackled. Kim raised his weapon and spun around.

"That all depends on what you have in mind." Stagar's voice filled the hold.

"How did you know?" Kim whispered.

"It's in his nature, a spider at the center of a web of plots and plans."

"Stagar," Epstine called out. "I did what you said, but now things are worse."

"You did magnificent, Mister Epstine. I'm proud of you. Now, let's listen to what Mister Rochez has to offer, shall we?"

"Good," Samuel began. "It's simple really. We hug close to the shield so the Loscar can't detect us. Then when they make an opening in the lockdown, we slip out."

"But..." Epstine interrupted.

Samuel spoke over him. "We use a satellite to mask the energy of a controlled thrust to put us behind a moon. From there, the far side of the planet and then the far side of the sun."

"Thrust and coast," Stagar said.

"Yeah," Kim added, "We go low energy during the coast and we'll be home free."

"Samuel, I'm impressed."

Kim walked over to Epstine. "So, it can be done?"

"Yes," the big man's eyes darted about the hold. "The energy output of the lockdown will dwarf us, and, and," he stuttered, "we can match their orbit on this side of the shield so we'll be in position when they open it up. I'd have to do some analysis back up in the lab. We can't stay too close to the field or a static charge could build up and disable equipment. No telling how bad it would be."

"Good. Now, who else do we need on this little venture?" Samuel asked. "Who else can we trust?"

"You can't trust anyone of this cut-throat crew." Stagar said. "We're on our own."

"No," returned Samuel, "that's just your perspective. Many of the men were not happy with the planetary destruction plan. I saw it in their faces."

"Maybe," said Kim, "But that doesn't mean they'll stand up to Lance."

Epstine whimpered at Lance's name.

Samuel faced Kim. "Some will. Lance has been bullying them mercilessly. A real chance to escape without having to bow down to the beast will appeal to many of them. Do you know which ones would be most likely to join in?"

"No, since Lance picked me as his new lieutenant, everyone is tight lipped when I'm around."

"Well then," Samuel clapped his hands together. "We'll just have to pick up people along the way."

"Along the way to where?" Epstine asked.

"To your lab, of course." He turned to Kim. "I'll need your sidearm; we may get into a fire fight. You take point, I'll bring up the rear. When we meet members of the crew they'll be friendlier to you."

They made their way up the stair and into the first corridor when they met two of the crew.

"What's up, Kim?" one said.

The other pointed to Samuel. "He's got him." Then he stiffened and raised his weapon. "He's armed. What's going on Kim?"

"It's alright," Kim raised his gun as well, but kept his voice soft, and stepped forward. "He's going to get us off this rock safely, and without blowing the whole thing up."

The men looked at each other for a moment and the second said, "And Lance is alright with this thing?"

"Lance hasn't been briefed on the plan yet," Samuel responded. "But his cooperation isn't necessary for this to work."

"Oh man, you're crazy," the first said. "You're going up against Lance, that's suicide."

"He's just another bully," said Samuel. "If we all stand up to him, he has no chance. Aren't you tired of being brutalized by that maniac?"

Kim spoke up. "He killed Harris, his friend, do you think he'll have any problem taking out the rest of us once we got back?"

"Not much of a choice," the second added. "Probably death later versus certain death now."

Samuel stepped forward lowering his gun. "It's only probable death now. How can he fight the entire crew?"

"So how many you got on your side Kim?"

"So far, just us."

"And, and Stagar," Epstine added.

The two men chuckled. "He's in hiding somewhere. I wouldn't expect him out till everything's resolved."

"Probably not," Samuel nodded, "but he has some resources at his disposal that will be useful."

The second man stepped up to Samuel and looked him over. "So, if we sign up with you, what are our chances?"

"Lance will want to make another missile. That will take weeks again. It is almost certain that the Loscar will arrive by then and you'll be dead by their hand, or living like savages, scavenging your living from this planet, constantly in hiding. If, on the other hand, we try this new plan, the Loscar will never know we were here."

The first man stormed over to Epstine and thrust his face in close. The Engineer tried to step away, but the man grabbed his collar and pulled him in. "Is this true?"

"Yes, yes. It should work, we, we're just going to verify it."

The second man looked Samuel in the eyes. "And what are we to do in this plan?"

"For now, spread the word. Convince others to move against Lance when the call is given."

"How..."

Samuel cut him off. "You'll know. It will be that obvious."

"Ok, we're with you for now; but, we won't do anything against Lance until we see something more substantial than three guys and your word."

"Good enough." Samuel gave a quick nod. "Send a couple of men to Epstine's lab once you're sure they are on board. We may have to defend it, and especially Epstine."

They picked up one straggler on the way to the lab. He had been on the bridge when the missile exploded. His black eye attested to his proximity to Lance at the time.

"You watch the door," Samuel said to him as they entered the lab.

Epstine mopped sweat from his face as he began working on his station.

Patting the pocket with the explosives Samuel surveyed the room. The single door made it defensible and Kim made good backup. Epstine would be safe. He moved to the door and scanned the hall, empty and quiet.

"Set your weapon on wide angle and bathe the hall if anyone approaches," Samuel said to the guard. "It won't kill them but they won't be able to stand it even for a second. We're expecting some support and it would be a bad welcome to cut them down."

The man nodded as he made the adjustments.

"I need to see to something," Samuel said turning to Kim.

The crackle sound of laser hitting metal broke his thought and he dove to the ground. "Fire!" he called to the guard. The low hum of continuous fire met with a cry of pain from the hall.

"What?" Kim asked dashing to the door.

Before Samuel could answer a voice boomed from the hallway. "Well, Roach, it looks like I've underestimated you again. I hope this won't become a habit."

"Lance," Samuel called back. "It doesn't have to end like this; there is another way off the planet."

"Oh, yeah, I heard your little plan. It's amazing what people will confess with their dying breath. I, of course, prefer my own. Once I take care of you, there won't be any interference with the next missile."

"Listen, Lance..."

"It was the grub, wasn't it? Some how you trained it to... what, cross some wires, plant a bomb? You really are quite bright. It's going to be one of my greatest pleasures to, I think, strangle you. There's something about watching the lights go out in response to one's own physical exertion."

Kim opened his mouth to respond, but Samuel held up a hand and whispered, "Best he doesn't know you are here."

"So, Roach, you going to come out and take it like a man, or am I going to have to come in after you?"

"Sorry to disappoint you," Samuel responded, "But I'm not giving up." Then he whispered to Kim, "take up position on the other side of the door and watch the other end of the hall." If he made a break for it, he could lead Lance and company away from the lab and Epstine. He could even make the missile bay and take out the armaments and if lucky, maybe Lance in the process.

"You don't get it," Lance hollered, "giving up is so much less satisfying."

"Kim, I'm going to try and lead them away. You..."

The guard cut Samuel off, "Grenade!"

Samuel dove at Kim, knocking him to the ground as a deafening roar tore through the air.

The intense heat burst into the room with the concussive force of the explosion. Samuel held his breath for the few seconds it took for the effect to end. Rolling over he ripped a blasting charge from his pocket and threw it out into the hall.

The pounding footsteps out in the hall came to a stop with the clattering of the device. "Two can play at that game," Samuel called as he retrieved the control from another pocket.

"Once again, you surprise me, Roach. But I don't see where we have many options here. If this standoff continues, we'll be sitting ducks when the Loscar arrive."

"That's up to you, Lance."

"No, I don't think so. You'd be happy to wait for them. It would save your revolting little grubs. But, that's probably not what the men want."

Lance called louder, "You men in there, are you willing to be taken by the Loscar? Because we can sit here for days or weeks like this. As long as the Roach has Epstine we're not moving!"

Samuel touched Kim on the shoulder. The younger man's wrinkled brow and roving eyes showed his deliberation.

"Bring him out, and we'll get back to work on our escape." Lance switched to a more relaxed tone. "Come on. Are you going to go with a half-baked plan that depends heavily on luck, or go with something sure fire?"

"The Loscar will be here sooner rather than later," Samuel called back. "The odds are you won't be able to build another warhead in time. So, who's to say which plan depends most on luck?"

"Ok, I tell you what. We'll cover our bets. If the Loscar show up before we manage to blast our way out, we go with the Roach's plan. It's a win-win. Just bring me the Roach and all will be forgiven."

Kim snorted.

"Forgiven? Lance you never..."

Bang, the sound of gunfire filled the hall. Someone opened up on Lance and his men. The cross fire outside the room became a dizzying array of lights and sound.

After a minute or so Lance yelled, “Ok, just remember, you all had your chance!”

Rapid footsteps faded into the distance as the weapons fell silent.

Chapter 25: Lance

Samuel looked around; smoke lingered in the air and the door rested on one hinge. The man stationed at the door lay motionless. Epstine cowered in one corner and Kim stepped over to his side.

"That could have gone worse."

"Yeah," Samuel shrugged.

Several of the men burst into the room. One of the men said to the others, "We've really done it now. I just hope we don't end up regretting it."

He stared at Samuel. "And you had better not be jerking us around, or you'll be the first to die." He paused for an instant. "You got that?" a pointing finger accentuated the phrase.

Samuel clapped his hands. "Ok then," and looked around the room again. "We need a couple of people to stay here and guard Epstine, and someone needs to get that man to the med bay."

The men stood still looking alternately between Samuel and Kim. They didn't come to life until Kim stepped forward and made assignments.

Walking over to Epstine, Samuel rested a hand on his shoulder. "That was the worst of it. From here on, things get easier."

Epstine looked in Samuel's direction, but didn't make eye contact. "You say that now, but wait until we're dancing on the under-belly of the energy field."

"Why, what's going to happen?"

"I don't know, I don't. There is no data on something like this to run a simulation against. I'm certain, though, that it will be a rough ride. Very rough."

Samuel patted his shoulder, "You can write a paper on it when you get back to civilization. For now, though," Samuel pointed to the equipment in the room, "try to find a way to keep us from being fried, please."

Helping him up, Samuel dusted off Epstine's shoulders. "There now," Samuel said and walked out the door and picked up the unexploded charge in one smooth motion. He needed to take care of the missile room before any more distractions cropped up. No matter their shortcomings, these were resourceful men. Left to their own devices on the planet they very well may come up with another way to destroy the place. He needed to get them as far away as possible but for that the ship had to be in full working order.

As he took his first step, Kim's voice called him back. "What about Lance?"

Samuel thought for a moment. "Break up the men in groups of 3 and hunt him down."

"He's in engineering," Stagar's voice crackled over the intercom. "He just took out the security feeds in there and the armory has been opened."

Samuel and Kim looked at each other at the same instant of realization. "He's sabotaging the ship!" Kim said.

Kim ran after Samuel. They dashed through several halls and up one set of stairs. As they reached the turn into the hall that led to engineering Samuel came to a halt.

Catching his breath he spoke quickly to Kim. "Weapons active, safety off." He checked his pistol.

Samuel grabbed the younger man's shoulder and looked intently into his eyes. "Fire on sight. Do not hesitate or he'll cut you down."

Kim's face scrunched up a bit as he looked at his rifle.

"Any of us will only get one shot. Lance is fast, efficient, and brutal. This is the way it has to be. Are you with me?"

Kim's features steadied, and then steeled. He nodded his head.

"You have the better weapon. When we get there I'll open the door. Be ready to fire."

Kim nodded again.

Samuel crouched and peeked around the corner. The engineering door stood closed. He moved out into the hall, hugging the wall and signaled for Kim to follow. The background hum of the ship muffled their footsteps. They reached the door with no surprises.

With his hand over the "open" button, Samuel watched Kim shoulder the rifle and aim down its sights toward the door. Positioning himself to cover a different angle, Samuel pressed the button.

With a whoosh the door swung open. The bright lights shone into all corners of the room. Lance wasn't there. Samuel entered, checking the area behind the door and working his way to the corners of the room. "What did you do?" Samuel muttered to himself.

As if in response Kim called, "Over here."

Crammed in among some cooling pipes and wire bundles were six land mines.

"There is a red light active on each," Kim said pointing.

Samuel wiped his hands across his face. "They're active and have pressure on them. Once the pressure is relieved, they'll blow."

"And blow up the ship?"

"No," Samuel examined one of the mines closely. "It would take a lot more than this to destroy the ship. These are strategically placed to cripple us." Samuel turned to face Kim. "We'd be grounded."

Kim swallowed.

"Stagar," Samuel called, "You catching all of this?"

"Yes, I'm working on the signal."

"The signal??" Kim asked.

"The detonation command will be sent on a set communication signal. The control module will be in contact with the mines. They are often set to deactivate if the signal goes away for a set period of time. If Stagar finds it, he can block out the detonation command. Then as long as the ship doesn't bounce around relieving pressure on any of these, we can defuse them at our convenience."

Kim looked over Samuel's shoulder. "How long to defuse one of these?"

"It's not my area of expertise, but I'd guess 10 to 15 minutes each."

"Hour and a half,"

"Or so," Samuel shrugged. They stood in silence for a moment examining the explosives.

Kim stiffened. "Do you feel that?"

Samuel glanced around and shook his head, "No, what?"

"There it is again."

Holding his breath, Samuel stood perfectly still. He felt different vibration through the floor, almost a rumble, very brief. He counted three of them a few seconds apart before they went silent.

Samuel lunged for the intercom. "Stagar, where is Lance?"

"I don't know," came the terse response. "I think I've found the signal, but it will take another minute to verify and duplicate."

"Look, Stagar, if he's willing to sabotage the ship this way, there is no reason to believe he won't set up a couple more for backup."

"We just felt some tremors in the ship," Kim said over Samuel's shoulder.

"Stagar, you brought the security system back up. That's how you found Lance here. Find him again."

"Yes, just give me a second."

Samuel and Kim stood staring at the intercom feeling for any more activity.

"Well..." Stagar's voice trailed off.
"What?" Samuel and Kim asked in unison.
"Lance has been busy."
"Can you be more specific?"
"He's blasted all the security feeds along his way. The starboard side of B deck is completely blacked out."
"Stagar, aren't the escape pods down there?"
Kim gasped. "Why would he..."
Samuel cut him off. "Have the men converge on B and get Thompson up here so that when the signals are taken care of he can disarm this junk."
"Kim, you and I will..."
His words trailed off at the sound of Epstine over the intercom. "Loscar, the Loscar are in the system, in the system, do you hear?!"
"Calm yourself," Stagar's voice lilted. "Take a deep breath."
"Stagar, they're here, here now. We have to get up to the shield, now. We're a black cat in the snow out here."
"Epstine," Samuel said firmly. "How long do we have before they are likely to discover us?"
"Oh, oh, I don't know. I don't know. They should be in orbit within, within, one hour. They may be able to detect us in half that time." After a brief pause Epstine added, "maybe?"
Samuel grabbed Kim by the shoulder. "We don't have time to disarm the mines. If the ride up near the shield is as rough as Epstine projects, the mines will go off in the first minute. We have to get the control from Lance."
"Stagar, we're going after Lance. Don't let anyone move the ship until we can confirm the mines are deactivated."
He didn't wait for a response but tore off down the hall with Kim in tow.
Samuel pulled up short as they arrived at the ladder down to B deck and turned to face Kim. "If you see Lance, shoot on sight. Don't hesitate; I know I've already told you. If you give him any chance at all, he'll cut you to ribbons.
"But..."
Samuel silenced him with a stern look. "We have maybe twenty minutes to deactivate the mines and get up to the shields before we're discovered. Shoot on sight."
At the base of the ladder, three narrow corridors broke off, one for each set of portside escape pods. Samuel pointed Kim towards the far left as he crept towards the middle.
The excellent lighting illuminated everything in the hall but bulkheads separated each pod's entry. Lance could be behind any of them. At the first, Samuel pressed himself against the far wall and leaned in, keeping the handgun trained on the obscured area. The first pod bay was empty.
He approached the second with the same caution. Peeking around the corner, he saw into the pod. It contained extra equipment, rations, and Lance's rifle.
A very faint noise came from behind him, like the rustling of clothes. He didn't have to turn; he knew Lance stood behind him. Realizing it was too late; he still tried to get the gun around. Before completing the turn, however, he felt his back slammed up against the wall with enough force to cause him to drop his gun and blank out for a second. When he came to himself, Lance's sneering face greeted him.
"Fine job you've made of this," Lance growled taking Samuel by the throat and pressing him against the wall. "You know, I really looked forward to savoring our last encounter, but time's a-wasting, and the Loscar are on their way, I hear."
Samuel gasped for breath as the fingers around his neck slowly constricted.

"One thing before you go, though, a curiosity. You've gotten what you wanted. The glorious destruction of the planet has been averted and the Loscar are here to safeguard your precious grubs. So, why are you helping these slugs by hunting me down instead of using an escape pod yourself, and leaving them all to their fate?"

"Because," Samuel sputtered, "With this crew left on the planet there is an unstable element that could raise havoc. Even without you, Stagar's willing to destroy the planet. When a group like this gets desperate, then there is no telling what they can do."

"Now there's the Roach that I've come to know. It's all about the grubs," Lance responded with a smile. "Goodbye, Roach."

As his windpipe closed up, Samuel grabbed at Lance's arms, pulled at the vice like grip and punched at his body. Nothing fazed the big man. The edges of his vision blurred. He kicked Lance in the legs to no avail. The blurriness crept in towards the center of his field of vision.

Reaching out, he grabbed at Lance's vest. In a pocket by his left hand he felt an oblong device, the mine control, he realized. A moment of clarity and calm filled his mind as he removed it from the pocket, brought it up to his field of vision and pressed the deactivate button.

The smile slid off Lance's face. Samuel dropped it into the open hatch of the pod they were by and pressed the launch button. Lance held him against the bulkhead with the button in easy reach. It took one second, one smooth motion and the mine problem dissolved with his sight.

His vision went black. The blood pounding in his ears let him know he still lived, for the moment, but it became harder to focus on any thought at all. He simply existed.

"Let him go."

He heard the words but did not understand, repeating them in his mind.

Then a pop and a ping sound echoed in his ears. It seemed familiar but he couldn't place it. The pressure around this throat ceased and he fell coughing to the floor. Laboring to get breath back into his lungs, he could do nothing but lay there.

"Kimmy, hold your fire," Lance said. "I'm glad to see you. I was about to go looking for you. What do you say, let's get off this boat? We let the rest of this scum fall prey to the Loscar."

"What?" Kim responded, "We're all trapped if we don't get to the shield in the next few minutes."

He heard a foot step near by.

"Kim, Kim, you really think that mad scheme is going to work? The Roach is playing you, he's playing everyone. He doesn't care what happens to you. He's only concerned with his beloved grubs."

Samuel's vision came back blurred, but he could make out Lance moving towards a figure at the end of the hall. "Shoot," he tried to yell, but he couldn't get even a grunt out. Lance steadily closed the distance between himself and Kim. If Kim didn't build up the nerve to shoot soon, then Lance would finish them both.

"Stay where you are, Lance. Lie on the floor and put your hands behind your head," Kim's voice had a tremble to it.

"That's hardly the way to talk to your friend and mentor. There's an easy way off this planet, but it's only for one or two. You can come with me. We take a pod down, sneak into the Loscar's camp and stow aboard one of their ships."

Breathing came a bit easier. Rising up on all fours, he shook his head, which restored most of his vision. Right before him on the ground lay his gun.

"And you said his plan was crazy."

"It is. You think he wants you to escape, to bring others to his pet planet. Look, I've stowed aboard Loscar ships twice during the war. It can be done."

Samuel looked up at Lance's back as the brute took another step closer to Kim. Lance didn't have his rifle. Stagar's stun gun hung from his hip and he probably had a knife or two on him.

Samuel checked the distance to the gun again, looked up to verify that Lance's focus remained on Kim, and flopped forward to the gun. Just as he did so, he heard the, "blap," of the stun gun and a shout.

With gun in hand he rolled on to his side and brought the barrel up. The business end of Lance's gun swung around. Samuel fired though he didn't have time to aim.

The big man lurched backward. Samuel brought the gun up higher to get better aim, but in that instant Lance dove into one of the escape pods. Before Samuel could stagger over to the pod entrance, a rumble announced the pod's launch.

Chapter 26: Escape

Samuel pulled himself up on the bulkhead and looked down at the port Lance escaped through. He was sure he hit Lance because Lance had staggered back; however, with his blurred vision at the time he couldn't tell how badly he had wounded Lance. It could have been fatal, or merely annoying. *An annoyed Lance is more dangerous than a dead one*, he mused.

Kim lay motionless on the floor a few steps away. Luckily, his first big mistake didn't cost his life.

Massaging his throat, Samuel walked out of the pod bay and found an intercom. "Stagar," he voice rasped out the word, "The mines are deactivated. Have Thompson turn them all the way off."

"Lance?" The name was question enough.

"Jettisoned in an escape pod, wounded, not dead."

"I see," Stagar said after a second. "The Loscar are on their way."

Samuel leaned heavily against the wall. "Yeah."

"Well?"

"Well, what?"

"You need to get up to the bridge fast and take charge."

Samuel closed his eyes and rubbed his temples. "Epstine knows the plan; he can tell the others what to do. Really, we all need to do as he instructs if we are to have any chance of escape."

"Epstine," it came out as a laugh. "Epstine is immensely capable in his own sphere, but who would follow him?"

"Any one who wants off this planet?" Samuel pushed the off button and made his way to Kim.

He rolled the young man over. Blood seeped from his nostrils, obviously, broken nose.

"That'll modify your looks a bit."

Looping his arms around Kim's body he dragged him over to the wall and propped him up in a sitting position. The flow of blood slowed.

Samuel sat beside him. "You and I have very little to do with what happens next. We're not the pilot nor the navigator nor Epstine and all his detailed calculations. No, we're just along for the ride.

"Still," he continued speaking to the unconscious man. "We should probably get up to the bridge, just in case Stagar tries something foolish."

Examining the nose again to confirm that the bleeding had stopped, he crouched down and with several heaves and some twisting, got Kim up on his shoulders.

"Great," he muttered as he shuffled forward. At the base of the ladder-like stairs he paused. Perspiration broke out on his face, his legs trembled and he breathed heavily. Twenty years ago he could probably have just run up the stairs with his load. His shifted Kim's weight and his back muscles protested.

"Alright," he said and sat Kim down against the wall.

Activating the intercom he called, "Medic, Kim got hit with a stun gun, come down to the port side escape pod bay with the equipment to wake him up."

He began to sit when another voice came on the intercom. "This isn't over yet, Roach!"

Samuel jumped at the sound of Lance's voice. The light on the intercom indicating a connection went out immediately.

He had watched Lance jump into the escape pod. Lance had no opportunity to sneak off into the ship.

"Stagar," he called into the microphone. "Lance just spoke through this intercom; can you trace it, read the log or something?"

"I don't know, let me check."

Samuel ran his fingers through his hair as he waited.

"We got a transmission from the ground a moment ago. That had to be him."

Feeling the mining charges in his pocket, Samuel asked, "Can you pinpoint the location and pepper the area with missiles?"

"Good thinking, Mister Rochez. However," Stagar paused, "The Loscar may be close enough to detect it. I'll check with Epstine."

"All right," Samuel wiped the sweat from his forehead, "but if you can, do it!"

Not only did Lance have something up his sleeve for them, he hated the thought of that butcher loose on the planet among the Home-kind. Lance had a grudge and enjoyed slaughter.

Samuel left Kim. A couple of minutes later he burst onto the bridge.

"Who's communications?" he demanded through heaving breaths.

The men looked at him and then at each other as if asking: "What's this about?"

Samuel raised his voice even louder, "Communications?" and steeled his glare on the group.

An average looking man with close cropped, black hair quietly responded, "Me?"

"Yes, you. What's your name?" Samuel took two strides to close in face to face. The other man stiffened, Samuel noted, but he didn't have time to be congenial about it.

"Intembe's my name. What do..."

Samuel cut him off. "I saw Lance leave in an escape pod. A few minutes later he called me over the intercom. Is it possible to access the intercom from outside the ship?"

Intembe squinted in thought. "Some hardware would have to be hooked in."

Samuel stepped aside and gestured towards the hall. "Show me."

Intembe looked around to the other men, but no one intervened. He started for the door.

"Today!" Samuel called, channeling Lance and the man broke into a trot.

The communications locker barely held two men with a bit of space between. Gray but antiseptic lights and controls filled the walls and one small console with a bench in front of it.

"Where would it be?" Samuel asked.

The other man cleared his throat. "It would be in one of three places."

He moved in and swung open a panel. "Wow, first try," he said.

Leaning over his shoulder, Samuel saw a rectangular box at an odd angle amongst the wires and boards. Intembe reached for it.

"Stop!" Samuel called. "Knowing Lance it could be rigged. Can you cut power to it without disturbing anything else?"

The other man looked back and shrugged. Pulling wire cutters from a pocket he reached in, examined the wires and cut one.

The two lights on the front of the box died.

"Good, check the other spots as well." Samuel leaned against the door jam as Intembe searched in other areas. "Do you think Lance had the technical knowledge to wire that device in?"

Intembe shrugged with his shoulders almost up to his ears, "I have no idea." He went back to his work. "Why, does it matter?"

If Lance didn't do it and no one confesses to it, then, however improbable, Lance would have a loyal follower on board. Samuel shook his head. He couldn't imagine anyone choosing Lance over freedom and life.

He stepped out into the hall and found an intercom out of earshot. "Stagar, are you monitoring?"

"I'm here," came the soft congenial response.

"Safe and secure with one foot on your web?"

"What is it?" Stagar responded in a formal tone.

"Lance linked together external communications with the intercom."

Stagar whistled.

"Does he have that kind of knowledge?"

"Lance picked up skills in a variety of areas. I always assumed it was because he didn't want to have to ultimately depend on anyone else; but, I haven't seen him work with communications."

"Did you or Epstine wire it in for him?"

Stagar paused. "You're thinking Lance might have a man on board?"

"It's possible. In the pod bay, after he left, he contacted me and said it isn't over."

Samuel sighed, "Watch your controls and check with Epstine."

Walking back to communications he called, "Are we all ..."

The floor fell below him and the ceiling tapped his head. Before he could react the floor came back up. He lay sprawled, stunned.

"Everyone strap yourselves down," Stagar's voice boomed over the PA.

"Come on," Samuel called to Intembe and started for the bridge. The next big tremor could occur at any moment.

Stepping onto the bridge he noted that no one had taken the command chair. He moved over to one of the empty support stations and strapped himself into the chair.

The navigator and helm moved with a fluid motion, almost as one being. They constantly talked to each other, exchanging codes, speaking the alien dialect of course management. Samuel wondered if it were their skill or Epstine's that kept the ship calm after the first big lurch.

Intembe entered the bridge holding a steri-pad to his head. He strapped himself into the communications station.

The main display flashed between static white, the dark of space, and the occasional satellite.

Epstine's voice came over the speaker and joined the code language of the others. That had to mean that the Loscar were close enough that they had to start worrying about being detected.

Samuel looked around the room. He hadn't gotten to know the men, didn't even want to know their names. Could one of them really be working for Lance now that they were free of him?

"Lance is on the planet," he called.

To their credit the pair guiding the ship remained fixed in their task. Everyone else turned to look at him.

"He took an escape pod down to the planet." Samuel pointed to Intembe, "he confirmed it. We're leaving Lance behind."

Samuel didn't expect shouts for joy or singing, but none of the men showed any sign of relief. The jostling of the ship and the tenuousness of their plan might have worn more heavily on their minds at the moment.

Minutes past, hours past, with them strapped into a constantly shaking ship. Occasionally a larger dip caused Samuel stomach to lurch. All the while the two men and Epstine continued their conversation. Their voices took on an irregular rhythm almost musical in tone.

Samuel's thoughts strayed to what Lance planned to do. There could be sabotage they didn't find. He went over in his mind the vital areas of the ship, wondering what signs would give them away.

The voices stopped. The broken pattern pulled Samuel from his deliberations.

"What is it?" some one asked.

"The Loscar have opened a hole in the lockdown. We're sitting under a satellite right at the edge."

The room grew silent except for the rattling of the shaking ship.

"They're coming through," Epstine's voice whispered.

Amid the flickering of the display three ships appeared, one oblong cargo ship and two sleek cruisers.

Epstine picked what would be the best time, when the ships hit the fiery section of atmospheric insertion.

The men resumed their song in hushed voices. The display screen cleared as they moved out from under the shield that had held the men prisoners for so long.

"Go!" Epstine called and the main engine roared to life. Even with their advanced technology Samuel felt a slight pressure on his chest from the acceleration.

The rumble of the main engine cut out after 5 seconds. For the next minute or two they would coast to the nearest moon. Everyone held their collective breath, listening for any indication of pursuit. A cruiser would take them out with a single volley from its main guns. With two they stood no chance.

The ship felt much more like a tin can floating adrift with the thought of the amount of firepower that could be launched at it.

Thirty seconds past and the men looked from one to another seeking reassurance that no one gave. Samuel didn't return anyone's gaze. It would be over soon, one way or the other.

A speck on the screen grew bigger and resolved into a large oval rock. It seemed from the view that it was falling onto them. Samuel shook his head. It was just another space rock like so many he had seen.

One minute and the moon filled most of the screen. It moved to one side as their path brought them to one side of it and then quietly behind. "Only a few more seconds to safety," he mumbled.

Everyone sat up and leaned towards the screen.

Perhaps Lance bluffed just to keep them on edge.

"What?" a voice called in alarm.

Samuel and everyone looked towards the communication console where Intembe gawked at an orange light.

"What is it?" Samuel asked.

"Someone's hailing us."

A light turned green. "And we're responding!"

At the same moment the pilot called out. "We're behind the moon."

"Intembe," Samuel yelled over the growing noise of the men in confusion. "Was it a tight beam transmission or a wide broadcast that we sent out?"

The other man slumped back in his chair. "Wide," he said grabbing his face with one hand and rubbing his temples.

"Shut up," Samuel hollered. "Someone, or something, onboard this ship just sent an open communication to the planet. The Loscar know we're here."

The color drained out of the navigator's face.

"Pilot, do we stand any chance at outrunning a Loscarian cruiser?"

He shook his head in response, "No chance at all."

"We're being hailed," Intembe said.

Samuel rolled his eyes and sat back. "Put it on the speakers."

"Unidentified ship, you are ordered to surrender and yield to boarding. Respond."

"Epstine," Samuel said into the com.

No response came. After a few seconds Samuel tried again with the same results.

"We could fly down and hide on the top of the shield like we did on the way out." Kim strode onto the bridge a little unsteady with his nose encased in a bandage.

Samuel thought about it for a moment. "Good idea, but I'm not sure we have the time. The cruisers should be out of lockdown in a few seconds.

"Ha, ha!" Stagar sprinted into the room and took up the command chair. He held a rounded oblong instrument similar to the device Samuel used to blow up the missile.

"Stagar, this is hardly..." Kim started.

Stagar pressed the com control on the chair and spoke to the Loscar. "You will recall your ships and stand down or be destroyed."

"No, it is you that will surrender this day."

Stagar signaled two of the men forward. "Hold him" he ordered and pushed them towards Samuel.

Attempting to lunge past the men Samuel yelled, "What are you playing at Stagar?"

The men wrestled him to the floor.

"Stagar!" Samuel pulled and pushed against the restraining weight.

Stagar ignored him. "Pilot and nav remain here. Everyone else search for Mister Epstine."

Clearing his throat Stagar activated the com again; "Scan the area roughly 150 kilometers southwest of your location. It will be difficult because of the Carlinium, but you should be able to pick up the signature of a nuclear warhead."

He paused for a moment. Samuel could almost see the invisible audience Stagar played to.

"That warhead is armed, active and encased in Carlinium." He slowed the delivery of the last three words. "Think about it. We engineered it with the greatest of care and craftsmanship. I'm told it will vaporize a large chunk of the planet, along with you."

Samuel struggled in vain. "Don't you dare. I swear..."

The remainder of Samuel's words were muffled by the gag Stagar stuffed into his mouth.

"Navigation," Stagar said smoothly. "Can you tie into one of Mister Epstine's sensors and see what the Loscar ships are up to?"

"No," came the response.

"Well, will you at least know when we are on the opposite side of the planet and can escape this solar system?"

The Navigator rubbed his chin. "Following the plan, that should be in about three and a half hours."

"Alright then."

Stagar rested his finger on the main button on his control and addressed the Loscar again. "I have my finger on the button. Do you choose life or death?"

The bridge seemed frozen in time as they waited.

"We have brought back our ships and are standing down. What is it you want?"

Immediately a collective sigh of relief swept through the remaining men.

"We weren't expecting to come across you here so we'll need some time to deliberate. We'll get back to you in about five hours."

Stagar paused with his finger over the com button. A smile slowly spread across his face. "And don't try to reach the device to deactivate it. We've left an operative on the planet. He called us after verifying you were in position. You may have picked up the transmission. He doesn't mind dying for the cause, so I suggest you don't push your luck."

With a click Stagar severed communication with the Loscar.

"Ok," he turned to Samuel. "Let him up."

Samuel rose slowly and pulled the gag from his mouth. He looked Stagar up and down. "Was that the warhead from the missile?"

"Yep," Stagar smiled at himself. "The missile broke up but the warhead survived."

"I'm surprised, and pleased that you didn't just blow them up without talking to them." Samuel smiled slightly.

Stagar held up the device. "What, with this?" Click, click, click, he pressed the button in rapid succession.

Before Samuel could react Stagar tossed the control to him.

"The warhead is alive and kicking. The detonator is shot."

"Wait," Samuel stood up straight. "You'd only know that if you already pressed it."

Stagar pursed his lips. "You win some, you lose some."

Flinging the device at Stagar's head, Samuel stormed out of the room.

###

Samuel waited in a dark corner of the escape pod bay. Stagar had done it. He pressed the button knowing the holocaust it would be to the planet. The failure of the detonation circuit is all that saved the Home-kind and all other life on the planet below.

The ship had passed the local sun a few minutes previous and would soon be out of the solar system. Samuel stood up and stretched.

Footsteps announced the arrival of someone.

"Thought I'd find you here." Stagar said.

"Goodie for you."

"Aw, now don't be that way. We both got what we wanted and Lance is stuck holding the bag. I'd say it is all for the better."

Samuel didn't respond.

"We'll be out of range soon, what are you going to do?"

"Ok, what are you thinking now?"

"Come on Mister Rochez. There is a reason you're skulking down here. You're going back."

Samuel leered at him and took a step closer. "And you're going to stop me?"

"I should, you know."

"But you can't." Samuel smiled.

Stagar squinted at Samuel. "Really?"

"You could call the men to back you up, but they won't get here in time. I'm ready to go now. You could try and use your legendary stun gun, but you'd need to be fast." Samuel turned to reveal the pistol on his hip. "You up for a quick draw?"

Stagar whistled. "You certainly seem to have everything covered. But you never know, there may be other ways."

"You mean this?" Samuel backed behind the wall around the pods and brought out a small metallic device with a few wires coming out of it. He tossed it to Stagar.

The other man examined it for a few seconds. "Well, you have been busy."

"Stagar," Samuel said with his hands on his hips, "it says something about a man that installs detonators in every single one of his escape pods."

"Well," Stagar shrugged, "can never be too careful. It's a shame Lance found his too. Must be losing my touch."

Samuel brushed past the other man and made his way to the escape pod he had packed.

Stagar gestured with a flourish towards the pods. "By all means, go, have a big old time. I just want to know one thing. How much time will we have before you turn yourself over? It takes a while to get to port, sell our load and change identity. It would be a shame to have the Loscar hunt us down before we finished all that."

"Ok," Samuel sighed. "I'll poke around the edge of the solar system for a few days and come in at a different angle and claim to be a survivor of some disaster. It will take some time longer than that to find out anything further. Rest assured you'll have the time you need."

"Well then, I guess we are done here." Stagar turned to go.

"What about Epstine?"

"Oh," Stagar tuned back and rocked on his heels. "We mustn't blame him. Even though Lance remained on the planet he still had a hold on the poor fellow. It's hard for cowards to handle threats."

Samuel raised an eyebrow.

"Don't get me wrong; he's a good man. One just needs to deal with his weakness. The same as most of the crew in one way or another."

"And Kwanso?"

Stagar raised his index finger. "Now, that boy has some potential."

"Yes, he does. Try not to damage him any more than you already have."

Samuel climbed into the pod. Rearranging the equipment he had loaded in, he settled into the seat.

Stagar came around to the door. "Well, goodbye Samuel Rochez. We'll probably never meet again."

Samuel looked up. "There is something you can do for me."

"What's that?"

"Give my share to Kwanso and send him home."

Stagar scratched his chin. "I'll consider it."

Samuel squinted. "Yeah, you do that."

"Oh, come to think of it, there is something you could possibly do for me."

"What's that?"

"If you happen to come across our mutual friend, Michael Lance, please tell him that the authorities are being informed of his illegal activities. If he does make it off that rock, he'll be one of the most wanted men in the galaxy."

Samuel smiled in spite of himself. "Goodbye, Stagar."

"Goodbye, Samuel."

With that Samuel closed the hatch and launched himself into space. He took one look at the ship as it shrank into the distance and then set a course around the edge of the solar system.

33758844R10086

Made in the USA
Charleston, SC
23 September 2014